The Girl in the Case

is the most recent novel by one of Britain's most respected suspense novelists.

'Convincing psychological insight and a high frisson count.' *The Sunday Times (Evil Acts)*

'*Evil Acts* is imbued from the start with a powerful and compelling atmosphere. Read it . . . but not perhaps when you're alone.' *Glasgow Herald (Evil Acts)*

'The mistress of unease on top of her form . . . everything the perfect crime novel should contain: plot, pace, original characters, all tightly controlled.' *Yorkshire Post (Wish You Were Here)*

'A creepy story in the du Maurier tradition . . . mind-blowing suspense.' *Daily Telegraph (Wish You Were Here)*

'She knows how to create an atmosphere of unease and incipient horror.' P. D. James *(Patterns in the Dust)*

'One of the classiest thriller writers around.' *The Sunday Times (A Life of Adventure)*

'Grips as tightly as the rope around the dead man's neck.' *Woman's World (Curse the Darkness)*

Also by Lesley Grant-Adamson
and available from Hodder and Stoughton paperbacks

Teach Yourself Writing Crime and Suspense Fiction
Wish You Were Here
Dangerous Games
Evil Acts

About the author

Lesley Grant-Adamson was born in north London and spent much of her childhood in the Rhondda in South Wales. She worked on provincial newspapers including the *Citizen* at Gloucester before joining the staff of the *Guardian* in London as a feature writer, then worked as a freelance journalist and television writer before becoming a novelist with *Patterns in the Dust*, published in 1985. *The Girl in the Case* is her thirteenth novel.

The Girl in the Case

Lesley Grant-Adamson

NEW ENGLISH LIBRARY
Hodder and Stoughton

First published in Great Britain in 1997 by Hodder and Stoughton
A division of Hodder Headline PLC
First published in paperback in 1997 by Hodder and Stoughton
A New English Library Paperback

10 9 8 7 6 5 4 3 2 1

British Library Cataloguing in Publication Data

Grant-Adamson, Lesley
  The girl in the case
  1. English fiction – 20th century
  I. Title
  823.9´14 [F]

ISBN 0 340 66022 8

Printed and bound in Great Britain by
Mackays of Chatham PLC, Chatham, Kent

Hodder and Stoughton
A division of Hodder Headline PLC
338 Euston Road
London NW1 3BH

For Jane McLoughlin

CHAPTER ONE

The smell of the forest is the smell of decay. On some days the breeze fans the sickly scent of blossom, sweetest shortly before it dies, but usually there are poisonous gases caused by wood rotting, vegetation liquefying and animals putrefying. There is always in the forest an over-riding smell of death.

The woman lay close to a path. Her body was likely to be noticed before very long although the icy spell of weather could delay the finding. She lay on her back, eyes half open and seemingly focused on a beech tree. The red flash on her padded jacket might signal to an observant passerby but the rest of her clothes were drab as the surrounding scene. Mud smeared both legs of her jeans which were new and deep indigo. A scarf of olive green wool hung loosely about her neck. Thick socks and boots, both caked with earth, were a rough match for the scarf.

Her dark brown hair masked one half of her face, except for the eye that feigned interest in the beech tree. A hectic flush to her skin made it appear she was raw with cold or over-heated from running. Whoever first glimpsed her would not say straightaway: 'I have found a dead woman.'

One curious thing, though. She was not wearing gloves. Her hands were clean and they lay palms uppermost with the fingers lightly curled. A squirrel ran down the trunk of the beech tree and squatted to watch her. A skeletal leaf drifted down and settled in her cupped hand.

The breeze that had brought it stirred scents from the forest floor. Pungent reminders of foxes. The sourness of urine. Unpleasant odours of wildlife and wild death. At 4.30, as day was fading, twenty-three primary school children trudged a path within thirty yards of the body. Although their teachers glanced nervously at the sky, glimpsed through a winter canopy of arching boughs, it did not occur to any of the children that their pace was so sluggish they risked being caught in the forest at dusk or that the forest might hold terrifying secrets. Too tired now for the skipping and shoving that had enlivened their first mile, they went steadfastly on, making wild calculations about the amount of money this sponsored walk was raising.

A little later Madeleine Knewton came by with her dog. Jay was running in front of her, foraging, longing for rabbits to chase. Coming to a fork, Maddy paused, cocked her head and listened for him. Agitated bird calls, and a rummaging in the undergrowth off to her right, proved he was taking the longer route. She pulled a rueful face, regretting letting him get so far ahead. Soon it would be dangerously dark for going the long way home.

'*Jay!* Here, Jay!'

But Jay chose not to notice and, knowing his stubborn nature, she wasted no more time trying to dissuade him. Breaking into a run, she set off along the path to the right. And so it was that she, too, avoided stumbling upon the body.

Street lights were on when Maddy eventually reached the village. Curtains were being drawn, doors were shut against the weather and she saw nobody in the street except for the driver of an empty school bus who raised a hand in greeting. Once the bus had died away she heard only the scuffing of her waxed jacket and the plodding rhythm of her rubber boots on the roadway.

She swung the retriever's lead in her hand, as useless as a riding crop when the horse has bolted. Jay preferred to reach home before her. No doubt she would find him posing on the doorstep, a withering gleam in his brown eye tantamount to asking: 'What kept you?' She would laugh at him and he would wriggle all over and they would be happy.

Rounding a bend near the post office, she discovered the road blocked by a lorry manoeuvring backwards into the lane that ran down to Mound Farm. The entrance, which was especially narrow, was flanked by two pairs of farm cottages. A prickle of annoyance spoiled her good humour. No one farmed at Mound Farm any longer, it had been turned into a road haulage depot. The village hated this and regulations appeared to prohibit it but the business was carrying on regardless. There were rumours of a councillor conniving with the owner.

The theme tune of a soap opera on Central television blared from one of the cottages. The other three were seldom occupied. As soon as there was a gap between the wall and the front of the lorry, she sprinted through. A big saloon car was held up on the other side. Peter Ribston, who lived in one of the new houses near the green, wound down his window and grumbled to her. He was fat, fifty, and his face had become furiously red owing to impatience and the heat in the car.

'We need another meeting, Maddy. This is bloody reckless. Look at him. An inch to spare.'

'Half an inch, more like.'

Scars on the cottage walls emphasised that drivers made frequent misjudgements.

Ribston said: 'I'll ring Beth when I get indoors. Strike while the temper's hot, eh?'

'Don't get cross with Beth. She's doing her best.'

There was space for him to pull forward now and she missed his final words as the engine revved. She decided to call Beth herself, either to prepare her for Ribston or to comfort her after the assault. She would make it amusing and they would laugh. Beth was zealous about curbing the lorries and it would be a pity if she grew dispirited because of all the complaints that were directed to, if not intentionally *at*, her. Angry people were not always careful who they wounded.

Maddy walked on down the sinuous village street of honey-coloured cottages. Porch lamps threw gentle light on cobbled paths and shrubby front gardens. A blue glow suggested television in thinly curtained rooms. When she passed the old barn a dog began to bark, as it always did when anyone went by. The evening was sweetened by fields of young grass, and only a couple of chimneys threaded the air with wood smoke as a reminder that winter was lingering.

She felt content. '*A Cotswold village in early spring,*' she was thinking, '*and there's nowhere else I'd rather be.*'

For the last few yards of the journey home she indulged in a sentimental view of the slumbering English village where neighbours were honest, friends were loyal and nothing went seriously wrong.

Her house, called Meadow Cottage, was set back a yard or two from the road and protected by a low wall. Automatic porch light had come on, a piece of magic she enjoyed every evening. Although the gate stood open, her dog was not lying on the doorstep challenging her with dawdling. Neither was he sniffing shadows in the patch of front garden.

Maddy stamped about to free her boots of mud, then finished off by using the cast iron scraper beside the step. The noise ought to have brought Jay from wherever he was loitering but there was no rush to meet her, no welcoming yap. With a shrug, she jiggled her key into the lock and went indoors.

Perching one-legged on the coconut doormat, she eased off her boots and put them on a slatted shelf to dry. It was a nuisance not having a rear access to the house. Worse, she was aware there used to be a right of way until a difficult neighbour had deprived her predecessor of it. But no, she refused to dwell on the petty trials of village life. Besides, if the house were perfect, it could never have become hers. Perfect houses – aloof from their neighbours and with garage space in addition to antique charm – were expensive. She had opted for eighteenth-century prettiness and vowed to ignore the inconvenience.

Maddy flung her jacket on to a hook, a hook it shared with a raincoat, a walking stick of dubious provenance, and a woolly hat unclaimed by a forgetful guest. The jacket, which had no loop, was precarious. Unless she balanced it correctly, its weight would drag it off. She kept meaning to do away with those hooks, kept meaning to smarten up the hall. The house lacked sufficient storage space for neatness. Upstairs the overflow from cupboards and drawers hung on the backs of doors. Downstairs it hung around the kitchen, awaiting reassignment. She lived in comfortable clutter and was happy with it.

The jacket lost its struggle and fell off. She let it lie where it landed, too busy tugging open the cupboard where she stowed shoes. The flagstones were so cold through her socks that she snatched at the first flat-heeled pair of shoes that came to hand. While she was fastening them, Jay came padding along the hall from the kitchen and nuzzled her.

She ignored the dog and called. 'Steve?' Until now she had believed she was alone in the house.

He answered from above, his words indistinct. Maddy stepped over the fallen jacket and ran upstairs, asking: 'Are you all right?' He had been unwell for the previous couple of weeks, or so she thought although he had denied anything was troubling him.

Steve was lying on the narrow bed in the small back room, dressed but with the quilt dragged across him. Running a temperature again, she supposed. A childhood in Africa had left him with a legacy of fever, that and some fancy stories. She studied him in the subdued light from the hall. Cadaverous features ensured he always looked like a delicate child in need of mothering. But this evening he appeared tense, pained, with his eyes screwed up and the green of the quilt casting an unhealthy glow on his skin. Maddy's hand stretched towards the light switch just inside the room but he stopped her.

'No, I don't want the light.'

Instead she went to him and felt his forehead. Hot. Clammy. He quivered at her touch. 'Is there anything I can fetch?'

She expected him to say no. While his physical frailty made a mute appeal for help and protection, his spirit rejected fussing. And there was, he had convinced her, nothing that *could* be done when he succumbed to a touch of fever. So she waited for him to say no.

'No, thanks. I'll try to sleep.'

'I'll bring you some water. You'll need water if you're sweating.'

He did not reply and she went out, drawing the bedroom door after her before switching on the landing light. Entering her own bedroom, *their* bedroom for much of the previous two years, she wrapped herself in a bulky cardigan and then fluffed up her duvet, just the part where it had been squashed as though one of them had sat on the edge of the bed. Either that or Jay had crept upstairs, illegally, to rest his head where he knew she slept.

As she was leaving the room, a light flashed across the ceiling and along a wall, making a chequer-board pattern of sixteen small window-panes. It would be another few seconds before the vehicle sped by but, as the road was twisting, the house had a clear view of a distant part of the village street. She heard the first sound of the approaching car; and while she was in the hall, stooping to pick up the jacket, it roared past her door.

Five minutes later she carried the water upstairs. Steve was asleep. She crept away, relieved and guilty to feel relieved. Her mind was made up, though. She wanted him out of her life, she had imposed a limit and she intended to stick to it.

Jay was taking an unusual lack of interest in her but this mild puzzle was solved when she looked for his feeding bowl and discovered he had been fed. Instead, she let him out of the back door and watched his yellow shape trotting through the gloom of the courtyard to the garden beyond.

Sometimes he preferred to linger in the yard, where she grew clumps of herbs between the slabs of Cotswold stone, and then she had to chase after him and shoo him as far as the garden.

Because he was being compliant this evening, she was soon free to telephone Beth about the latest lorry complaint. Beth's telephone was answered by a machine. Maddy hung up, realising there was no point in leaving a message since she did not know what, if anything, Peter Ribston had done.

She took a bowl of lasagne from the fridge and put it in the oven to heat. A particularly dull evening stretched ahead of her as Steve was on his sick bed and she had already ducked out of the only social event on offer: drinks in the pub with Malcolm and Gina Winterson, bothersome newcomers whose role in village life was touting schemes for improving the community. Most people believed their schemes would wreck it. Village gossips honed rumours to discredit their efforts.

They had taken early retirement from the travel business and had time on their hands. Maddy's solace was that she had not sold them their house. At the time, she had been disappointed when the property was put in the hands of another agent but it had turned out to be worth every pound of lost commission to know that no one could blame her for the Wintersons.

Although she thought of ringing a couple of friends, to see whether they were also under-occupied and eager to chat, it was too early to do so. Instead, she flicked through the morning paper and confirmed there was nothing she cared to watch on television. She spun the paper across the table, pretending disgust at its failure to promise her entertainment, then sat chin cupped in hand, a parody of boredom. Her predicament seemed funny. She tried out a sigh or two, aiming for ennui but achieving exasperation.

Her failure made her jump up laughing, only to clap a hand over her mouth in case she woke Steve. Noise from the kitchen was readily relayed to the bedroom above.

Whenever she took a telephone call in the kitchen, she wandered away to another room with the handset rather than imagine him overhearing.

'That sums it up,' she thought. 'I'm sharing my home with a man from whom I want secrets. I've cut him out of my emotional life but not thrown him out of my house. No wonder it's more difficult than when I was married to Dave or living with John. When those relationships collapsed, everything went, *bang*. This shading off is hopeless. *I* can't move on, and he *won't* make any move.'

Her thoughts, seldom so articulate when Steve was the topic, clouded into the usual miasma of guilt versus responsibility. This time it was his guilt and her responsibility but it was regularly the other way around.

As it was her house, she was the one who had suggested they live together. There was no ducking her responsibility for that. By then she had known him a few months and thought she was in love, but quite soon she discovered it had really been loneliness.

They had met one summer, on a lawn at a Sunday lunch party given by one of her friends in Oxford. Steve arrived late, accompanying an extrovert acquaintance of hers called Janine who was notorious for being late. Maddy had been attracted by his quiet manner and attentiveness, all the more pronounced when seen alongside Janine's antics. Few of the men Maddy knew were good listeners. By the time it occurred to her that listening was a deft way of avoiding having to talk yourself, it was too late. Janine had gone to Scotland to be married to a man in the oil industry and Steve was living at Meadow Cottage.

The telephone rang putting an end to reflection.

'Maddy we need you.' Her friend Nesta sounded typically flustered. 'You haven't eaten, have you?'

'I'm heating a lasagne but . . .'

'Oh, forget that. We've got something far more interesting on offer. Ten minutes?'

'Er . . . yes. Fine.' She tacked on a thank you, but it was too late. Nesta had hung up.

Maddy turned off the oven, scribbled a note inviting Steve to heat up the lasagne if he wanted supper, changed her comfy cardigan for a smarter one, added an Indian silk scarf, slipped a torch into the pocket of her jacket and hurried out of the house. It was ten minutes fast walking to Nesta and Graham's house, thirty seconds of it spent traipsing up their curving drive. She had not been there for about three weeks, too busy with other people and other outings, although they were close.

Park House stood four-square at the top of the rise. In daylight its rear windows enjoyed long views of woodland and river. At the front were two bay windows which faced lawns and the thick hedge concealing the house from the road. It was not a big house but it was designed to look like a miniature version of a grand one. Close up, the years of neglect were revealed in flaking paint on window-frames and stained stonework where drainpipes had proved unreliable. Once or twice Maddy flicked on her torch to avoid potholes on the path, but otherwise the light from the uncurtained kitchen drew her confidently on.

Running a professional eye over the property, she thought: 'Comfortable stone family house set in mature gardens and orchard.' Should she squeeze in Victorian? Or was it Edwardian, anyway? Turn of the century was apt but the phrase was too long.

Then she was in the porch, pushing open the front door and calling out a hello. Graham stuck his head out of the kitchen and waved her in. His greying hair had tightened in damp curls as though he had rushed out of the shower rather than the kitchen.

'Maddy, come and get hot and bothered and tell us what you think of this.' She noticed he was wearing the red striped apron which meant his wife would be wearing the green. They both preferred the red.

As Maddy entered the kitchen he jabbed a spoon into a bowl and held out a sticky dob for her to taste. Nesta, poking at something in the oven, looked fiercely hot with her red hair and flushed skin. There were blemishes on her forearms from touching a plant or product that stirred up one or other of her allergies. Seeing Maddy, she swung the oven door shut, wiped her hands down the green apron and poured dark wine into tumblers. If the household boasted wine glasses, no guest had ever glimpsed them.

Maddy, nibbling the gooey concoction, murmured an appreciative 'Mmm', and asked what it was exactly that she was eating. She slipped off her jacket, which the Collinses had been too preoccupied to think of taking from her, and dumped it on a stool.

Graham rattled off the ingredients with Nesta interrupting to point out that the key was the coriander. Then he said he wasn't convinced the wine would not overpower it. Nesta asked Maddy's opinion. Maddy gulped a mouthful and said 'Mmm' in a considering way.

She shooed a cat off a chair, loosened her silk scarf, and sat down at the kitchen table. Its jaunty French oil-cloth cover was hardly visible beneath all the cookery books, notebooks, crockery, pans, jars, and bottles that littered it. Carefully, she moved Graham's camera and two spare rolls of film, to make space for her glass plus the plate of samples her hosts would inevitably hand her.

Being called in to help the Collinses was different from being invited to supper but no less entertaining. The pattern of these evenings was that she would be fed extraordinary inventions, and afterwards would repay them by telling comical anecdotes and they would all be merry until it was late.

In a while, after much tasting, adjusting of seasonings and three-cornered deliberations, the meal was pronounced ready to eat. Nesta swooped on the table and cleared the debris, dumping it on the dresser instead. Meanwhile, Graham produced hot plates and mismatched cutlery. Then Nesta carried over the serving bowls. Maddy was always surprised that, after all the sampling, there was anything left to serve.

There was a short pause while Graham aimed his camera at the serving bowl and then it was time to eat. Once he had recharged their glasses, he raised his in a teasing toast: 'To Maddy, our favourite guinea pig.'

The guinea pig wondered what the readers of the glossy magazine would make of the haphazard way the '*sparkling new recipes created by our brilliant food writer Nesta Collins*' were created. Graham's published credit was restricted to '*photographs by*'. She also wondered how readers would react to a photograph of the Collinses' kitchen while they were inventing, in place of the usual coolly beautiful picture of a dish. Herself, she had been rather astonished at the amount of faking that went on, raw food often photographed in place of cooked food that had lost texture and colour.

'To Maddy,' echoed Nesta, and drank deep.

When she had first come to know them, Maddy had taken Graham to be considerably older than Nesta but he was one of those men whose hair had greyed when he was young. By contrast, Nesta had kept her fresh young face and it was only her broadening hips and vanishing waistline that gave away her real age. They were both in their early forties, a few years older than Maddy herself. They were liked in the village and when Maddy heard them referred to as dotty or arty it was said with affection.

Before they could eat, Graham had to go in search of a serving spoon. As he handed it to Maddy, a door closed somewhere in the house. She raised a questioning eyebrow.

'That will be Linsey,' said Nesta, and Maddy noticed a slight tightening of Graham's features.

Before she had time to ask who Linsey was, a woman opened the kitchen door. Linsey stopped so abruptly on the threshold it was like watching someone slam into a sheet of glass. Maddy smiled a hello and Linsey clasped her hands together and bowed to her. She was tall and angular, dressed in a girlish manner too young for her thirty or so years: long straggling hair and a full cotton skirt down to her ankles. Below the skirt Maddy spotted dingy running shoes. Linsey spoke rapidly to Nesta, bowed again and fled.

'You may well ask,' began Graham heavily although Maddy had not said a word.

Nesta cut in. 'She has nowhere to live so she's helping out around the house for a while. That's all.'

'We hope that's all,' Graham added.

Nesta directed her words to Maddy. 'Linsey came here looking for my aunt. She used to know her and hoped she could help.'

Graham was exceedingly sceptical. 'That's what she told us. Of course, with Nesta's aunt having been dead for the past six years we couldn't check, could we?'

Maddy looked from one to the other. 'You mean she's a complete stranger?'

'Yes,' he said.

'Not exactly,' said Nesta. 'One of my cousins in Charlbury says she remembers her. She thinks Linsey's mother used to work here. Cleaning, I suppose.'

Maddy began to share Graham's reservations. 'Where has Linsey come from?

Nesta said: 'India. Or Goa, rather. Isn't that India now? I know it used to be a Portuguese colony.'

'An *asram*,' said Graham. 'That's the real answer, the one that counts. It doesn't matter a damn where it was. She lived in a commune with one of those religious cults.'

Maddy was thinking: '*Oh, of course, that explains the clothes, the bowing, the strangeness of her.*'

Nesta defended Linsey. 'She takes it very seriously.'

Graham raised his eyes to heaven, probably not Linsey's heaven. 'Darling, you're making it sound like a virtue.' And to Maddy he added: 'You know what they say, Maddy: one man's religion is another man's delusion. Well, Linsey's brainwashed. She tells us she's heard "The Truth". What that means is she refuses to hear anything else, so our simple requests fall on profoundly deaf ears.'

It was Nesta's turn to look askance. 'Graham, you don't *make* simple requests, you challenge her faith. If you were less combative . . .'

'Me!'

'. . . and accepted that she likes to do things in a different way from us . . .'

He made a wide-eyed appeal to Maddy. 'I don't give a damn what Linsey does, all I ask is that she stops interfering in what *we* do. She dictates how we ought to run our house, our lives, how we should feed ourselves . . . Did you realise the food we cook is saturated with passion and ignorance? That our free-range hens are prisoners? Maddy, that woman has a batty rule for everything and relishes telling us we're breaking each one of them. As if we *cared*.'

Nesta was flapping her hand in a 'calm down' gesture, having heard his objections so often they bored her. But Maddy was fascinated because the Collinses were seldom at variance. They worked as a team and were remarkably compatible in the rest of their lives. Now, suddenly, here was a bone of contention, a hint of fissure beneath the perfect surface of their marriage.

Quite apart from that, Linsey seemed a most unsuitable person to be caught up in life at Park House. Maddy was curious to know how long she had been there but, as any question would revive the argument, she checked herself. Luckily, the answer came up in conversation later while Nesta was searching for her new bowl. Graham remarked that it was one of the first things Linsey had taken.

Nesta bridled. 'She hasn't taken it. Not in the sense of stealing it. She's simply moved it from the kitchen and put it in her room.'

'Along with the new towels and the new . . .'

Nesta interrupted. 'We don't need a catalogue. Linsey has to have things to use and I said I'd find her what she needed.'

'Darling, she's been here less than two weeks and there's nearly as much stuff in that flat as we've got in the rest of the house. Which is interesting when you consider she claims to eschew possessions.'

'Oh, but she does,' said Nesta, unintentionally funny. 'She avoids having to buy her own and she uses ours.'

On that they agreed and the wrangle petered out in laughter.

Half an hour later, while Graham was making coffee, Nesta showed Maddy how Linsey had imposed her personality on the tiny flat on the ground floor of the house. They did not march in but stood in the doorway, to make their inquisitiveness seem less of an intrusion. Maddy had seen the flat previously, during the time Nesta's mother lived in it before going into a nursing home. Once they realised she would never be well enough to return, the Collinses had decided to let the flat for some much-needed extra income. Instead, Linsey was living there free.

The room reeked of incense. Statuettes of oriental gods were dotted around, and lengths of Indian fabric were draped over furniture. Nesta's missing bowl was displayed before a shrine and from it trailed fronds of buttery winter jasmine, snipped from the shrub that struggled up one wall of Park House.

Through the open door to the bathroom a block of bright blue caught the eye. One of the new towels. Maddy pictured Linsey cross-legged before her joss sticks, making supplications to unpronounceable gods and supremely confident in The Truth that had been drummed into her in the *asram*.

For a woman with nothing to her name, Linsey had a comfortable berth. All the unattractive old-fashioned pieces, which formerly furnished the flat, had been ejected or shrouded in drapery. Apparently, The Truth did not foster asceticism.

A distant telephone rang.

Nesta asked: 'Might that be Steve, wondering where you've got to?'

'No, he wasn't working this evening.'

'Oh, I assumed . . . Then I ought to have invited him, too.'

Maddy reassured her. 'He had a touch of fever and went to lie down. I left him sleeping.'

Nesta hesitated before asking: 'Is he still working in Oxford, at the coffee bar?' The questions sounded critical.

The reply was wry. 'It's gone on a long time for a stop-gap, hasn't it?'

'You'd have thought a proper job would have come along by now.' He was thirty-one, he had qualifications but had never worked at a real job.

She closed the door of the flat and they moved away, talking about Steve and others like him who were unlucky in the job market. As they reached the hall, Graham flung open the kitchen door.

'The phone . . .' he began. 'It was Malcolm Winterson . . .'

Maddy groaned. 'Grumbling that *you* didn't go to their meeting either?'

But Nesta had registered the grim look on his face and knew the call was nothing trivial. Urgently, she went to him. 'What's wrong?'

'They've found a body.'

They stared.

He said: 'In the forest.'

'Who?' It was Maddy who spoke.

'Malcolm didn't say. He was ringing to warn us because we're isolated here.'

Maddy felt a physical reaction, revulsion creeping the length of her spine. And the warmth had gone out of friendship. Graham and Nesta touched each other for comfort. Their eyes met. Maddy was abruptly on her own, as so often in her life. Outside there was danger. She shivered.

CHAPTER TWO

Maddy's car was held up in traffic on her way into Woodstock next morning when her colleague rang.

'Ken here, Maddy. Have you got the local radio on?'

'Morning, Ken. No, what have I missed?' She turned down her Delius tape to hear him better. Ken was softly spoken.

'A murder in Wychwood.'

'I know a body was found in the forest yesterday.' Her stomach clenched for fear of what he might tell her.

'They're saying the victim's a woman from your village.'

'Did they give a name?'

'Jean Dellafield. Mean anything?'

She relaxed. 'No, I've never heard of her.'

Vehicles began to move. 'Ken, I've got to go. See you later.'

It was a horribly dark morning and it seemed to have grown darker. As she drove on, alongside the grey stone boundary wall of the Blenheim Palace estate, she pondered the surname. Not a common one and neither did it belong to any of the families rooted in that part of Oxfordshire.

She was first in the office because Ken was going straight to a meeting with a client. Having gathered up the mail, she piled on his desk and then listened to messages on the answering machine. There was one from a Mr

Watkins complaining that Rigby March and Rollitt had not advertised his house in that week's *Oxford Times*; one from a woman requesting details of a flat which *had* been in the advertisement; then one from Ken's girlfriend who dared not ring him at home because his wife was not supposed to know of her existence; next, a fretful one from a woman whose house nobody had wanted to view in eighteen months; and finally a terse one from Nesta Collins.

Maddy rang Nesta first. The line was engaged. She spent the next minutes riffling through the post, thinking about the way the alarming news had reached Park House the previous evening. According to Graham, the Wintersons had stayed on at the pub after winding up the inaugural meeting of their campaign for a reduced speed limit through the village, and so they were there when a local man came into the bar and said he had noticed the police arrive. After that the Wintersons had set about warning anyone they considered vulnerable.

Well, perhaps they were right about Park House hidden behind its thick hedge. And it had probably been sensible for Graham and Nesta to walk Maddy home rather than let her make the journey alone. Even so, she wished the bearer of bad tidings had been anyone but a Winterson because it was too easy to construe their suggestions as officiousness. She hated being bossed about by them or, far worse, being made to feel they had saved her life.

The second time she rang Nesta the telephone was answered instantly.

Nesta said: 'Maddy, they've named the dead woman.' Her voice was tight.

'I know. But I've never heard of her, have you?' She felt foolish adding the question when Nesta's voice had given away the answer.

'Actually, Maddy, you did know her.'

'Jean Dellafield? I'm sure I didn't.'

'It's Beth, Maddy.'

Shock made her splutter disbelief. '*Beth* . . . But . . .'

'Her name was Jean Elizabeth. That's where the Beth came from, her second name.'

'Then she isn't actually married to Chris Welford?'

'Only living with him. Dellafield is her name. *Was*, I mean.'

'I . . .'

But she had nothing to say and after a moment Nesta filled the gap. 'I'm sorry, Maddy. I know it's an awful shock for you but I decided it was better you heard it from one of us.'

Maddy swallowed. 'Yes. Yes, you're right. Thank you for thinking of it, Nesta.'

A young mother was parking her push-chair outside the office window. Maddy watched her reassuring her baby that she would not be long and then opening the glass door.

Quickly she said goodbye to Nesta.

'*Not Beth*,' she was thinking. Over and over: '*Not Beth.*'

The young woman who had come in was short and dark like Beth. But she lacked the bright intelligence of Beth's brown eyes and her jaunty step. She looked drab whereas Beth had been vibrant.

She was asking after new houses in villages near the railway line. 'My husband's commuting.'

Maddy did not grasp where he was working. She went automatically to a filing cabinet and took out particulars of modern developments in two villages.

'*How can Beth be dead?*' she was thinking.

The woman glanced through the pages and began to ask questions. Maddy answered, still on automatic, adding something about the ninety-minute rail journey to Paddington from Charlbury. The woman was giving her a curious look. What had she said? Something nonsensical, judging by the doubt in the woman's eyes. No more questions were asked, the woman turning instead to look through the window at the baby and saying: 'Oh dear, I'd better go to him.' She used him as an excuse to escape.

Afterwards, Maddy noticed the woman had left the papers on Ken's desk. She snatched them up and put them away.

Then she took papers from another file and stared at them for a long time as if they might disprove what Nesta had reported.

Beth Welford had asked Maddy to sell her cottage. Three weeks ago it had been valued and photographed, the written details prepared. Beth had declined to have a board on the building and had decided to have the property advertised for the first time in the agents' monthly magazine, the March issue due out next week. She had signed a form giving the company Maddy worked for sole rights to sell it for a limited period. Maddy stared especially hard at the signature on that form. Beth Welford.

Now her client was dead and Maddy was being asked to believe she had really been Jean Dellafield all along. It wasn't just any client who had died, it was one who lived in the same village as her, campaigned with her against the lorries and shared her attempts to undermine the Wintersons' schemes. Maddy had known Beth well. Most people in the village would say that, too. But who had they really known?

As the initial shock receded, Maddy discovered her predominant emotion was neither sadness nor horror but bewilderment.

The police called at Meadow Cottage five minutes after Maddy arrived home that afternoon. She was in the bedroom, stripping off her suit and blouse and pulling on jeans and a sweater when they began ringing the bell. Jay barked at them until she let them in.

There was a mumble of names and a flashing of identity cards – Detective Sergeant Laing and Detective Constable Dodd – and then they were in the kitchen with her. She would have preferred to take them into the sitting room but she had to let Jay out into the courtyard and they followed her through.

For a second or two she lingered, checking he was heading for the garden and not proposing to do anything unforgivable to the clumps of herbs in the courtyard. When she closed the door she found Laing, a thickset Glaswegian, leaning against the dresser and Dodd, the sharp-eyed Londoner, sitting at the table with his notebook ready.

'Nice dog,' said Laing.

'I'm fond of him.'

'We've been told you took him for a walk through the forest late yesterday afternoon.'

'Yes, we were there from about five-thirty.'

'Which route did you take yesterday?'

She began gesturing as though the walls had become transparent and they could see Pipers Lane a hundred yards south of her house, then the footpaths skirting the fields and leading into the trees on the high land.

Once he had written it down, Dodd nodded for her to go on. Maddy said: 'When we got into the forest I took a path to the right and planned to do a fairly short circular route.'

Laing asked whether that was what she normally did.

'It depends on the weather,' she said. 'Yesterday it was getting dark early and, of course, it was worse in amongst the trees.'

'Why didn't you come home the same way, across the fields and up Piper's Lane?'

'I was going to, it's easily the shortest route. But, unfortunately, I'd let the dog get ahead of me and he chased off along another path. He went out to Hawksnest Copse . . .'

Laing cut in. 'Sorry, could you explain where that is, please? We're not too familiar with the area.'

Maddy pulled a couple of Ordnance Survey maps from a pile of papers on a shelf and spread them on the table. 'We need two to see the village as well as the forest. Look, here's Wychwood Forest. And this is the way Jay and I went.' She trailed a finger along dotted paths.

'In that case, you came out of the wood at a more northerly point than you entered it.'

'Yes, and so I had to go this way home.' Her finger sketched the following stage of the journey.

'Right, I've got you now. That's why you were seen walking the length of the village street.'

'And without a dog because he went across country and raced me home.'

'And won,' suggested Dodd, glancing up from his notebook.

'He invariably does.'

There was a pause while the three of them studied the map: the broad green patch that signified the forest, the brown scattering of farms and hamlets on the hill below it and the three bigger villages along the blue of the River Evenlode.

Maddy asked in a small voice: 'Where was Beth?'

Laing placed a nicotine-stained forefinger on the printed forest. 'About thirty yards south of where these two paths cross.' He allowed her time to think it before he said: 'You were close.'

'If I'd gone the way I'd planned, I would have . . . Or the dog could have . . .'

'You were close, Miss Knewton. And it's possible you were there soon after she was killed.'

Maddy covered her mouth with her hand and recoiled from the maps.

He said: 'She was strangled and left lying under the trees.' He answered her unspoken question. 'We don't think she was raped or anything like that.' Then: 'We need to know what you saw and heard on your walk.'

'Nothing's occurred to me yet. Nothing unusual, that is.'

'We'll take it from the beginning. Everybody you saw and everything you noticed after leaving the house.'

Maddy turned to the sink and filled a kettle. 'All right, but I've just got home and I need some tea. Have you been drinking it all day or would you like to join me?'

Although they had indeed drunk numerous cups during the day's interviews, they accepted. While she made it they talked to her about other things. Inconsequential as the exchanges were made to seem, the pair were hoovering up information.

'Live here with your husband, do you?' Dodd abandoned his seat at the table and strolled about to stretch his legs.

'I'm divorced but a friend lives with me. Steve Linton. He's at work now in Oxford.' She reached for the teapot.

'Unusual garden,' Dodd said, looking into the courtyard. 'Is it you or your friend Steve who does the gardening?'

'I grow the herbs, he's in charge of the rest.' For once she was glad there was no view into the garden beyond. It would not have taken two detectives long to notice that Steve was worse than lax about caring for the garden.

Then Laing's Scottish accent came in. 'What does he do in Oxford?'

Maddy was used to fudging this one. 'A friend of his owns a coffee bar. He's involved in that. Would you mind passing me those mugs, on the hooks at your end of the dresser?'

Laing, lounging against it, was neatly distracted. There would be no need for her to spell out the dreary facts of Steve's working life. With care the sergeant lifted down three mugs and set them on the table.

Dodd, still gazing out of the window, asked: 'What hours does Steve work?'

Inwardly Maddy groaned. What was the point of forcing the details from her? She said truthfully: 'Sometimes he's there from mid morning to mid afternoon and sometimes from the afternoon into the evening. This week he's working late.'

Pouring tea into the mugs she added: 'I knew Beth quite well, you know.'

Quickening interest on their faces told her they had not realised. She followed up rapidly: 'We were allies in the fight to stop lorries from the haulage depot disrupting the village. Beth was especially good at it. She was collating complaints from people – not just in this village but in the other two as well because they are nearly as badly affected as we are.'

But while she was speaking she saw the interest fading in the men's eyes and she ended lamely: 'I expect people have already mentioned all that.'

Laing leaned across to take one of the mugs. 'They all say that's how they knew her. Otherwise nobody seems to know much about her.'

Maddy winced. They were making her feel she had let them down. 'She was planning to move away from the village.'

That caught their attention. Laing said: 'You're an estate agent, right? With Rigmaroles?'

Everyone reduced the dignified Rigby March and Rollitt to that jokey sobriquet.

Maddy nodded. 'In Woodstock. Beth asked me to sell Church Cottage.'

'Did she say why?'

She frowned, struggling to remember exactly what Beth had told her. 'My impression is they were having to move because of Chris's work. That's her . . . the man we thought was her husband. He's a sales rep and he works away a lot. But I can't say whether she gave that as the specific reason or whether I deduced it. She took me by surprise, you see.'

He saw immediately. 'Because her campaigning had made it look as though she was committed to the village.'

'Exactly. She loved it here.'

Dodd sat down again and resumed writing.

Maddy said: 'But I can't tell you anything about Chris Welford. I saw far less of him because of his work. Maybe he isn't the type to pitch into a campaign, anyway. I can't tell you whether he loves the village.'

'Or whether he loved Beth?'

She shook her head. 'There's nothing I can tell you.'

'OK,' said Laing, gesturing to her to sit down. 'Let's go over your walk again.'

Routine, she thought. Question and answer. How many people with only the most tangential connection with the case would the police interview, how many cups of tea would be drunk by these two and their colleagues on the case, how many notebooks filled, how many lies told to conceal embarrassments before the killer's identity became clear? If it ever did. The English village was a place where secrets were hard to keep but truth was elusive.

Maddy asked whether the police knew of anyone else who had been in the forest while she was.

'Twenty-three seven-year-olds and two teachers,' said Laing.

'Raised £25 for a wildlife charity. *If* all their sponsors cough up,' added Dodd.

The police established their incident room in the village hall, displacing a playgroup and thus annoying the Wintersons who protested that matters should have been handled more sensitively. The under-fives, however, were not alarmed to discover policemen in their room instead of toys, and explained to each other that the men were actors making a television programme. No cameras? Well, they were practising before the cameras arrived. The children's logic was unassailable. They knew that you saw policemen in pairs, even in a big city like Oxford, and that the only time you saw lots was on the telly.

Over the next few days the trickle of gossip, begun when a man blurted to a barman that a body had been found in the forest, flowed faster. People made extra journeys to the post-box and the shop in the hope of picking up news. Trade improved in the pub which became interesting as the place where the story germinated. Other people were less evident in their quest for tidbits. They used their telephones.

Steve said to Maddy: 'You can't stop walking the dog because of what happened to Beth. Jay doesn't understand, he expects to go out as usual.'

'I know he does but I haven't the heart to take him up to the forest.'

'You mean you're afraid to go yourself.'

'No, not afraid. Not since the police started hinting they know who did it. But the idea of going up there is repellent. I don't want to be tramping around in my usual carefree way within yards of where she was killed.'

'It's not as though she's there now. The police might have yards of incident tape up there, but there wouldn't be anything frightening.'

Maddy put on her waxed jacket and called Jay. 'Sorry,' she said, and it was not clear whether she was speaking to the dog or to Steve. 'We're going down to the river.'

They passed two people in the street: an elderly widow in a trench coat who believed her dry-coated old dog reserved a special welcome for Jay as a fellow retriever; and a long-haired youth reputed to be camping in a barn. The youth smiled, said hello and went on his way.

The woman settled down to chat and the dogs indulged in ritual sniffing. 'The police went to Peter Ribston's house, you know, Maddy. They were there for ages.'

Maddy suspected the woman lived directly across The Close from Ribston. She tried to play down the significance of the visit. 'They're interviewing lots of people. They came to see me, too.'

'Ah, but that's because you were in the forest that evening. You were seen walking home, with the dog's lead but without Jay. Peter Ribston was home late that day, you know, and he was very agitated when he arrived.'

Maddy no longer had any doubt about the clear view across The Close, from one modern picture window to the other. Luckily, Jay was losing interest in the other dog and ambling away. Maddy said a hasty goodbye and trotted after him.

Peter Ribston, she was thinking, had definitely been agitated when she had seen him but that was because he was furious at being held up by a lorry. She smiled, believing it a good thing she had already described her encounter with him to the police.

At the junction of the lane and the village street Maddy hesitated and checked for lorries. There was neither sight nor sound of one so she let Jay go loping ahead down the lane. A net curtain stirred in the window of one of the cottages which kept being grazed by the lorries. As Maddy passed the back garden, Mrs Spencer, a woman of venerable age and owner of a collection of frayed blouses, called to her. Naturally, she wanted to speak about Beth. Everyone did. The murder had ousted all other topics.

They talked over the wall, swapping platitudes. In the background Mrs Spencer's television chattered.

She brushed wisps of silver hair out of her eyes and appealed to Maddy. 'Will *you* be doing it now? Arguing with the council to get the lorries stopped?'

Maddy said it had not been decided who would take over Beth's role. 'We'll be meeting soon to discuss it.'

'She came to see me, you know.'

'Yes, she was very good.'

But Mrs Spencer did not mean Beth had called to encourage her. 'She was here the day before she was killed. She'd been down below to see him.' An arthritic thumb jerked in the direction of Mound Farm, the haulage company and Rex McQuade who owned them.

Maddy tried to picture Beth confronting McQuade in his lair. She could not manage it. He was a bombastic man who wore braces and vivid striped shirts over a beer gut. Beth had been five foot two.

Mrs Spencer said: 'She reckoned she'd found out he was going to tear down one pair of these cottages and widen the lane.'

'Demolish them? How could he do that?'

'He'd have to buy them first. They're leased from the estate so it could be done without me or the other occupants having a say. Beth said that once he'd got them he could make the damage worse. Push them right over, if he wanted. She said she'd been to tell him she'd heard he was planning this and he didn't deny it. He told her to keep her nose out.'

'Did they have a row?' It was difficult to imagine: Beth a small bundle of energy standing up to the mountain that was McQuade.

'She said he threw her out. I know she can't have been with him very long because I saw her walking down and she called in to see me on her way up. Angry, she was. Bursting to tell someone.'

Jay began to bark and Mrs Spencer encouraged Maddy to go after him. 'They've got some nasty dogs minding Mound Farm these days. You don't want him getting into a fight down there.'

Maddy skipped down the lane, calling Jay who came loping to her, happy to obey on an occasion that gave him an excuse to turn away from the monsters snarling through the chain-link fence. There was a footpath leading away to the left and Maddy and Jay were equally happy to take it.

The path was muddy, forcing her to watch her steps. When she glanced up and the scene ahead flooded into focus, she caught her breath at its lambent beauty. Flashes of white flecked the inconsequential river running through fields of tender grass and a march of willows. A heron objected to Jay's presence and lifted off on indolent wings. The dog gave token pursuit as the bird beat downriver to where flags bloomed in summer.

Maddy, tracing the heron's flight with her eyes, took in the rising curve of shadowed land across the river. The shadow ended in a deeper one, the near black of the forest crowning the hill.

A breath of bitter air flowed downhill and engulfed her at the very moment she remembered Beth's murder and how close she had come to discovering the savagery. Tears welled. She had not cried for Beth. Her feelings had been a jumble of anger, distress and bewilderment but she was not a weeper and the tears had not come. Now she let them spill over her lashes and burn her cold cheeks.

'Poor Beth,' she was saying in her head. 'Poor Beth.' But even as the refrain was running on she knew she meant something else. Her tears were also for herself, for the other walkers in the woods, for everyone who lived in and cared for the villages. Her tears were because everything had been spoiled.

Jay, barking some way off, roused her from her misery. Maddy dabbed at her tears and ran downriver after him. She slipped on mud, caught her balance, tripped again. Her brimming eyes were telling lies about the path, the

whereabouts of the dog, about everything. In a shimmering
world, her judgment was awry. Skidding again, she slammed
into a willow and smeared lichen on her hands and her
sleeve.

'Jay! Jay!'

But the dog was off on adventures of his own and when
she registered another of his barks it was yet more distant.

Another icy breath. The breeze teased her hair until the
warmth was shaken out of it. It dried her face and left it
stiff with the salt of weeping. Maddy stuffed her hair down
inside her collar and hurried on, shouting now and again to
a dog she trusted to ignore her.

'If he's to give me any protection, I'll have to keep him
on a lead,' she thought.

Protection? Jay had been offered her as a pet, not a guard
dog. He was for company and for walks – not that he was
much good at providing company *on* walks. The murder was
casting him in a new role. All the boundaries in Maddy's
life had been shifted by one brutal act. Her freedoms were
curtailed and her choices ever after would be coloured by
the knowledge that murder was not an abstract thing that
happened elsewhere. Although Beth was the girl in the case,
as Detective Sergeant Hart had called her, she was not the
only victim.

Shadow eased down the hill and smothered the highlights
on the stream. Willows went from delicate green to spectral
grey. Orange lamps flickered in the village. Maddy jogged
along an alternative path leading towards the lights. '*Never
mind Jay, he can find his own way home. He always does,
so what's the point of fussing about him?*'

She worried that she did not know who else might be out
in the dusk and the lonely cold, who might be prowling the
countryside in search of another victim. She felt foolish to
have made herself vulnerable, and she grew cross. For the
sake of her own safety, would she have to forgo walks?
Would she have to anchor Jay to his lead whenever she
left the cottage?

She drew close to a garden thick with evergreens that

overhung a wall and darkened the footpath. Her nerves were on edge but this was the shortest route home and she took it, steeling herself to sprint through patches of blackness where an assailant might lurk, to head into the blind bends that might conceal a man who hated women and wished them harm. A new refrain was echoing in her mind: *'The quickest way home. The quickest.'*

CHAPTER THREE

Nightmares. He suffered nightmares, battening down the truth.

They were guilt. They were fear. They were secret. Whatever it cost, they had to be kept secret.

He taught himself to be wakeful without disturbing the sleepers, the lucky ones whose rest was tranquil whether they deserved it or not. He learned not to cry aloud the pain that woke him. When he failed, he told lies. A toothache. A twinge. A physical explanation to mask the mental agony.

Now and then he suspected he was going mad, making it up and making it worse. It grew increasingly difficult to sift real from imaginary, to remember which events he had lived through and which were the embellishments of nightmares.

What had he done, actually *done*? He could not say. Things had happened in a confusing flurry of scenes in which he had a part and yet no part. At the time, he could not interpret them. Later, he dared not.

But the dreams cast up his demons into view. Sometimes they gave him the role of chief actor. Sometimes he was a voyeur on the sidelines, a peeper through foliage, a sneaker among trees who saw what he should never have seen. The constant image was the girl on the grass, twisted in sleep. A hand, which might or might not be his hand, reached out and touched her dress.

The touch was electric.

It was the touching that woke him, with a screaming in his skull that was a child's scream, the girl's scream. In the most desperate dreams the shriek was translated into his own, real, terrified cry.

His face in the mirror was scratched. Sweat drenched the hair that fell over his forehead. He was forcing himself to stay awake, risking sleep only when alone, because he was afraid the nightmares would voice his terrors.

He knew how to keep secrets. He was isolated, estranged, wary of questions and closeness. The past had done that to him. Foolishly, he had hoped to shuck it off by playing at normal life but the rules of the game defeated him. He could not sleep, he could not think, he could not live as other people lived. He dared not confide or share. He felt himself to be a shadow, a colourless thing that was there but not there.

When his hand reached out and touched her garments, as she lay still as the forest, he knew his separateness to be profound and cruel. The nightmares, the screaming, plagued him.

CHAPTER FOUR

Chris Welford was the epitome of an anguished husband making a televised appeal for help in finding his wife's killer. Dishevelled, and casually dressed because he would not be going to work until the case was solved, he made false starts, weighed down his simple message with jargon and left sentences flapping open-ended.

He sat behind a table on a rostrum, hands trembling on the white cloth. Beside him was a senior police officer who spoke first, reciting a concise statement about Jean Elizabeth Dellafield's death and the paucity of information the police had about it. The man fielded a couple of questions from journalists who were anticipating a link to a dramatic case in the neighbouring county. Then the camera swivelled to show a close-up of Chris Welford.

'God, he looks awful,' Maddy murmured. He was a poorer, rougher version of the neat and confident salesman she knew.

Steve did not tell her to hush but he hunched forward in his chair, which amounted to the same thing.

'If anybody knows anything then I want them to . . . I mean, the police need to have all the . . . no matter whether it's any good or not . . . I mean, it's what they need . . . what we all . . . her family and her friends and me. Somebody must have seen something. Heard it maybe . . . She was . . . Well, she must have screamed or . . . But nobody's saying

anything. Not yet. I mean, the police have got to trace him.
Whoever did it . . .'

He seemed to be going on forever, going nowhere. It
was a speech without purpose except to fill the screen
with the ravaged features of a man whose bereavement
was incomprehensible to him. Maddy was silently begging
the policeman to chip in or the camera to swing away or one
of the journalists to have the humanity to interrupt and save
him. But there was no saving of Chris Welford.

Maddy flounced across the room. Steve repeated the
hunching. She wanted to rush out of the house for fresh
air or upstairs to the comfort of her bedroom. What they
were putting Chris through was terrible. She could not bear
to witness it but she could not bear to miss it. The dreadful
performance held her fascinated.

As he wept, the camera filmed the top of his head, the
patch that would be bald before he was much older and
the thicker floppy hair that quivered with each wrenching
sob. The camera waited. The journalists were quiet. The
police did nothing. An eternity passed before the producer
replaced the image with a man in a studio describing a road
scheme.

Maddy cried: 'That was a disgrace! Did you see how they
treated him? After everything he's gone through since Monday, they had to do *that*. They were exploiting him . . .'

Steve gave the slightest shrug. 'He asked to be allowed
to make an appeal. That's what they said.'

'He can't have meant them to do *that*.'

'He offered to help by making an appeal.'

'I don't believe it. Nobody agrees to being made a public
spectacle.'

'What were they supposed to do? Wait until he dried his
eyes and try again?'

'Yes. No! Cut it, I suppose. How does having him
maundering on improve their chances of finding out who
killed Beth?'

She intended the question to be rhetorical but Steve
answered. 'People will remember it.'

'Oh, they'll do that all right. I shouldn't think *I'll* ever forget it.'

She was tempted to add a highminded remark questioning how many licence payers actually wanted to see people unravelled by grief, when Steve startled her, saying: 'They think he did it.'

'Not *Chris*.'

'Husbands are always the first suspects. And the most common culprits.'

'But we're talking about *Chris Welford*. He's one of the mildest-tempered men in the village. One of the unlikeliest . . .'

But the whole business was unlikely. Beth had been popular which made her an unlikely victim. The murder happened in an especially friendly village which made the location unlikely.

Maddy reminded herself that she hardly knew Chris, certainly not well enough to advance opinions about his temperament. He frequently worked away from home and was not active in the lorry campaign. They did not have mutual friends. Although her instinct was to defend him, her grounds for doing so were weak.

Steve changed the television channel. A man in climbing gear was giving an account of a tree-top protest against the felling of a wood by road builders.

Steve said: 'What's going to happen to the lorry campaign now you've lost Beth?'

'No one's indispensable.' She felt disloyal saying so.

'Have they asked you to take over her work?'

'We haven't discussed it yet.'

'But I thought you'd been talking to Robson. Didn't he ring yesterday evening?'

'Ribston. You mean Peter Ribston.'

'That's him. Stocky man with a high colour. Lives in one of the new houses by the green.'

'Yes, he phoned me but it wasn't to cajole me into collating complaints about McQuade's lorries. In fact, I have an idea he'd rather enjoy doing that himself.'

'What did he want, then?'

'Oh, it was silly really. Peter was annoyed because someone told the police he was agitated when he drove home on Monday evening. Apparently, he took exception to the way the pair who interviewed him kept harping on it. He wanted to be sure I'd support his explanation about being in a fury because a lorry blocked the road.'

'And you did?'

'I promised him I'd already told the police.' She laughed. 'I *could* also have told him who got the police excited about his state of mind that evening.'

Steve raised an eyebrow.

She added quickly: 'Of course, I didn't say a word.'

'Not one of the Wintersons?'

'No, they're in the clear this time. Besides, I don't think they whisper behind backs. No one accuses them of that. We're scared of what they might say to our faces.'

'Your friend Nesta wasn't always keen on Ribston, was she?'

Maddy stood up and stretched her arms above her head, careful not to graze knuckles on the low ceiling. 'No good guessing, Steve. I won't play.'

'Which must mean I've got it. Nesta shopped him.'

'No, she didn't.'

'I can just imagine her doing it.'

Maddy yawned. 'Only because you have a good imagination. Believe me, Steve, Nesta has said not a word against Peter Ribston.'

'I remember her being quite caustic. He was mouthing off about grants for doing up old houses and she decided he'd got wind of Graham's plan to restore Park House. Remember?'

'That was nonsense. Graham didn't apply for a grant.' Nor, she might have added, was there much evidence of restoration at Park House.

'Doesn't prove Ribston was wrong, though, does it?'

She yawned again, not interested in breathing life into a two-year-old misunderstanding between Ribston and the Collinses. But Steve would not let it drop.

'Nesta objects to him because he lives in a brash new house in a development she didn't want built. And Ribston resents her because he's mortgaged above the plimsoll line while she lives in inherited splendour.'

The 'splendour' of Park House was a running joke between Steve and Maddy. She laughed. 'If only Graham had the wit to apply for a grant . . . But he never will.'

She let Jay out for a while before they went to bed. The dog stood in the band of yellow light that fell from the doorway, sniffed the air but then shuffled about the courtyard. Did he understand the grass in the garden would be wet after a shower?

'Go on, Jay,' Maddy urged with a note of despair.

He disregarded her and peed on a clump of thyme.

Ten minutes later Steve joined her in the kitchen. Jay was indoors and more or less forgiven, and Maddy was grappling with the door.

'What are you doing?'

'Locking up.' Her voice was distorted with the effort of forcing the bolt across.

'But you never do.'

She jiggled the bolt into the socket, just a little way because they were both painted up.

'Perhaps this is why I don't. Because it's impossible.'

'Stand back.'

He took her place and jerked the bolt another quarter inch. Rather than admit it was impossible, he offered a logical reason for not achieving more, the way men do.

'We'd better leave it there if we want to be able to get out again.'

Maddy missed his sly smile. Jay had come to watch what they were up to and she was bending down, smoothing his rich golden coat. The dog was a useful distraction when there were things she did not want to say or notice.

It did not suit her to explain to Steve how vulnerable Beth's death made her feel. Neither would she let him in on the secret of her tears and fears on the walk by the river.

She had to remain strong and cleave to her plan to get him out of the house during the spring.

'Once the better weather comes,' she had said the last time they discussed it. She was too kind to throw him out in winter when it could be true he had nowhere to go. He had talked of a better job lined up in the spring. She realised it had gone unmentioned for weeks, that it might no longer be a prospect and that it was conceivable it had never existed beyond Steve's wilful imagination. But she did not care: she had told him she would not throw him out until the better weather, the spring, and whatever means he contrived of clinging on to her and the comforts of Meadow Cottage, she would be implacable.

To admit, meanwhile, that the murder had left her afraid of being alone or that she lay awake listening for murderous housebreakers would hand him the perfect excuse for staying.

A car's headlights chequered the wall at the foot of Maddy's bed. Yellow rectangles took flight, careering across her ceiling. Like a flock of frightened birds, she thought, or cloudlets harried by a gusting wind. How had it been when the cottage was new? Had the lamps of eighteenth-century carts created similar effects or was the phenomenon due purely to the power of modern headlights?

To turn her window into playful shadows, a vehicle had to be some way off. She lay very still and strained to hear it: first a faint movement of the air; then a barely perceptible thrumming; gradually a bolder sound, identifiably wheels on tarmac; a great rush of noise as the car sped past; and then the sequence reversed until there was, once again, nothing.

Maddy opened her curtains and sat on the edge of the bed, a vantage point for looking down the village. A few indolent clouds hung beneath a meagre moon. Street lights in the village centre had gone out, switched off automatically at midnight to save electricity. She guessed an orange blaze was someone's security light. Without it she could not have made out the dark bulk of the church tower, the black shape of the overgrown hedge hiding Nesta and Graham's house, or the snaking road that . . .

She caught her breath as a figure appeared on the road. Craning, darting to the window, she peered hard but the moment had gone. She was too far away and her sighting had been fleeting. One instant she thought she saw a person on the roadway and the next there were shadows and an empty pool of porch light.

'It was a dark blob in the middle of the road. I didn't see it come from left or right, it appeared in the centre of the road. I had the impression it was an upright figure moving towards me.'

For all she knew, the thing was a dog or a fox. Distance and poor light made it impossible to be certain of anything. She willed the creature to be travelling her way and to materialise around the bend near the cottage. Ten minutes later she drew her curtains and went back to bed.

She lay, alert for footsteps that did not approach and for cars to bring her window-panes to life, but silence lay heavily on the village. She thought about the people who might be moving around at night. There was a strange old man who no longer recognised the difference between reality and delusion, and sometimes dressed and went out to wait at the bus stop at two in the morning. An elderly woman who shunned her neighbours had taken to creeping into their gardens in the early hours and leaving rotting vegetables on their doorsteps. A young girl in The Close was known to be a sleep walker who once covered a quarter of a mile in her dressing gown. And there was the long-haired student, making a point about low grants by living in a barn. He was rumoured to do all manner of odd things at any time of day or night, although Maddy could only say she often saw him when she walked the dog.

Her mind began to trail along a familiar sequence of ideas that put sleep beyond reach. From guessing about the figure on the road, it was an obvious step to thinking about the man who had left Beth dead. The thought that simmered in her mind was that not only had she narrowly missed discovering the body but she had stood a very strong chance of meeting the killer.

'I would probably have recognised him,' she thought. 'If he lives anywhere in the valley, we would have recognised each other. And then . . .'

She shied from picturing the worst, preferring to imagine a chase that ended with her bursting into the village street and being safe. Had Beth run or been denied the chance? The police had not said anything about that. The widow from The Close had told Maddy a friend of hers had overheard a man in the pub saying there was no sign of a struggle. Beth, or so the village gossips had decided, had been slain without putting up a fight.

Maddy imagined the police conferring about unreliable alibis and implausible explanations but interrupted by the crusading Wintersons who were upset at the children's playgroup being ousted from the village hall. Good and evil, the solemn and the frivolous, always co-existed.

She counted the number of cheers that would go up if the Wintersons were taken in for questioning. Of course, there was no chance they were guilty of murder or anything worse than interfering, but she totted up plenty of decent people who would enjoy having them under lock and key for a day or two.

From the Wintersons her mind hopped three decades to a childhood spring in another part of the country when ice thawed on a pond, a dead dog bobbed to the surface, and the nicest farmer in the district confessed: 'I shot him.' She could not say why the deed had been done but she remembered well the peculiar intensity of interest that spread through the valley. The general feeling was summed up by a murmur of 'There's more to it than meets the eye'.

Perhaps the grown-ups had not troubled to tell her what more there proved to be or maybe the valley continued to puzzle over it. She decided to ask her mother the next time she visited her. The subject was too cumbrous to tackle in a letter or on the telephone. Her mother was a poor letter writer who did not respond to anything in the letters she received, nor did she hear well on the telephone. Maddy believed she refused to hear well because, as she had once snapped at her, 'Australia is so far away, how *can* you expect clarity?'

The notion of leaving Exmoor for Australia had been Maddy's father's. For years now he had been an invalid but there was no talk of them coming home. When Maddy spoke to him on the telephone she heard an Australian she did not know.

From the dead mongrel in the Somerset pond she began to think about Jay snoozing downstairs in the kitchen. He had been John's last gift to her, possibly the only genuine one because the others had a knack of appearing among the items on his credit card bill when she helped him out with a cheque. Jay had been offered as a tremulous puppy when he was put into her arms.

'Snatched too young from his mother,' she had objected. The golden head had reached up and a tongue had touched her ear.

John had set her mind at ease. 'The bitch has five others and rejects this one.'

What she had since learned about Jay's nature suggested the mite had been tenacious enough to have insisted on his turn at the teats.

John had survived for three weeks after Jay entered Meadow Cottage. By then the puppy had come to regard the kitchen as his territory and was growing confident about finding his way around the courtyard, although several clumps of herbs were too high for him to see over. But then there had been The Disaster, as Maddy called it. John's former girlfriend reappeared in his life, rich from a divorce and seeking him out for fun and frolics. Maddy asked him to leave but they were speaking simultaneously. He was telling her he was going.

Stonily she had watched him pack, the girlfriend at the wheel of a sports car at the gate. Within hours of The Discovery and The Row, he was carrying the last of his belongings out of Maddy's house. As the door slammed

LESLEY GRANT-ADAMSON

behind him, her wax jacket fell off the hook where it
balanced with a walking stick. For a couple of seconds
she let it lie on the flagstones while she resisted picking
things up after John, as he had so annoyingly expected her
to do. But then she was seized with the compulsion to tidy
up this final thing and be truly finished with him. She ran
to the jacket.

Jay got there first and snuggled into it, yapping, tucking
himself into a sleeve which he transformed into an animated
sausage, and giving her a much needed laugh. Obviously, he
believed she was about to take him for a walk. When else
did he see her in that old jacket?

Laughing, struggling to extricate him, she tried to persuade him otherwise. And then it occurred to her that he
was right and a walk *was* the thing to do. Better than moping
in the lonely house, better than pouring a drink to salve her
feelings. She lifted his lead from a hook and jiggled it until,
through the cloth of the sleeve, he recognised the sound
and came wriggling backwards into view. Maddy clipped
the lead to his collar, pulled her jacket on and opened the
front door. John and his fast-driving, fast lady love were
long gone.

She had looked round the hall before closing the door.
The house was all hers again just as she imagined when
she bought the place. It was her security and a part of her
identity. She had enjoyed sharing it but it was important
that it was hers. The shock of The Disaster was raw and
she expected it to be a long time before she dared to
share again.

The puppy had tugged at the lead, coaxing her out of the
house. She drew the door shut and faced what was left of
the afternoon. Shadows of leaves pranced on the roadway
and the puppy sprang about attempting to catch them. He
made her laugh then and several other times as they took
the path towards the forest.

They walked along it only a short distance because he
was too young for a lengthy outing and his progress was
impeded by discoveries. By the time they turned for home

he had enjoyed his first encounters with numerous local insects, plants, birds and a cat, and he had been petted by half a dozen people in the village street.

Back home, he bounced straight through to the kitchen as soon as his lead was unclipped. Maddy heard him rooting about. Once her jacket was hung up Jay scampered to her and tilted his head in a query. As she spooned food into his dish she heard him pattering in the sitting room, on the stairs, in the bedrooms and bathroom. He conducted a tour of the courtyard.

'John isn't here,' Maddy said when he came indoors and licked her shoe. 'He hasn't left anything here. Except for you.'

Which, of course, had made it harder for her to forget him.

From remembering John, Maddy's restless mind moved on to Steve. They were unlike in most ways. John's busyness versus Steve's laziness. John's flair and determination opposed to Steve's capitulation in the face of adversity. John's robustness against Steve's cadaverous frailty. She suspected one of Steve's initial attractions had been that he seemed too lethargic to cultivate a mistress while sharing her bed.

Even so, the explosive ending of her affair with John had made her especially cautious about Steve. She had taken a conscious decision to keep her antennae aloft for hints of duplicity but she was too relaxed by nature to stick to it. Besides, she wanted to forget John's betrayal, not keep checking for a repeat performance. Had Steve resembled John, she would have been wise to keep up her guard. As they were utterly different, she rapidly came to believe it was pointless.

Lying in bed mulling it over, Maddy spotted one similarity that had developed between her two lovers. It was not as strong a trait as secrecy and she put it no higher than Steve showing a reluctance to bother her with details. The prime example was that he hated discussing the coffee bar. Because he found it demeaning to be a waiter, he avoided mentioning the place. Maddy hardly knew what hours he was on duty or where he went when he was not.

She hoped he was looking for work: writing letters, attending interviews and following up any contact that might result in a better job. But if she pressed for information he grew moody and sometimes stayed away from the cottage. All the fun had been squeezed out of the relationship. She knew he was taking advantage of her but when she tried to discuss it he had stormed out.

Steve had done so three times. He had slunk back while she was at work, assuming he could take up residence again as though nothing had happened. He was right because she was tender-hearted. Her antennae had twitched so severely the last time that she had wrung from him an agreement that they should part amicably before the time came when they could only do so in bitterness.

'And so,' she whispered into the darkness of her bedroom, 'here we are, under one roof but with our lives tracking separate stars. Soon – oh God, let it be soon – when the warmer weather comes, I'll have to force the issue. Pack his bags for him and dump them at the coffee bar? Give him the bus fare to Oxford? The train fare to London? I'll have to give him *something* to set him on his way. And why not? I'm the one who's always done all the giving, so why change now? Nesta's right: the only thing I haven't given him is the push.'

Like most people who knew them, Nesta had long been convinced it was all Maddy ought to have given him. Weighed down by family affairs, her roots in the valley, Nesta was automatically dubious about people who seemed to float free. Steve had troubled her from the outset with his deliberate vagueness about his origins. She liked to be able to label people: town or country, rich or poor, cultured or ignorant, honest or not. She failed to coax him to tell her anything directly and what she learned via Maddy she distrusted.

Maddy had reported that his family came from a village in Warwickshire and had lived in a series of African countries while he was growing up. Nesta required clarity. Which village in Warwickshire? What was his father's job which, presumably, had kept the family on the move? Which particular countries and for how long? Once it was clear she would not be told, her mistrust intensified.

'But, Nesta, you have Graham,' Maddy had said, making light of her friend's determined defence of her. The Collinses, and Nesta especially, had a tendency to be over-protective. 'You have Graham and I have adventures.'

'*Adventures?*'

Maddy was ready to justify and to elaborate with a comical story to turn the moment to laughter, her usual way of dealing with gloom.

But they were interrupted and the subject dropped. It lay there between them, ready to be picked up any time. Every so often, Maddy rehearsed an argument in her head. She heard herself remarking she had tried marriage and rejected it or rather it had rejected her; and as a result she had taken to adventures. She conceded they were mild adventures compared to other people's but insisted she felt fortunate that her life had not been touched by drama or its extreme, tragedy.

Maddy pulled the duvet up around her neck, made herself comfortable, remembering Ken telling her during one of their many quiet times at Rigmaroles: 'Love, according to the Greeks, is the child of chaos.'

In her life, she thought, it was the other way round.

CHAPTER FIVE

Ken was in the office, playing overnight messages, when Maddy arrived. A woman asked why her daughter's house was not selling. A man wanted to know how much money his former wife's house had fetched. Ken's young girlfriend pleaded for a phone call.

'Heartbreaker!' said Maddy, pushing him aside so she could borrow his paper-knife.

Ken grinned and reset the machine. 'Your turn or mine?'

'Yours. I made it yesterday.'

On average three days a week he claimed not to remember.

'Did you?'

'Yes, *and* went running through Woodstock to buy the milk we'd forgotten.' That was unarguable. She smiled as she slid the blade beneath an envelope flap.

Ken shrugged and went into the tiny kitchen. There was the sound of tap water, a plastic clunking, increasingly frantic hissing and, eventually, the aroma of coffee. By then Ken was purring into the telephone to Sarah, or was it Sally or Susan? He went for younger women whose names began with S. It could not be said his calls to their offices were confidential, merely that Ken spoke in a confidential tone. Women whose names began with S. seemed to enjoy that.

Maddy sorted the mail, made calls in response to letters

and took a selection of house details from the files to post them. Ken was still entertaining Sarah or Sally. Maddy poured the coffee, making faces at him as she plonked his cup and saucer on his desk.

He dropped his voice yet further and said in a winding-up tone: 'Sorry, I've got to break off. We're getting busy.'

After the briefest pause he hung up.

'Busy!' Maddy's laughter derided him.

'If only, eh?' He drank his coffee. Then, pretending pomposity: 'I think I can squeeze a few minutes in my frantic schedule for you to give me an update on the murder case.'

'Did you see Chris Welford on the regional news last night?' She hoped he would say yes so that she could skip all that.

'No. Enlighten me.'

She did, toning down the wretchedness of the performance and saying nothing of her own disgust.

Ken echoed Steve. 'I suppose they've decided he did it. It's usually the husband, isn't it?'

'It'll be especially rotten for us if he did. Victim and killer from the same community.'

'Now come on, Maddy, all you've told me is what was on the box. I want the inside stuff. What are they saying as they gather round the village pump?'

'A lot of nonsense. Speculation.'

'People must have an idea which way the police are thinking.'

'Yes, lots of ideas but they're hot air. I haven't seen a policeman since a pair interviewed me. They aren't mingling, Ken. They're either tucked away in the playroom . . .'

'The what?'

'The room the playgroup uses in the village hall.'

'Oh. Where did the kids shove off to?'

She made a warning thrust with the paper-knife. 'Don't *you* start. We've already got our own resident troublemakers saying eviction is blighting the tiny tots' lives.'

Ken rubbed his hands with pantomime glee. 'That's what

I love about villages. They're *terrible*. Pretty to look at and all that but they're dens of wrong-headedness and spite.'

'Ken . . .'

'Have they started whingeing yet about the notoriety knocking thousands off the value of their houses? They will. I give them a week. No more, a week.'

Maddy flung down the knife. 'Can I get back to work now?'

'No, you're still bottling it up. Let it go, Maddy. You'll feel better if you talk about it.'

'*I* feel fine, Ken. I'm not the one suffering from rampant curiosity.'

'Tell me and then I won't have to ask again. Your late client and her husband, what do the good village folk say about them?'

'There's a story about them having rows but nobody's sure where it came from.'

'Neighbours? The ones with a tumbler against the party wall?'

'No good, Ken. Church Cottage is next to St Mary's. On the other side there's a gap separating it from a shop.' She recited the words she had written when preparing details for the sale of Beth's house.

'Sounds nice, Maddy. Wonder whether you'll get any interest now.'

'But am I meant to be selling it or not, after what's happened?'

'Wait and see whether the husband's charged.'

'It must be the last thing on his mind, but perhaps I ought not to assume.'

Ken's eyebrows danced up his forehead. 'You're going to ask him?'

'I might. Delicately.'

'Ho, *very* delicately, I should think. "Excuse me, Chris, but am I right in thinking that if you get life you won't want to hang on to Church Cottage?" Well, perhaps you'd better not use "hang", Maddy, but . . .'

'All right, all right. That isn't *quite* what I meant.'

'And what, pray, did you have in mind?'

But the telephone rang and saved her from inventing an answer.

A friend, one of her colleagues from another office, had a query about a property on Maddy's books. It was no surprise when, instead of ringing off, Cathy demanded the latest gossip about the murder. Maddy gave a full report, including the alleged rows and the reversal executed by the dog-owning widow who had previously been poised to arrest Peter Ribston but was now convinced of Chris Welford's guilt. Maddy added that she knew for a certainty three of the bits of tittle-tattle were wrong. Cathy did not have time to listen to corrections and rang off.

Ken said: 'That story about the police finding no evidence of a struggle. You didn't tell me that.'

'Cathy asked me. Ken, I don't know the truth of this stuff. I can only parrot what people are saying. I suspect the truth escaped a long time ago. All we have is a stream of rumour.'

'OK, I accept that. But if it's correct it suggests she was either pounced on by an attacker she didn't see or else by someone she knew and wasn't afraid of.'

Maddy shuddered. 'You're as bad as Cathy. Where do you two get these theories?'

'Cathy said it, too?'

'When she rang the other day. She said it was crucial to know. For the police, she meant.'

Ken nodded. 'Quite so. The husband, then. Your friend Chris.'

She opened her mouth to object but realised she was reluctant to disclaim Chris. Instead she picked up the telephone and tapped out a number.

A machine answered her. After some electronic music Nesta, sounding as though she were watching her kitchen go up in flames, raced through her speech.

Nesta's gabbling had left a long gap before the tone. Maddy was undecided whether to leave a message. Suddenly another voice came on. 'This is also Linsey's number. If you have a message for her please speak now.'

Taken aback Maddy managed: 'Um . . . I'm ringing Nesta. Or Graham. Either of you. Could you ring me, at the office? It's about the herbs. Bye. Oh, sorry, it's Maddy.' And she hung up before she became even more incoherent.

Ken was looking in the mirror as he put on his hat. He had bought it in Moscow, before The Fall and ahead of the Russian winter. He was inordinately fond of it.

'I'm off to see that old hotel on the Stratford road. I've got this, in case you need me.' He waggled his mobile phone at her before slipping it into his pocket.

'Fine. I'm around until three when Mrs Morris wants another tour of Dunflirtin.'

This was a red brick bungalow in an area where buyers demanded stone. Ken had bet Maddy she would not shift it. It was, she had begun to fear, one of his safer bets.

He said: 'If the Peglers would just call that damned bungalow Number 34 they would have sold it a year ago. Haven't you thought of telling them that?'

'Many times,' said Maddy through gritted teeth, and watched him go jauntily down Woodstock high street, tipping his fur hat to everyone he met.

She guessed he would not return until after lunch. He had a flair for making a long outing out of a short one and the mobile telephone presented him with great opportunities. Once upon a time, several years ago when she had first gone to work with him, he had felt obliged to call her to check whether anything had happened during his absence. These days he waited for her to contact him if necessary.

It rarely was. Business was depressingly quiet. Maddy took calls from people who were fed up because they could not sell or from other people who were fed up because they could not afford to buy. Perhaps it was not wholly surprising Ken avoided ringing.

Maddy entertained herself by looking at the wall map and working out where he might go after the hotel. She rested a forefinger on the black rectangle that signified a building about five miles up the road to Stratford-upon-Avon. It was virtually on the outskirts of Enstone village. Then her finger fluttered above the map, picking a likely route for a man avoiding hurrying back to Woodstock. Where did his Sarah or Sally work? He would almost certainly fit in lunch with her or another friend.

The door opened and a young man with horn-rimmed glasses and coppery hair came in, bringing with him a blast of cold air. He seemed about twenty, too young to be a buyer in a pricey area. Was he going to try and sell her something? Was he a student seeking help with research? He loosened the yellow wool scarf that hugged his throat, a signal that he expected to be with her for some time.

'Hello. How can I help?' Maddy asked, moving away from the map.

'I'm interested in houses near Evenlode.'

Unbidden, Belloc's line, which Ken occasionally recited at her, popped into her head: '*A lovely river all alone . . . forgotten in the western wolds.*' What would the poet make of it now the villages of the valley had been invaded by Wintersons and haulage companies? Not quite so lovely. Not quite so forgotten.

Making conversation, drawing out information to help her assess his potential as a buyer, Maddy ran her eye over the leather jacket, the cord trousers with smooth patches where the pile had rubbed away, and the battered shoes. He was not dressed like a man with enough money for a house in the valley but people did not necessarily wear their wealth. Besides, the warm clothes they dragged on when the weather was bitter were usually not their smartest or newest. Looked at in that light, he was wearing what was sensible. Thick-soled shoes and a jacket that resisted the cold.

She felt a flicker of amusement at her own cheek in summing up people by appearances. How would *she* rate when she was out of her office suit and wool overcoat? The cuddly jumpers and jeans, the venerable waxed jacket and scuffed boots would definitely count against her.

'Have a chair while I go through the file.'

He plumped for Ken's instead of the small one that visitors usually sat on.

'Houses near the river go quickly,' she said over her shoulder.

Obliquely, she was advising him that owners got their asking prices without a battle. Unless he had done his research by reading advertisements he might, once he had discovered the sums involved, have to lower his sights and buy a house in Witney for a quarter of the price. Lots of people did that.

He did not follow up her point by inquiring about prices. It was as though they were of no consequence. She put details of three houses on the desk and returned to the file. She was still finding it hard to believe in him as a genuine enquirer and was inclined to think that, rather than choosing a place of his own, he was gathering details for a parent who was planning a house move.

So she rehearsed the ways young people acquired money. He might have come of age and been allowed to dip into a family trust. He might have inherited. His parents might be buying a house for him or he might be marrying and his wife's parents might be paying. He might have won the lottery or come up on the football pools. Oh, there were numerous ways . . .

Maddy held up some pages. 'Two of these are in the higher price bracket. Small country houses with a few acres.'

Although she expected him to let her put those away, he stuck out a hand. After a cursory glance he dropped them on Ken's desk. 'What are the others?'

'This one's a modern house at . . .'

His expression convinced her he did not fancy that. 'And this one's a cottage in a village street. It's small and very pretty but there's no parking space and it has a patio instead of a garden.'

Experience had taught her it was fair to stress the disadvantages of Candlelight Cottage before people were beguiled by the photograph. Lack of car space and garden had seen five buyers change their minds after drooling eagerness.

He reached for that one. Unbeguiled, his interest was again momentary. He gave a smile that might have been sheepish. 'I'd heard . . . Well, I thought you had a cottage for sale near St Mary's.'

An alarm bell rang in her skull. She did indeed have one but she did not know whether she ought to be trying to sell it. Yet a sale which started out as an enquiry in February might not be completed until summer. If the horn-rimmed young man really was a prospect, and a good one if he were a first time buyer whose transaction would be uncomplicated, she ought not to let him slip her grasp.

Maddy frowned, uncertain how to handle this. 'Ye-es,' she said, letting the doubt reveal itself in her voice. 'But I'm not sure whether the owner wants to go ahead at present. Let me take your number and call you later.'

He asked her to ring the owner straight away. Maddy tapped Chris Welford's number.

The phone at Church Cottage rang out, allowing her time to wonder whether she actually wanted to have this slightly mysterious young man living in what had been Beth's home.

Just as she was lowering the handset, a cracked voice spoke. Maddy found herself faltering, too. It took a couple of confused seconds before she was understood, saying: 'Chris? It's Maddy Knewton here. About selling your house.'

'Oh. Hi, Maddy.'

'I'm sorry to bother you.' Very sorry. The call was a bad idea. Worse, she had at her elbow an earnest young witness to her discomfort.

'What did you say you were ringing for?'

'Your house. I need to know whether you want to sell it.'

'*Sell* it?

'Yes because Beth . . .'

'Beth . . .

'The thing is, Chris, I need to know. As soon as you're

ready to take a decision, I mean. About whether you want me to sell it.'

His telephone slammed down.

Abashed, she struggled to conceal what had happened but knew it was wasted effort. Although her visitor was pretending to be absorbed in the details of the pretty house without car space or garden, he could not have avoided hearing.

'Sorry,' she said. 'That was rather a muddle and I didn't get the answer we wanted.'

She felt a callous fool for having contacted Chris, especially as she had been so appalled by the way broadcasters had treated him.

The young man was cajoling. 'Let me see the details, anyway.'

'Sorry, I'm not in a position to offer them yet. It's important the owner gives the go ahead.'

He looked bemused. 'The owner must have done, otherwise why would . . . ?'

The door burst open and Mrs Morris, the woman who was dithering over whether to buy Dunflirtin, heaved her enormous weight up the step and waddled into the room. It was several hours before her appointment and she was plainly burdened with news.

Maddy made a split second decision. While greeting Mrs Morris and gesturing her to a chair, which the woman overflowed lavishly, Maddy thrust at him the details of Church Cottage.

'Just to glance over, mind,' she said.

Mrs Morris had begun talking. Her voice was on a scale to suit her body. Ken swore her laughter threatened to crack windows and warned that if she bought Dunflirtin she would huff and puff and blow the house down.

To Maddy's amazement Mrs Morris suddenly slapped her hands on her rheumatic knees and declared: 'Maddy, love, if they'll take that stupid name off the gatepost, I'll buy it.'

Maddy squeaked surprise. 'You will?'

'I said to Jack – my brother, you know . . .'

Yes, Maddy knew. He was the usual sounding-board for his sister's opinions.

'. . . "I've got it, Jack," I said to him. "I know what's holding me back. It's that name," I said. I might be an old fool, Maddy, but I couldn't abide having to tell people I lived at Dunflirtin. Writing it on forms. Seeing it on envelopes. It would get me down.'

Cautious, Maddy remembered that previously Mrs Morris had been convinced that the boiler-house obstructing the view from the kitchen window would get her down. Likewise the creeping buttercup strangling the rockery. Ditto the street lamp positioned to prevent the bedroom being completely dark. And also the bathroom that was too cramped to contain a decent airing cupboard; the wood block floors that required polishing; traffic noise from the new road slashing through the fields; and goodness knows what else besides. Mrs Morris had a habit of being got down.

Maddy gulped. 'Have you really made up your mind to have it?'

She was afraid she might awake from slumber and discover the imminent renaming of Dunflirtin to be naught but a dream.

'Yes, Maddy, I'm definite.' Beaming triumph set all five chins wobbling.

'Well, hooray,' said Maddy. And smiled at her a moment, giving Mrs Morris time to say it was all a joke; giving herself time to wake to reality. Then, when nothing happened, she went on: 'I'll let the Peglers know, shall I?'

Mrs Morris nodded. Excessive wobbling.

Maddy reached for the Peglers' number, and that was when she noticed that her other visitor had disappeared. She hardly blamed him because he had lost her attention. Mrs Morris was too much in every way. By her volume, both physical and vocal, she dominated. And, anyway, on this occasion she had said what Maddy had waited months to hear. No, she would not be hard on herself for letting the young man slope off without a farewell.

Half an hour later, after she had spoken to a pair of

jubilant Peglers and had assisted a resolute Mrs Morris down the step into the street, she scooped up the papers from Ken's desk and returned them to the file. With a flash of anger she discovered that the details of Church Cottage were missing.

The petty theft upset her, coming on top of the débâcle of her telephone call to Chris Welford. She was unsure what to do about Chris. Make a placatory telephone call? Go to see him? She decided she ought to go because such damage was more easily mended by talking face to face.

Weeks later, when she thought about this day, she tended to overlook Mrs Morris's pivotal role in it. Many things happened, which were uncomfortable at the time and turned out to be worse, and it was easy to forget the Peglers' unbounded delight and Mrs Morris's joyful conversion from waverer to decision-maker, let alone Maddy's own satisfaction at a deal made. To crown it, she had also won her bet with Ken.

The first thing that swept Mrs Morris out of her mind was a telephone call from him to say he had crashed his car at Chipping Norton.

She nearly blurted: 'Whatever were you doing in Chipping Norton!' Instead she managed: 'Oh, no! Are you all right?'

'Had a nasty jolt. Too soon to say what it's done.' Sparing with words, he winced at each one.

'Where are you?'

'The hospital in Chippy.'

'Are they keeping you in?'

An agonised pause. Then: 'Don't know.'

'Ken, is there anything I can do? Phone your family?'

He ground his teeth through a longer speech. 'All taken care of. Car, too. Afraid I left you to last, Maddy. Sorry. You must have been wondering what had become of me.'

She had not. She had been imagining a tête-à-tête in a country pub with a Sarah or a Sally, a Susan or a Sandra.

She said: 'Don't forget to let me know whether they send you home or keep you.'

'Promise. Anything happen while I was out?'

She edited the day down to one bright moment. 'One thing. This will put a smile on your face. Mrs Morris made an offer and the Peglers accepted it.'

'Good grief. Are you sure?'

'Totally sure. The widow Morris imposed one condition and the Peglers agreed to it.'

Ken rallied sufficiently for a joke. 'They agreed to move the bypass?'

'They agreed to stop calling the bungalow Dunflirtin.'

Ken began to laugh but it rapidly changed to coughs and groans and he spluttered an apology and hung up.

Maddy stared at the receiver in her hand. 'What is it about me and phones today?'

She checked Ken's diary. He had written down an appointment for six that evening. A man called Watson was expecting him at Felden Farm for a valuation. Watson's office number in Oxford was noted as well as the farmhouse. Maddy rang to see whether Ken had cancelled the appointment. A grudging secretary said not. Maddy explained about the accident and asked her to say that she would keep the appointment instead of Ken.

The woman sighed. 'All right, *if* I hear from him, which I probably won't. He's out at a meeting all afternoon.'

'Does that mean he'll go straight home afterwards?'

There was a sarcastic laugh. 'I wouldn't know. He doesn't tell me about his private life.'

Maddy conjectured a time when he had. She said: 'I'll leave you my mobile number in case he needs to reach me after I've left the office.'

With the deepest reluctance the woman echoed the number, adding: 'Not that I expect he'll get it, mind.'

Ringing off, Maddy wondered whether the piece of paper was winging its way into a waste-bin. Or whether Oxford's most recalcitrant secretary had bothered to write it down.

Everything went wrong. She was caught in heavy traffic, made a wrong turning and tried to cut across country. Signposts were missing or else obscured. Drivers familiar with the lanes zipped along at dizzying speeds while she, mindful of Ken's calamity, crept. All the while she was expecting her telephone to ring and Mr Watson to complain she was late.

The sky darkened. Wind rolled down the hills. She blundered from one unmarked crossroad to another, stopping a few times to check her map, losing time and losing heart. When her car clock was reading six-thirty, she pulled into the gateway of a field and cut her headlights. A black pool, created by a couple of lofty trees and a crooked wall, swallowed her. Beyond it the valley was shrouded in half-light. Maddy scanned for lights from isolated houses, fairy lights on a pub, signs of a village on her side of the valley. There were only slanting fields of greyness sinking towards night.

She resolved to ring Watson and beg directions, although it would hurt her pride to admit the delay was entirely due to her mistakes. Then she discovered her telephone battery was dead.

Maddy was flinging the useless telephone onto the rear seat when she became aware of a man creeping up behind the car. He was by her rear bumper, nearly close enough to grab her door handle. With frantic movements she snapped the door lock and lunged to secure the passenger side. His shadow fell across her but she was already letting in the clutch and lurching the car up the road.

Her breath came in angry rasps. She was angry with him for scaring her, and angry with herself for being lax. Why park with the doors unlocked? Why set out with dud batteries when a mobile telephone was her only protection? Why get lost? This part of the county was her patch, she ought to do better than this.

Shunting her anger to him again, she glanced in her mirrors to see what he was doing but the lane behind her might have been a void. Her world was shrinking fast and would soon extend no further than the bleaching beam of her headlights.

She approached the next junction too fast and slithered

to a stop with the car jutting into the other lane. She turned left, pulled in when she had moved a few yards away from the junction, and stopped.

'Calm down,' she said aloud. 'It was nothing. He was probably walking home, that's all.'

But he would have been in the centre of the lane if that were true. He would have had no cause to get close to a vehicle in a gateway, no need to loom beside her and terrify her.

The argument ran on in her head. 'Forget it. If he was coming to the car it was probably to ask whether you needed directions. It doesn't matter what he was doing, it was a scare but it's over.'

'*Except that it isn't over. I'm lost. I can't find the client and I don't have a phone.*'

'You've been at this job for years and nothing bad has happened. There's no reason to imagine it will now.'

'*Huh! I've never had a client murdered before.*'

And that is where she stuck, with the idea that Beth had been killed in a lonely country place a few miles away and her killer was at large.

Maddy peered around carefully. Barren winter fields with the colour leached from them. Stone walls reduced to black strands cast over the land. She continued her miserable journey.

Not long after, as she was trailing up a hill, a village glinted to her right. She had given up Felden Farm and aimed to get her bearings in the village and head home. But, as she slowed at the lane to the village, a dash of white caught her eye. A fingerpost pointed up a track climbing the bank on the other side of the road. Black lettering read: Felden Farm. Maddy made the awkward turn up the farm track.

Her professional interest surfaced. It promised to be an attractive old Cotswold farmhouse, the sort of thing for which there was always an enthusiastic market. She understood Watson owned the house but not the neighbouring farm. Although, if he had a couple of acres and a bit of stabling . . .

Maddy pulled into the yard in front of the house. In daylight there would be long views but, disorientated, she was not confident whether they were to the south or south-west. Wind whipped the car door, bumping it against her shin. It tugged her coat and made a frenzy of her hair. As she fought her way to the porch, the valiant creeper that survived on the front wall lashed at her.

She tucked herself into the shelter of the porch and felt for a bell. It eluded her but she found a knocker and thudded it half a dozen times. Truth seeped in slowly. She stamped back to the car for a torch.

Maddy pressed it against the glass of an unfurnished room. Soot had fallen down a chimney and spattered bare floorboards. She played its beam along a hall, as far as uncarpeted stairs.

Watson was not late home. He did not live at Felden Farm. Nobody did. Nobody had done so for a long time.

CHAPTER SIX

The tension struck Maddy as she opened her front door. Jay came into the hall, head down and tail hardly daring to wag a welcome. Voices started up in the sitting room, awkwardly, as though they had broken off when they heard her.

'It isn't like that.' Steve was emphatic, a man despairing of convincing the person with whom he is arguing.

'Hi!' Maddy called, pausing to pat the dog. No one answered her.

She heard Nesta, attacking but too low for her words to carry.

Then Steve again. 'It doesn't matter that *you* don't understand.'

'There's no need to . . .'

They stopped as Maddy appeared. She was bright, pretending she had not caught their drift.

'I'm *so* glad to be home. You wouldn't believe what sort of a day I've had.'

She went towards Nesta to hug her but Nesta's face was taut.

Steve said: 'Where have you been, Maddy?'

She swivelled to look at him, his hair anyhow, eyes blazing a challenge.

'Working,' she said simply, to defuse the row.

Nesta said: 'I got your message and I . . .'

Steve repeated: 'Where have you been?'

Nesta pushed on. '. . . I wanted to . . .'.

With coruscating sarcasm Steve said: 'Nesta says she's come to photograph herbs.'

Caught between them, Maddy raised her hands to placate.

'Look, I'm sorry I'm late but I haven't been gallivanting around in the dark for the fun of it.'

Nesta relaxed a shade. 'We were worried that we couldn't get hold of you on the phone. Graham felt one of us should look in. I asked Steve to try your mobile but he said it wasn't answering.'

He interjected: 'It *wasn't*.'

Maddy confessed, making light of it. 'I was lost in the deepest Cotswolds and the phone was dead. When I stopped to look at my map I got into a ridiculous state because I noticed a man in the road. It's the Beth thing, it's really shaken me. I'm seeing murderers lurking everywhere. I was even scared walking the dog by the river the other day.'

Nesta said: 'Hardly surprising. You shouldn't visit out-of-the-way places on your own, especially in the dark.'

Avoiding the ramifications of it having been Ken's appointment, Maddy said: 'It goes with the job, Nesta. If a client asks me to meet him at his house, I have to.'

'Well, I hope you make a fat commission out of this one.'

'Oh, he wasn't there. The farmhouse was empty, my nerves were in rags and I had to find my way home. Let's have a drink, shall we, while I tell all?'

'No, thanks,' Nesta said quickly. 'I must get home now I know you're safe. Graham will be . . .'

She was edging out of the room as she spoke. Steve's scowl eased into a smirk. Maddy showed Nesta out.

Before vanishing into the night Nesta pointed to an egg box on the bench in the hall. 'Oh, I brought you a few eggs. Not a full box, I'm afraid. The hens aren't too enthusiastic at this time of year.'

Maddy took the box into the kitchen. She had left half a bottle of wine in the fridge but it was now standing empty beside Steve's dirty plate. Maddy opened another bottle, tossed ice cubes into a glass and tipped wine over them.

This was not at all what she wanted. She wanted companionship and comfort, warmth and someone kind enough to hand her a drink and put a meal in front of her. She had spent a wretched evening, was exhausted and needed to be cared for. Instead there was Steve. A couple of times he spoke to her from the distance of the sitting room but she ignored him.

She put his plate into the dishwasher, wiped the table and checked in the fridge to see whether he had eaten her supper as well as his. Yes. He had done it before. It was easy if you were too lazy to cook rice or pasta to supplement the meat or vegetables. Suppressing a sigh, she opened the box of eggs. Four. Her supper would be a plain omelette.

Going upstairs, to change out of her suit, she could see directly into the bedroom Steve used. He had not straightened his bed. Clothes were tumbling from a chair. Magazines and shoes littered the floor. It was a serious mess. The room smelled rank and she was tempted to throw open the window and let the sharp wind scour it. Instead she bit her lip and hurried to her own room.

When she had changed she noticed how reluctant she was to go downstairs. Avoiding him. Scared of him. Hating having him in her house.

Suddenly she reached the end of her patience. She dashed down and into the sitting room where he was slouched in an armchair, not doing anything, not drinking the glass of wine on the table beside him and not even troubling to look at her. He was just there and the sheer fact of his being there was more than she was willing to accept.

'Steve, I want you to leave.'

The hurt little boy look came over him. 'We've talked about that.'

'I mean now.'

'*Now?*'

'Well, not this minute. Not exactly. Tomorrow.'

'Oh, come on, Maddy. You can't expect me to move out tomorrow.'

'I can.'

'No. I'm not going.'

'But Steve . . .'

'It's the worst possible time.'

She folded her arms, looked resolute. 'Steve, every time we talk about it you say it isn't a good time.'

'There's a murder hunt on. What's it going to look like if I go in the middle of that?'

She frowned. 'Oh. You think it would look suspicious? As though you were running away?'

'It's the way people think.'

She attempted to rescue her plan. 'I'll say I threw you out.'

But he could see he had undermined her certainty. 'I'll go as soon as the police charge someone. Not before.'

Maddy hesitated long enough for him to be sure of his victory.

'He's made a fair point,' she was thinking. *'There's no sense in having the police haul him in.'*

She began calculating the odds on Chris Welford being charged before the week was out.

On Friday morning Maddy went to see Chris Welford. He was haggard but a surge of indignation lent him fresh vigour.

'I wonder you've got the nerve to come here.' He gripped the edge of the door, poised to slam it in her face.

'Chris, I'm sorry about yesterday. I've come to apologise.'

'And to ask if I want to sell.'

She wished he could bring himself to let her in. Passers-by were watching the confrontation.

'No. Well, it's because Beth . . .'

He coiled for attack. 'That's what you said. Because Beth's dead you're anticipating me selling up.'

'*No.* That's not what I meant. I'm not touting for business.'

'That's what it sounds like.'

'Please, let me explain.'

But he did not invite her in and she had to do her explaining on the doorstep.

'Beth asked me to wait until the next property guide . . .'

'I don't understand.'

'Sorry. I'm not making myself clear.'

'No, you're not. You keep mentioning Beth and selling.'

'I need to find out whether you want to go ahead with selling the cottage. Beth asked me not to advertise it until the next property guide comes out, and that's next week.'

'Sell this cottage?'

'Of course I expect you'll say no, in view of what's happened . . .'

'Sell it?'

'. . . but I can't act on my own initiative. Without Beth, it has to be your decision.'

He swayed and his grip tightened on the door. Maddy put out a hand, afraid he was going to collapse.

For a long moment he studied her. Then: 'Did you say Beth was going to sell the cottage?'

Her heart sank. 'You were moving because your job was taking you away.'

But as she spoke she knew it was untrue. His devastated face proved it. Maddy watched him struggling to believe the hurt Beth had meant to do him.

She said a few words to round off the conversation and allow her to escape. It hardly mattered what they were, he was too stunned to listen.

Realising he was bound to have questions later, she left her business card. 'Call me when you're ready to talk, Chris.'

Aghast, she retreated. The woman who walked the retriever waved at her as she drove by. Peter Ribston hooted his car horn. But she was oblivious. Instead of driving on to Woodstock she pulled up outside Meadow Cottage.

Steve was drinking tea. He half-rose as she flung herself onto a chair across the kitchen table from him.

'I've had a sickening conversation with Chris Welford. God, I can't believe how appalling it was.'

'I thought you were in Woodstock.'

'I had to see him first. Could you pour me one?'

He weighed the teapot in his hand, added a splash of hot water from the kettle, swished it around and poured.

Maddy said: 'Beth asked me to sell their house and I've just discovered he didn't know.'

'Did you find a buyer?'

'No.' She outlined what had gone on.

He said: 'That must have been one hell of a conversation you two just had.'

Maddy's eyes flashed. 'It isn't funny.'

'I'm not laughing. I'm picturing you . . .'

'I know what you're doing. And it isn't funny, Steve.'

There was a maddening hint of amusement in his eyes. Maddy avoided it by looking down into her mug. Reading the leaves. Divining her future.

After a moment he said: 'They weren't the cosy couple you like to think. Cosy couples don't sell the roofs over each other's head.'

'Mmm. I'm afraid you're right.'

'And therefore they probably were having the rows everyone's gossiping about.'

Maddy preferred not to pursue that. It would lead to criticism of Nesta whom he liked to accuse of fomenting rumour. Remembering Ken's remark about villages being hotbeds of wrong-headedness and spite, she added: '*Mischievousness, too*'.

Aloud she said: 'I wonder why Beth owned the house? Most couples share.'

'It's badly cracked, isn't it? The facade of the Welfords' happy relationship?'

Maddy disliked the way he persisted. Although he was scathing about scandal-mongers in general, he was taking pleasure in whipping up rumours about the Welfords. It

68

was depressing to think he was doing it for the sake of contradicting her. Rather than take him up on it, she grimaced at the clock.

'I shall be late all day because of this.'

'Have you got much on?'

'Oh, the Felden Farm mess to sort out. An appointment to show a woman a flat. Plus whatever I can squeeze in of Ken's work.'

'Where's the flat?'

'Netherlands.'

'Isn't that where Douglas Martin lived? The Thirties film star?'

'Yes. Ken says it had a reputation for wild showbiz parties. But when Fiddlers, the property developers, bought it three years ago it was nearly derelict. They carved it into over-priced bijou flats.'

'Are they selling?'

'Several have but the owners keep them for weekend retreats. Not quite what the planners intended.'

She carried her mug to the dishwasher but it was full of clean crockery from the load washed overnight.

Steve said: 'I was going to empty it.'

He was getting worse. The tiniest effort seemed too much for him. She wondered whether the fever was continuing to affect him, causing debility and confused thinking. Perhaps she ought to remind him they were going out that evening.

'We have to be at the Collinses' at half-seven, Steve. You will make it, won't you?'

'Wouldn't miss it.' Wide-eyed innocence, defying her to lecture him about being nice to Nesta.

As she drove to Woodstock she tuned the radio to a romantic intermezzo. What would it be like, she wondered, to make one's living writing soul-stirring music? Dreaming about it occupied her mind for the rest of the way.

During the day Ken rang from his hospital bed to report three fractured ribs. Cathy rang from Witney to ask after Ken, and so did colleagues from other branches. Mr Pegler, a determined little man with a military bearing, came on the line and announced in his rich Cotswold burr that he had unscrewed the Dunflirtin name-plate and created a pale patch. He sought Maddy's advice about repainting the gateposts.

Knowing how easily Mrs Morris was 'got down', Maddy thought it wise. 'It couldn't do any harm, Mr Pegler.'

'I've got a can of paint and a free afternoon so I'll press on with it before the rain comes.' An old countryman, he always had an eye for the weather.

Mr Watson was not in his office and his secretary excelled at unhelpfulness. Maddy vowed to waste no more time on Felden Farm.

Superficially, the Netherlands outing was a success. Felicity Fisher, a glamorous company director in patent high heels, made enthusiastic remarks. The view from the windows! The colour of the walls! The quality of the built-in furniture! Oh, everything earned a word of praise! But Maddy noticed the puckering forehead and pursed lips when the house was 'further from the road than I expected', and 'I suppose those Alsatians belong to someone who lives here'. Maddy doubted that delight in Netherlands would last the journey to London.

Fortunately, Ms Fisher had not inquired why Alison Black, the vendor, was selling months after moving in. One reason was that it felt remote during the week when the weekenders were away. Another was the dogs who had held Miss Black at bay until their owner arrived. He was hoping they would catch a genuine wrongdoer one day because it would justify his case for guard dogs at Netherlands.

The dogs were also the reason Rigmaroles was handling the resale instead of the company who marketed the new flats. Nervy Miss Black was adamant she had been promised there was a covenant restricting the ownership of pets. Her story was that when she protested about the trio of Alsatians, no one referred to them as pets. They had become guard dogs, and there was nothing in the covenant about those.

After Netherlands, Maddy drove Felicity Fisher to the railway station in Oxford. It seemed an elaborate courtesy but, in fact, Maddy needed to visit her head office a little later. She used the spare time buying replacement batteries for one of her radios and decided, on a whim, to drop into the coffee bar where Steve worked. She hurried along Cornmarket Street, weaving through pedestrians, breaking into a run for a few yards now and then.

'Must be six months since I was in there,' she thought, as she waited to cross a traffic-clogged street.

Between vehicles she caught flashes of a pub, a bookshop, a men's clothes shop and a florist's. The coffee bar was further along, in a position that was frankly less favourable for passing trade. She recalled Dennis, who owned it, telling her he intended to create a niche for a coffee bar in that location.

When there was a gap in the traffic, pedestrians surged into the road where they met and eddied around those surging in the opposite direction. A minute later, Maddy was outside the coffee bar. It was closed. A card in the window said it was supposed to open from 8.00 in the morning until 11.00 at night. Shielding her eyes with her hand, she peered in.

Blond wooden furniture. Chrome light fittings. All pristine and elegant but nobody was in the kitchen or at the counter where the espresso machine perched. Disconcerted, she moved away.

In the shoemender's next door there was a queue and a clamour of machinery. She did not wait. On the other side of the coffee bar were offices. Solicitors' offices. She might be recognised. Estate agents and conveyancing clerks swam in the same pool and someone would grasp her problem: where was Steve when he was supposed to be working in the coffee bar?

A clock struck the hour. She had mistaken the time and risked being late for her meeting. Breaking into a trot she set off in the direction of Rigby, March and Rollitt.

The meeting was a routine gathering of staff to discuss developments in the market and how the company should respond. Business had been in the doldrums for ages but Clive Rollitt, the senior partner, always announced an upturn. Maddy avoided catching anyone's eye while he was speaking lest mirth erupt. As negotiators' incomes depended in part on commission they were not misled by his optimism. For political reasons he wanted it to be true. For practical reasons they knew it was not.

Ken was on the agenda, too.

Clive said to Maddy: 'I'm sure you can handle Woodstock until he's fit.'

Maddy agreed. A problem might arise if Ken stayed away for another three weeks because she was planning a holiday but she did not prolong the meeting by sending everyone down that conversational path. Clive had already let the meeting drag on, ensuring she would be caught in the rush hour.

Jay was scrabbling on the flagstones when she eventually got home. He flew through the gap as the door began to open. Desperate, he cocked a leg against the wall of the house. The stream of urine left an ugly stain. Then he came tail-wagging to her.

Maddy stroked his head with one hand as she hung her shoulder bag on a hook in the hall.

The back door was locked although not bolted. She had tried to persuade Steve to bolt it by day as well as at night but he did not see it as a sensible precaution while a killer was on the loose.

She called out. No reply. She ran up a few stairs until she could see into his room. On this occasion she took no pleasure in having the house to herself because Steve was invited to the Collinses' and she was keen to prise out of him the truth about his work at the coffee bar. She was ashamed to remember how she had once dismissed Graham's suspicions.

Maddy was pulling garments out of her wardrobe, matching up shirts and blouses and rummaging for shoes to go with them. Jay, taking advantage of her current mood, had boldly accompanied her into her bedroom. When she eventually noticed him, nuzzling the pink and green bundle that was her favourite skirt, she gave him an absent-minded pat.

She wanted to wear the skirt for a change. Winter clothes had been worn for too long and everyone was bored with them. Nesta and Graham would have some smart people at Park House this evening. Well, 'people from London', which made Maddy imagine them to be smart.

Leaving Jay to patrol the landing, she shut herself in the bathroom.

'Soon he'll hear Steve's key and he'll bark and race downstairs.'

But she had heard no barking by the time she stepped into the shower. Afterwards, drying herself, she concentrated on listening for sounds from the kitchen or from the bedroom where Steve might be hunting down a suitable shirt to wear on his enforced evening out.

When she had rubbed her hair dry and came onto the landing in her towelling robe, Jay was flopped there. He opened one eye and lifted his head as she stepped over him.

'Perhaps I missed a phone call.' She checked the answering machine. There was no flashing light signalling a message. On impulse she pressed number three on the telephone's memory which automatically dialled the coffee bar number.

When she had designated the coffee bar one of the handful of numbers stored in the memory, she had done it as kindness to reassure Steve of his importance to her. He had argued it was unnecessary but she had insisted. She had seldom used it.

A few times she had failed to get through and he had explained there was a problem with the line. On other occasions he had answered, rather than Dennis or anyone else. He had been curt, discouraging, creating the impression he was putting on an act for those overhearing his end of the conversation.

'Where Steve's concerned, everything's an act.'

Or to put it the way Nesta had: 'He's a sham.'

'Sham or not, you're needed now.'

Maddy turned to go upstairs and in that instant felt the sensation of being watched.

With a sharp intake of breath, she clutched the robe closer to her, holding the neck so that it no longer gaped and exposed pink cleavage.

The courtyard was dusky grey near the house, deepening to night where light from the uncurtained window failed to penetrate. She got it into her head that a man was spying on her from the gateway to the garden. She flicked off the kitchen lights, bolted the door and then approached the window. No movements, nothing to encourage her to believe she had seen a face in the gateway.

The fridge started up. Maddy looked at the luminous hands of the wall clock and fled.

'A fine guard dog you are!' she chided, stepping over the dozing animal.

Two minutes later she was dressed and ready to leave. The waistband of the pink and green skirt nipped her and she eased it once or twice, vowing to starve an inch off her waistline.

She hovered near the telephone. Ring Nesta to say she would be late? Or the coffee bar on the off chance it had opened? Both, perhaps.

Jay kept nudging her. He wanted a walk. It occurred to her that taking him was not a bad idea. Nesta and Graham would be generous with the wine and leading a dog home made better sense than driving. She did not fancy walking anywhere without an escort.

He threw himself into paroxysms of joy as she reached for his lead. Within seconds he was towing her down the lane.

Every so often she looked round, hoping to spot Steve striding to catch them up and fearful of seeing instead a spying figure. The feeling of being under observation revived at every blind bend and corner round which an attacker might spring. Jay's calmness was a comfort. Surely a dog would warn her if anything unpleasant were about to happen? Wouldn't he stop, raise hackles, issue a menacing growl, bare his teeth and display the classic signs that meant 'don't come near'? She realised she had never known him do any of those things except to menace cats.

As they approached Piper's Lane he strained to lure her towards their riverside walk. She won the tussle but after a few yards he seized on a fresh idea and wanted to take a footpath. Again she fought him and won.

'This is becoming a tug of war. I'll be exhausted when we get there.'

Across open land she saw her porch light but no lights from her windows. Then the road twisted and the cottage was out of sight.

No Steve, no pursuers. The only person on the road was Maddy, uncharacteristically nervous and accompanied by an energetic dog who could not understand why he was on a lead. Beth's death had changed her attitude to her freedom. For the sake of feeling secure, she was conceding it inch by inch. Matters that had not previously troubled her were now important. Bolting locked doors, for instance. Carrying her telephone everywhere. Keeping her dog beside her.

'Jay would warn me, wouldn't he?' Doubt circled. *'I'm not deluding myself, am I? He's alert to danger and prepared to protect me, isn't he?'*

But he was only John's gift to her, a pet rather than a guard dog. Would he necessarily recognise danger if they met it? Beth had not put up a struggle, apparently because her killer was a man she knew. A dog could be tricked as badly as Beth had been. And Jay was the type to run off and have a good time instead of coming to her when she yelled.

The long hedge of Park House loomed. The dog's pace quickened. This time when he chose to deviate from the village street she let him have his way. By the meagre light of the moon, they marched up the pot-holed drive. Jay picked a safe route and neither of them put a foot wrong.

Two unfamiliar cars were there. Maddy hauled on the lead and brought Jay to a halt. She eased her waistband before strolling the last few yards so that nobody would guess at the helter-skelter pace of the earlier stages of her walk.

CHAPTER SEVEN

The Collinses' attempt at a formal dinner party entailed opening up an ill-favoured room burdened with Nesta's aunt's heavy brown furniture.

Maddy had a foretaste as Linsey, the lodger from the *asram*, ushered her into the hall with smiles and much bowing and bobbing. Each bow and each bob released a gust of incense from Linsey's flapping garments. She had improved her appearance. Her hair was newly washed, her mouth was a painted rosebud and her eyes sparkled from pools of kohl. A long green silk scarf was draped across her throat. Behind her its ends copied each bob and bow.

Linsey's welcome was feigned surprise. 'Maddy!'

'Hello, Linsey.' She added a reflex: 'How are you?'

Linsey leant her head to one side and gave little shrug. Maddy feared she was about to be told. Wriggling out of her jacket, she thrust it at her.

Linsey reverted to smiling. 'Let me take your . . .'

'He's called Jay.' Maddy pushed the lead into her hands, too.

'. . . dog,' said Linsey, the smile collapsing.

Through an open door Maddy saw two women and a bulky man poised halfway between a dining table and a fireplace, seemingly unable to make up their minds where to settle. A short woman with tall hair appeared to be wearing an orange woollen dress topped by a warm wrap. The other was in thick trousers and a jacket. As smoke billowed towards them, they edged away from the fireplace and nearer the table. The woman in orange coughed.

Graham poked his head around the kitchen door and hissed at Linsey who dumped Maddy's jacket on a chair and rushed at him with Jay.

Maddy heard an exasperated: 'What am I expected to do with this dog.'

And Graham's simultaneous: 'You've been at the onions again.'

Linsey tossed her head. Two wands of green silk also tossed. 'I can't keep him here.'

Graham looked beyond her and nodded to Maddy.

Linsey said: 'Where shall I put him?'

'In your room,' said Graham with malice.

'*No!*'

'Has the lord taken against dogs now? As well as onions?'

'But . . .'

Graham snapped that if Jay were left in the hall he would escape the next time the door was opened. He shunted his attention to Maddy. 'Feel like giving a hand?'

The kitchen was as thick with steam as the other room was with smoke. Nesta, wearing the red apron, was stirring a pan. She grinned at Maddy. 'This isn't as chaotic as it looks.'

'Yes it is,' said Graham. 'Linsey's expunged all trace of onions from the house. Can you believe this? Two chefs without an onion between them? Apparently, Lord Bakshish took against them and so it's Linsey's duty to steal ours and destroy them.'

Nesta gave him a 'Not now' look. Then: 'Why don't you take that tray into the dining room, Graham?'

He picked up the tray. On it were several pottery dishes containing unusual nibbles which Maddy deduced were Collins inventions. She held open the door and snatched a view of Linsey and Jay sulking in the hall.

Nesta put a lid on a pan, turned off the heat and offered Maddy the spoon to lick. 'Enough seasoning?'

Maddy employed the appreciative Mmm that was so

useful on her visits to the Collinses' kitchen. She dropped the spoon into a bowl of washing-up water in the sink.

'Nesta, I have to apologise for Steve. He's either going to be late or not come.'

'Oh?' Nesta's eyes narrowed. Bustling about, checking pans and counting plates, she was patently alert to Maddy's news.

Maddy interpreted her curiosity. 'No, I don't think he's left me. He went to Oxford today and hasn't come home yet.'

'Perhaps he forgot about this evening.' Nesta did not seem disappointed, she had only ever wanted him to balance the number of males and females.

'I reminded him.'

'Tried phoning the coffee bar?'

'I didn't get through.'

Picking up a telephone, Nesta said. 'Give it one more shot. What's the number?'

Maddy recited from memory. Nesta keyed in the figures, then shook her head. 'I'm getting the unobtainable signal.' She invited Maddy to do it herself.

Nesta tipped the contents of two of the pans into serving dishes and put them in the oven. Beside her, Maddy was listening to the unobtainable signal.

Nesta looked up. 'There's a directory in the hall, if you want to look it up.'

But Linsey and Jay might be out there. Jay would be excited to see her and Linsey might be annoyed with her.

'No,' she said. 'Let's forget about him.'

Nesta whisked off the apron and flung it down on the table on top of crockery, cookery books and notebooks, a camera and a bunch of daffodils.

'Oh, the flowers!' She cast about for a jug.

'Here let me do that.' Maddy knew where to find scissors to snip stems and she guessed which vase was a suitable height. While Maddy arranged the daffodils, Nesta was brushing her hair and slipping on a pair of earrings from her skirt pocket.

'Listen,' Nesta said, 'before we join the others . . .'

Maddy waited apprehensively.

'Glenys is the editor we need to impress. Marcus, the man she's brought, isn't her husband which is a bore because the husband's a nice man whom we know.'

'Is Glenys the one in the orange dress?'

'Yes. The other woman is May. She has a kitchenware business in Oxford and she *has* brought her husband, Rod. Unfortunately, the two couples don't seem to be getting on. If you could be poised to intervene if anything contentious comes up . . .'

Maddy winced.

'You're the only one I can ask, Maddy. The other locals – Patsy Kimball and Peter Ribston – well, you know I couldn't brief them.'

With a sinking heart Maddy promised to do her best.

Nesta said: 'If they hit on something they're happy to chatter about try and keep them at it. OK?'

Maddy handed her the daffodils and followed her out of the kitchen.

While they had been talking Ribston had arrived and, minutes after, Patsy Kimball. To Maddy's mind, Patsy was the epitome of good grooming: sleek hair, varnished finger-nails and a neat figure in clothes which always appeared brand new. Most women felt at a disadvantage in the same room as her.

The villagers greeted each other like dear friends, a way of establishing their special status. Graham then introduced the outsiders who established *their* special status by discussing variously difficult journeys to Park House.

'Maddy walked her dog here,' said Graham, inviting the outsiders to laugh at such quirkiness.

Patsy, a vicar's daughter and a solicitor living close to the church, said: 'Do you know, a man took his dog to mass at St Mary's last Sunday.'

But as none of the others were churchgoers they did not share her wonder and the subject lapsed.

Nesta invited them to sit at table, promising food shortly.

A puff of smoke pursued Ribston as he crossed in front of the fireplace. Glenys, coughing, set her towering hair a-quiver. Graham marched over and kicked a burning log.

Then he took up the challenge of seating people so that they were not next to their partners but not next to people of the same sex, either. The table was round and big enough to seat ten at a squeeze; but it was canted. The tilt made the tumblers (there were definitely no wine glasses at Park House) look funny when wine appeared to run uphill. Linsey managed a clever trick when she ladled the soup: it flowed to within one eighth of an inch of the rim once the bowls were set down on the slope.

They were all glad of the soup. The room was achingly cold. Maddy regretted her pink and green skirt but could not decide which she coveted more: Glenys's ensemble of woollen dress plus cosy wrap or May's thick trousers and jacket. Patsy Kimball had also made the mistake of wearing clothes that were pretty but too thin. Maddy noticed her tweaking her collar to make it stand up.

A few topics were picked at and discarded over the soup. During the hiatus between courses, Nesta disappeared to the kitchen and Graham played jolly host. That meant he did all the talking with the result that, when the door slid open an inch and Nesta's finger beckoned him, conversation foundered.

'Tell me,' said Glenys breaking the silence, 'about your murder.' Gold bangles clanked along her arm as she reached for her tumbler. Maddy worried that metal must feel terribly cold on bare skin.

Peter Ribston had a story to tell. 'It was a damned funny thing. The police knew I'd arrived home late and all het up that evening. What they didn't know was why, so I suppose they had to check it out. Fair enough, it's their job. A girl's dead and they've got to catch the culprit and quick. But I didn't care for their attitude. I mean, they pretty well said my explanation – that I'd been held up by a lorry blocking the road – wasn't credible. Not local, you see. Don't know how those lorries get to us.'

Several voices mumbled agreement or sympathy. Glenys rested her cheek on her hand, sending the bangles skimming to her elbow. 'What happened then, Peter?'

'Well, there we were, with them trying to find out why I'd been in a state; and with me struggling to work out who'd reported me. A nosy neighbour's my best guess.'

'Who?' The interjection came from May Finch, the kitchenware woman. She had a well-modulated voice but had barely spoken, leaving Maddy fantasising that her tongue was frozen.

Ribston replied: 'A busybody with nothing better to do. And there I was, answering damnfool questions for hours.'

The villagers noted the exaggeration. Hours? But Glenys enjoyed the tale. She asked him: 'Wasn't there anybody who could back up your story?'

He swung a grateful smile in Maddy's direction. 'Yes, Maddy here. We met by the wretched lorry, did we not?'

She remembered his florid face, dusk falling and his determination to telephone Beth. Remembered, too, her own decision to warn Beth. But neither of them had spoken to her. Beth was already dead.

Eyes were on her. Glenys was coaxing information. Maddy told her own story, the one about meeting Ribston by the lorry and mentioning it to the police when she was interviewed. She excised the part about her abortive telephone call to Beth and her reluctance to leave a message on a machine. Anyway, she did not have to say much because he interrupted, ostensibly to add fascinating details about his own experience. Maddy understood it was actually to prevent it becoming clear that she had verified his story long before he discovered he needed her.

Patsy Kimball then told her story, about one of her colleagues being Chris Welford's solicitor. 'The police have suspected him from the outset.' She was hinting at special knowledge. Nobody was mean enough to remark that a husband was usually the first suspect.

Then Graham rushed in with bottles of wine and a torrent of apology for having failed to fetch them up from the cellar earlier. 'But I've wiped the cobwebs off,' he said, keeping up his act of jolly host.

Maddy cringed. Park House had no cellar. She wondered where the bottles had actually been. In the fridge? In a wine warehouse bag in the back of the car? Oh, dear. She looked surreptitiously at her watch. The evening was young. There was time for all manner of gaffes before liqueurs. She did not doubt they would be pressed to drink liqueurs.

She was lucky, she decided, to work in a job where everyone knew what the subterfuges were, and therefore they were useless. How terrible it must be to do what Nesta and Graham were attempting: to reinvent yourself to impress people because that was your only chance of getting commissions and without them you faced penury. Oh, dear. Poor Graham. Poor Nesta.

He refilled the tumblers. Glenys drank. Clunk, click of gold bands. Maddy wondered whether she was habitually a heavy drinker or was anaesthetising her throat against the smoke and her flesh against the cold. As Graham moved around the table the little draught he raised tugged at the fire and drew smoke down the room.

Glenys was concentrating on what Marcus, the man who was not her husband, was saying: a tale about a murder that took place during his army days. He had done National Service, he was old enough for that. Glenys was younger. And her husband? Maddy planned to ask Nesta later.

May drew a finger along a stain on the mahogany veneer. Maddy supposed the veneer had become clouded because the table had been kept in a damp room. This room? It was a serviceable piece of Victorian furniture and worth paying to have the underpinnings mended so the top sat level and having the veneer repaired. Couldn't you make clouded veneer come good again? Didn't vinegar have something to do with it? But none of her ideas were any good, Maddy realised, because Nesta and Graham could not pay.

She felt Graham at her side, pausing in the pouring of the wine to whisper. Luckily, a clamour for details of the army court martial drowned Graham's plea.

'Would you mind popping out to the kitchen?'

She made her move while everyone was concentrating on Marcus's story, querying, challenging, demanding confirmation that they had heard him aright.

'Oh, surely not!'

'He *can't* have.'

'Do you really mean he . . .'

'Well, that's incredible!'

She found Nesta and Linsey at loggerheads. Nesta, livid, was saying: 'Of all the selfish . . .'

'It is forbidden.' Linsey lounged against the dresser, lower lip jutting.

'You know how important this evening is to us.'

'They're stupid people. It's demeaning for me to be a slave to them.'

'All I'm asking you to do is to serve the food.'

'Huh, such bad food. With mushrooms and onions . . .'

'You're not required to eat it, Linsey. Carry the serving bowls into the dining room . . . Oh, Maddy.'

Maddy's smile encompassed them both. She registered Linsey was lacking the green scarf.

Nesta put two covered dishes on a tray. 'It's a bit heavy, Maddy. Think you can manage?'

'As long as someone opens doors.'

Linsey was implacable, leaving Nesta to do it. In the hall Nesta seethed: 'I'll kill her. I swear I will.'

'May I watch?'

And then Maddy was in the dining room where everyone was chattering about Beth Welford's murder again. She made two further trips to the kitchen before they were all seated around the table and enthusing about the Collinses' wonderful food. Linsey did not put in another appearance and Maddy was demoted, or maybe promoted, from guest to helper.

She wondered what Linsey had done. No doubt she was guilty of recalcitrance and of bad timing in choosing this particular evening to stand on her principles. But Linsey issuing reprimands because the Collinses were wickedly using garlic, onions and other foods 'of the low order' was nothing unusual, so Maddy assumed matters had gone further. After a while she became aware that the delicately balanced sauce she had sampled on Nesta's stirring spoon was not being offered. And also . . .

Patsy was saying: 'We had no idea they meant Beth. None of us knew Jean Dellafield was her real name.'

People with full mouths grunted agreement. Ribston was first to swallow. 'Gave us two shocks instead of one. First the murder, then the realisation we knew the victim.'

'A customer in my shop,' began May, 'said there was a Dellafield in a murder case once before.'

Eyebrows lifted.

'When?' asked Ribston.

'Where?' asked Glenys.

May said: 'I forget.'

Disappointed faces were on her. She frowned in concentration, cross with herself.

Patsy helped out. 'It was Stratford.' In case anyone mixed it up with the others – Stratford, London; Stratford Tony; Stratford St Mary; Stratford St Andrew; or Stony Stratford – she gave its full title. 'Stratford-upon-Avon.'

'What happened?' Glenys again. She nodded a thank you as Nesta offered her another helping of vegetables, then hitched her wrap around her shoulders.

Maddy realised she had not heard Glenys say anything complimentary about the food although she had twice remarked on the wine. *'But she's gobbling it down. That must be a good sign.'*

Refreshingly, Patsy brought a lawyer's precision to the telling of her tale. 'A teenage girl was found dead near the river. The police believed they knew who killed her and they charged a man. But the evidence wasn't strong enough and the case was stopped.'

'Nesta can't have meant this.' Maddy sighed as the subject of murder was fanned to life every time it threatened to die. She was unsure how to fulfil her promise. Keep the

topic going? Repeat her hopeless attempts to move them on
to something less unpleasant?

During one pause she tried to shift them to history, by
asking whether they realised Wychwood was the remnant
of a vast forest where the Plantagenet kings hunted. But
Ribston made a sour remark about it having lost whatever
cachet it had once claimed and added that one of his
neighbours, who was trying to sell a house in The Close,
was worried about the effect the murder might have on
property prices.

There was some jousting about whether Beth had been
raped as well as strangled, but those whose information
came on the grapevine soon deferred to Patsy and her
colleague's insider knowledge. Maddy privately doubted
that the correction would be broadcast on the grapevine,
too. She expected the information that Beth's gloves had
apparently been stolen would, though.

Over coffee and, yes, liqueurs Maddy was trapped by
May's bear-like husband, Rod. He had begun as quietly
as his wife but as the drink went down his capacity for
talk had increased. He had the kind of carrying voice
well-suited to a judge or, with less education, a barrow
boy. May, probably anticipating his transformation to raging
bore, was ignoring him. She was locked in conversation with
Glenys's man.

Glenys was toying with her bangles, patting her lofty hair
and drinking. The group had broken up into little knots of
conversation. Was she listening to anyone in particular or
to nobody?

Before Maddy worked it out Rod was bellowing in her
ear: 'The thing is, you can't buy a decent stockpot for love
nor money. So I said to May, "If you want to make a
few bucks, my girl, you could do a lot worse than import
them." "Mail order," she said. "No, a shop," I said. "Oh,"
she said, "I don't know that I'm the shopkeeper type." "Not
the same thing," I said, "Not when you're talking about
specialist kitchenware." Anything in the foodie line, you
know, Maddy, it's not the same thing as shopkeeping.

May agrees now, of course, now I've steered her into it. If it hadn't been for me . . . And the shortage of stockpots . . .'

Maddy was grateful when he broke off to acknowledge Graham topping up his glass. Her face ached with smiling, her head was tired of nodding.

She recognised a similar strain on Patsy's face. Patsy was hearing Glenys's man's opinion of London restaurants. 'These days you can't get in unless you know somebody, it's got that bad. It's the tourists, you see, Patsy. Any place worth going to is packed out with Japanese, French, Italians . . . Unless you know someone, you won't get a table. It's a scandal but what can you do? Except turn away the tourists.' He interrupted himself with a phony laugh. 'Well, no, I don't suppose you *could* do that. That would be classed as racist, wouldn't it?'

He cocked an eyebrow at Graham across the table. 'Often wonder why you and Nesta don't go into the restaurant game.'

Graham's weak smile accompanied a shake of the head. 'Too much hard work.'

'But you'd raise the capital, I'm sure. Who do you bank with?'

The question astounded Graham. He went blank. 'Nesta, which bank do we use?'

'Lloyds. In Chippy. Why?'

Marcus had heard. 'Oh, you bank locally, do you?'

Graham sensed a cooling off, a reassessment of his ability to raise the loot and run a restaurant. He fixed his jolly host smile in place and asked whether anyone would like more coffee before they went home. Nesta, he knew, would tell him off about that word 'home', which implied that the hosts were anticipating the guests' departure even if the guests were not.

His hint worked perfectly and the two couples from further afield started chattering about the best routes at that time of night.

Soon they were in the hall, handing round coats and saying

goodbyes. The outsiders said must-meet-agains to people whose company they had not enjoyed. And the villagers said see-you-soons to each other because it was inevitable they would do so.

Glenys and Marcus were first to drive away. May and Rod followed their tail-lights down the drive. Patsy whisked her sports car after them. Maddy's dog followed Patsy. He brushed past Graham and Nesta in the doorway and fled into the night.

A chorus of '*Jay!*' brought Maddy from the kitchen at a run.

The tableau by the door made questions superfluous. She soothed Nesta who was inclined to blame Graham. Graham was all for blaming Linsey for releasing the dog at precisely the most dangerous moment.

Peter Ribston guffawed. 'Your escort's gone without you, Maddy.'

Although they had spent much of the evening dissecting murder cases, it took him a full minute to stop finding it amusing. When he finally grasped her predicament he insisted on taking her home.

'Peter, you're forgetting you didn't come by car,' said Nesta.

He denied forgetting. 'I meant I'll walk her home. It's hardly any distance, is it?'

And so it was that Maddy set off with Peter Ribston. He was hardly the ideal companion. Emboldened by alcohol he walked too close and his conversation became risqué. But he was company on a potentially hazardous walk and that was what she required. Besides, she knew his reputation for drunken pawings and accused herself of being over-zealous in finding fault. The stumble that had him grabbing her arm could have been genuine. Avoiding pot-holes could account for his closeness on the drive.

His conversation was another matter. Maddy pretended to miss the *double entendres* and the innuendos. She did what she had failed to do at supper and steered the conversation. Lorries. Village matters. Anything that let her do most of the talking. Side by side, their twin torch beams bounced along the village street.

Abruptly his stopped and hers bounced a yard or two on its own. His voice became a stage whisper. His arm wavered into the darkness. 'What's that?'

'*Pink elephants,*' she thought before whispering: 'Where?'

He drew level with her. 'By that tree.'

'Can't see anything.'

'Look. A long pale streak. *There!*'

He was right.

They had to decide what to do. Maddy was dubious about his capacity for rational judgment. Her own brain, clearer than his by far, was not at its sharpest. She summed up the options. Most tempting, they could hurry up the road without investigating what lurked near the tree; but in that case they would spend the rest of the journey looking over their shoulders. Alternatively, they could investigate and hope they were not given a nasty surprise.

He said: 'If we don't clear this up now, I've got to face it again on my way back.'

To her shame she had not thought about him returning alone. 'All right. Let's walk towards it and see what happens.'

He did not move. Neither did she. Then she said: 'One thing, Peter. I want us to look, not do anything else.'

'Like what?'

'Fighting.'

'*Fighting*? Good God.'

'Right. Just as long as we're agreed. We're going to look, that's all. We're not going to get involved in, well, in anything.'

They exchanged a glance, each gauging the other's readiness to move. Maddy drew a deep breath. 'Come on, we'll walk steadily forward.'

Ahead of them the thing leaned around the tree, withdrew, peered again. The uncertainty was nerve-racking. Maddy wished she could cling on to Ribston but she dared not encourage his boozy advances. Screwing up her courage, she reminded herself she had coped when someone watched her from the garden and she had survived the walk to Park House. This time she had an adult male to protect her. She wished she could rid herself of the suspicion that he was as faint-hearted as she was.

'*Men don't have an equal right to be scared,*' she thought. '*They're seldom the victims of prowlers. They don't go through life knowing themselves to be designated prey.*'

She let resentment at Ribston's timidity spur her on.

Because of the angle of approach, whatever waited by the tree was obscured for part of the way. Ribston said: 'He might have gone.' So he was also assuming it to be a man.

He flapped his arms to indicate he was going behind the tree and wanted her to go round the front. Seconds later they were shining torches on each other and running beams of light down a long green silk scarf trailing from a branch.

'Linsey's,' said Ribston.

'Nesta's,' said Maddy who had a deeper understanding of the ménage at Park House. 'Can you lift it down?'

Maddy expected it to be snagged because every breath of wind had sent it dancing alongside the tree trunk. She put out a hand but he was twirling the scarf, coiling it. She hated him playing with it, fondling it, making it into a noose.

'Let me take it,' she said, stupidly nervous. She felt safer once it was in her pocket although nothing had changed. If he intended to throttle her, he was powerful enough to whip it out of her pocket whenever he chose.

'Why do you suppose Linsey put it up the tree?' she asked, to spark a normal conversation.

'To upset Nesta.'

'Yes, it'll achieve that. But do you think there's anything in the cult rules about green scarves?'

They speculated on the cult rules. Maddy calculated that the subject should see them to her door but he suggested a short cut.

'The footpath saves walking round the bend in the road.'

'I know,' she said, suppressing irritation. The man was a virtual newcomer.

He veered towards the stile where the path joined the road.

'No, Peter, I don't want to go that way.'

'Eh? What's wrong with it?'

She sought a plausible excuse. 'Er . . . my shoes. These are my best shoes. I'll wreck them if I go climbing stiles and tramping along footpaths.'

She trusted it was too dark for him to see her sensible shoes, chosen for the walk to and from Park House.

He conceded with a grunt and began to move away from the stile, but a leg folded beneath him and he yelped. Maddy rushed forward.

It was not the greatest surprise of her life. To her he had always looked like a man primed for a heart attack. *'But not here. Not now,'* she prayed.

He was on the ground, rocking with pain. Maddy was striving to remember First Aid. Shouldn't he be lying flat? Head on one side, her jacket beneath his head, something of that order?

She heard herself murmuring: 'Oh God, what can I do?'

Pain had sobered him. He snapped at her. 'You can get out of my way and let me stand.'

No heart attack, then. Prayers answered. But . . .

'Peter, what's happened?'

'My ankle. It's gone again.'

Relief made her gabble. 'Oh, you're not . . . I was afraid . . .'

He struggled to his feet, one hand on the wall to take his weight. When he transferred some to his left foot, pain made him suck his teeth.

'No good. I can't walk a step. It won't improve until it's strapped up and I can rest it.'

There was a pause while they both swore silently. Then Maddy offered to run home to fetch her car.

Frustration made him sarcastic. 'The reason I'm here is that it's not safe for you on your own. Remember?'

'Well, I could . . .'

He guessed. 'And if you go to Park House you'll have to pass that place where we found the scarf. We *know* something weird was going on there.'

'Linsey . . .'

'Did you see Linsey hanging around?' He allowed sufficient time for her to realise she had not. 'Well, there you are. It might or might not have been her skulking. No, you're not to risk going anywhere on your own, Maddy.'

'In that case, I'll have to help you to walk.'

'Which are we nearer to now? Park House or your place?'

'Park House,' she said, rather than reopen discussion of the short cut over the fields. 'Come on, let's see what you can manage.'

Progress was pathetically slow. After a few yards they stopped and bandaged the ankle with the green scarf but it made no difference.

There were no cars to flag down. Once a fox crossed the road and an owl flew out of a tree. Lights were off in the cottages they skirted and Ribston announced he would rather stagger on than ring people's doorbells at dead of night.

'You ought to buy a mobile phone,' he said, leaning more heavily on her shoulder than she found comfortable. 'Then you could send for help in a crisis.'

Maddy ducked telling him she had left it at Park House in the confusion, along with Jay's lead.

Pain and indignity were making him tetchy. 'If Steve had shown up as he was supposed to, none of this would have happened.'

'I'll remember to tell him that.'

She had a number of things to tell Steve, whenever she caught up with him. Blaming him for Ribston's bust ankle came a long way down her list.

CHAPTER EIGHT

Saturday morning. Maddy lay awake listening to birds playing in the creeper outside her bedroom window. Lengthening days were persuading them to behave as if spring had arrived. A draught sharp as a blade cut across her neck and she hauled the duvet up higher. But it was no use. She was fully awake and, however much she resisted mulling over the previous evening, memories were seeping in. She might as well get up.

The evening had left her a legacy of chores: return Ribston's car, borrowed after she had helped him hobble to his house; deliver Nesta's scarf; and collect the dog's lead and her mobile telephone.

She pulled on her dressing gown and went on to the landing. The door of the small bedroom was open giving her a view over the courtyard. Frost dusted the tufts of herbs. The harsh winter was unending.

Steve had not returned. Maddy yawned and went downstairs to make tea. Jay wagged his tail against the table leg. Thud. Thud. Thud.

'Don't dogs feel that? Doesn't it hurt?'

He took up position by the door. Dogs were lucky, she thought, unlocking it and battling with the bolts. They never had to make conversation, let alone reason and justify, and providing their wants were simple, they were usually met.

After grunting effort she undid the top bolt and let Jay out.

He sniffed the air, walked part way across the courtyard and dithered.

'Go on, Jay,' Maddy urged. 'Garden.'

He hesitated, one paw off the ground then set off at a trot through the gateway.

Thankfully, Maddy shut the door and made tea. She hugged the mug to her. The central heating had come on a few minutes ago and the floor was cold through the espadrilles she wore around the house instead of slippers. She sat at the kitchen table, rested her feet on the staves of her chair to keep them off the stone, and laced her fingers around the mug.

'The sooner I get Peter's car to him, the better. The fewer people who see it outside here, the less gossip there'll be.'

Dread spurred her on to shower and dress. She called Jay indoors and inflicted on him the indignity of a lead improvised from string. Then there was the bother of getting him into Ribston's car. He was content to explore it but, she swore, his nose wrinkled in distaste at the smelly residue of tobacco smoke. Whatever his reasons, he backed out and there ensued a struggle she was not confident of winning. Eventually she fooled him into jumping onto the rear seat and she trapped him by shutting the door before he realised his mistake. Jay whined for most of the journey.

She wanted to zip along to The Close but Saturday morning brought its special hazards. Weekenders whose cottages stood on awkward bends were emptying their cars after the early morning dash from London or Birmingham. Riders were clopping along the lanes in clouds of horsey steam. Dogs, who had been constrained in town flats all week, were flying into the road to celebrate their freedom. Small children were doing likewise.

In the heart of the village the postman was hefting his sack from door to door. A cleaner was sweeping broken glass off the pavement outside the pub. The vicar was unlocking St Mary's. A couple of thinly clad girls were hopping about outside the village shop, willing the blind to shoot up. The village was more or less awake and facing the day.

It was different in The Close. Twelve houses snoozed. Maddy switched off the engine and let the car coast to the kerb. But there was really only one person she cared not to disturb and that was Peter Ribston who, in all probability, was awake with the pain of his injured ankle. She tiptoed to his door, dropped the keys through the letterbox, then hurried away with Jay chewing the stringy lead.

By the time she and Ribston had parted company the night before they had been disgusted with each other. He had shifted from blaming Steve for the fiasco and settled responsibility on her. Maddy was convinced the worst of it was his own fault. If he had kept to the road . . . if he had not drunk too much . . . if he had let her seek help rather than stagger along beneath his weight . . . Outside Park House he had announced there was no sense in stopping when The Close was near.

'But, Peter, Graham would run us both home.'

'The Collinses are probably in bed by now.'

'No, they'll be clearing up.'

'Can you see a light?'

'No but . . .'

She had been about to say their lights were never visible from the road but he had cut her off with: 'Well, there you are.'

So Maddy had finished up in Ribston's house, telephoning home in the hope that Steve would fetch her.

'Peter, I'll have to borrow your car,' she had told him, and watched every conceivable objection parade across his face. Might she not get a taxi? Stay the night? Dig out somebody else who would lend a car?

As his car keys were visible, she had helped herself. 'I'll bring it back early, I promise.' She had gone before he could mount further selfish, unreasonable protest.

No, she was in no hurry to see him again.

Jay tweaked the string to the left and drew her obliquely across The Close and out onto the village green. The woman who swept up the glass waved at her. Two shivery girls were coming out of the shop, clutching a pint of milk and a loaf of sliced bread. A paper boy was waiting to go in, returning his empty bag. Two women, one with a dry-coated retriever, were chatting by the postbox. Maddy said a friendly hello and got by without breaking step.

She overheard: '. . . and he said Beth Welford had discovered more than was good for her about McQuade and his lorries, so I said . . .'

The gossip flowed through the village. A trickle, a stream, it had become a torrent. Bits of information flashed by like leaves in a mill race, so fast Maddy was not always sure what she had heard, so fleeting they were as swiftly forgotten. But some things stuck. Beth had been raped; she had stumbled upon a businessmen's conspiracy; she had been on the point of leaving her husband; she had been slain by her husband, her lover, at random by a stranger.

Maddy reached Park House as Nesta was pouring coffee. Nesta was nasal, an allergic reaction to something she had touched or eaten. The kitchen was deep in dirty crockery and pans, as though a tide had washed through in the night and deposited it all. Having let Maddy in, Graham resumed his position leaning against the dresser. Maddy shifted a cat and some grubby tea towels off a chair. She pushed a serving bowl aside so that there were a couple of inches for her to put her mug on the table.

Nesta, tired and wan, looked round hopelessly for space to sit and then joined Graham by the dresser. Maddy narrowly stopped herself offering the chair she was using herself.

'That was a good evening,' Maddy said brightly. White lies. What good was the truth?

Nesta yawned and Graham shrugged. Maddy heard herself offering to help clear up.

'That's sweet of you, Maddy,' he said, in a tone which suggested he was about to add 'No, thank you'.

Nesta leaped in. 'Another pair of hands would be marvellous. Bless you, Maddy.'

'*Damn,*' Maddy thought. '*Why do I do this sort of thing? I'm far too busy.*'

Aloud she said: 'It'll cost you a slice of toast, though. I had to leave home without a crumb.'

'We could all do with toast,' said Nesta. And she trawled among the flotsam and jetsam for a loaf, a knife and a board, butter and honey.

Maddy stacked the crockery until it covered less than half the table. Graham cleared bundles of this and that from a stool and a chair. In a few minutes they were having breakfast.

Maddy regaled them with an embellished account of her night's travails. While she was telling the story about the mystery figure lurking by the tree, she drew the green silk scarf from her pocket.

She passed it to Nesta. 'It's rather snagged, I'm afraid.'

Nesta ran it through her hands, inspecting the damage. 'I didn't think I'd see it again.'

Graham said: 'That thieving bitch.'

But Nesta put up a half-hearted defence of Linsey. 'She doesn't see it as theft, Graham.'

He choked. '*I* do. *We* do. That's what counts, isn't it, Maddy?'

She laughed, reminding them there was a comical side to it. 'It certainly would be if it was *my* things that were going missing.'

The door bell rang. 'Post, probably,' Graham said, going out.

Nesta was stroking the scarf. 'He bought me this on holiday once. He said it was the perfect colour for a redhead.'

'How did it fall into Linsey's hands?'

'Because her hands were going through my wardrobe. I didn't know she'd taken it until she started wafting around in it yesterday evening. I told her to take it off at once and give it to me. You know the rest.'

'She stopped helping you and the scarf disappeared.'

'Graham says she's brainwashed, her mind's gone and there's no use reasoning with her. I hoped that with a bit of encouragement she could settle down to an ordinary life and be less trouble to herself and everyone around her. I was wrong.'

Graham brought three envelopes and a package which contained a book of recipes compiled by an actress. Several of the photographs illustrating it were his.

He flicked through the pages, snorted disparagingly a couple of times and dropped the book down amidst the clutter. 'Nobody understands how to crop a picture these days. They're all fifteen years old, editors. Did you know that, Maddy? It's the only qualification for the job. You see it in advertisements in the publishing press. "Editor required. Heaps of responsibility. No experience necessary. Must be fifteen years old."'

Nesta, who had heard this one before, winked at Maddy. 'He's pleased, really. You wouldn't think so but he was quite pleased they wanted his photographs.'

A silent figure came to stand in the kitchen doorway. Linsey pressed her palms together, bowed, touched her hands to her face in self-absolution and bowed again. Nesta and Graham visibly geared themselves up to cope with her. Here she was, smiling the ingratiating smile that had won her admittance to their home, and either one of them would cheerfully have wrung her neck.

Linsey said: 'My friend is coming here today. I would like you to let him in, please. He will be here at three this afternoon.' She made a further bow and was poised to withdraw.

Graham spoke harshly. 'Just a minute, Linsey. We want a word with you.'

'I have to be at the temple, Graham. I can't stop now.'

'Stay right there,' he said, advancing on her.

But Linsey gave a coy bow and scuttled away. Unless he were to run after her, grab a handful of floating garment and reel her in, there was nothing to be done. He clenched his jaw. The front door banged.

He gave a sigh that ended in a growl. 'If I could pin her down long enough I'd tell her she's a greedy little magpie and I'd chuck her out of my house. The thing is, Maddy, how do I catch her?'

'We could,' said Nesta, 'lock her out. Leave her own possessions in a bag on the porch and prevent her getting into the house.'

This was obviously not a spur of the minute idea. Graham's features relaxed into a mischievous grin. 'I love it. What do you think, Maddy? Would it work?'

She was cautious. 'I'm not an expert on the little magpie. I can't guess how she'd react.'

'Unfavourably,' said Nesta. 'Very. That's how.'

Maddy pretended to be weighing it up. 'How unfavourably? Forced entry? Bricks through windows?'

As she spoke she glanced outside. Linsey was striding across the garden, scattering hens, her long skirt sweeping the grass and loose hair streaming in the breeze.

Nesta said: 'She threw away a sauce yesterday evening. Did you realise, Maddy?'

'The one I tasted? Yes, I wondered why I didn't see it on the table.'

'That's why. I demanded the scarf from her and she retaliated by refusing to serve the rest of the meal. First she carried two of the serving bowls outside instead of into the dining room, and emptied them into the bin where we collect scraps for the fowls. I caught her pouring the sauce down the sink.'

Maddy was scandalised.

Nesta said: 'That's when Graham begged you to come. I didn't dare leave her because she'd have destroyed everything else, too.'

He interjected: 'Well, she did also do away with the rabbit *confit*. If you want to know whether it was any good, Maddy, ask Jay.'

Her gasp was drowned by Graham running on: 'She doesn't admit to spite, of course. Oh no, she assured Nesta she was saving us from several kinds of sin.' He rolled his eyes skywards. 'Every dreadful act she's perpetrated since she came here has been done for our own good. The property that's been stolen, the garden produce that's been destroyed, the food that's been contaminated – all for our own good.

I tell you, Maddy, if I thought locking her out would put an end to it instead of being the start of a vendetta, I'd be nailing up the doors right now.'

Maddy wondered whether a better approach might be to find another place for Linsey to go. 'Somewhere she'd prefer to be. Ideally, she'd have to believe it was her choice and not yours.'

'Another flat?' said Graham. 'Spoken like a true estate agent, love.'

There was too much teasing for them to explore the idea.

While Graham was clearing up in the dining room – cold ashes to cart outside before he made an attempt to rectify the smoking chimney – Nesta and Maddy tackled the mess in the kitchen. Up to her elbows in suds, Nesta said: 'We have versions of the same problem, don't we? Unwanted guests.'

'You've reminded me I ought to ring mine.'

Without success she tried the cottage and then the coffee bar. Jay nudged her legs as she dried the dishes. Nesta asked: 'Where was the dog when you eventually got home last night?'

Maddy frowned. 'In the courtyard.'

'Really? He must have devised a way of getting in at the back.'

'I know. I'll take a look at the boundary wall when I get home. Last night I was too tired to be other than pleased he hadn't run off.'

She chose not to share her suspicion that a figure had watched her from the garden gateway but Jay having got into the courtyard proved a man might have done so, too.

An hour later, with the dog on his proper lead and her telephone in her pocket, Maddy set off home. A class from the riding school came by with a jangling of harness and a creaking of leathers. Once they had gone she let the dog run free. He went home like a dart.

A police car was parked outside a weekenders' cottage.

A net curtain stirred in Mrs Spencer's cottage across the lane. Her television shouted.

'*They have to question our temporary residents, too.*' Maddy answered the question she assumed was running through Mrs Spencer's mind.

Murder affected everyone, she thought, however peripheral they were to village life. She wondered whether all the weekenders were going to be quizzed this Saturday or whether there was anything special about these two. Over the years she had exchanged the occasional word with them in shop or pub but they did not mix in the village. She pictured them making much of this incident once they were in the city. 'You wouldn't believe what happened to *us* this weekend . . .'

A car pulled up beside her, grounding her flights of fancy. Gina Winterson was issuing instructions. 'Maddy, if you see Ruth Pye make sure she knows I've changed the route of the children's walk, will you? We're taking them along the river not through the forest. Well, after what happened up there . . .'

Maddy thought: '*You're no longer a travel company rep, so please drop the bossy tone.*'

Mrs Pye and all the little Pyes lived a few cottages away from Maddy's. Gina had come from that direction.

Gina said: 'I've called at her house and left a note. There's nothing else I can do, is there, as she hasn't got a phone?'

'Afraid not.'

Maddy bridled. The Pyes were too poor to have a telephone. Some people were. They did not do it to hamper the arrangements made on their behalf by the likes of the Wintersons. But Maddy left it all unsaid. Her irritation with Gina hurried her along the lane and home. Jay was waiting on the doorstep, apparently satisfied at being first again.

Maddy went straight through the house and into the courtyard. The gate into the garden was open. As she headed towards it, the memory of those anxious minutes in the kitchen was sharp.

'Come on, Jay,' she called, to scare off a lurker. He chose

to linger, sniffing the winter savory. Maddy did not move until he had loped to her side. She waved him through the gateway ahead of her.

Her garden was the meadow that gave the cottage its name. Shrubs flourished near the walls and, in relatively sheltered spots, there were two beds where a few flowers and vegetables grew, Maddy mixing them together as cottage gardeners traditionally did. Although this was never a good time of year for a garden, what she saw was particularly dismal. Not only had it been too cold on such an exposed site for the earliest and bravest plants to stir themselves, but the garden had not been tidied up in readiness for winter. Grass was shaggy and matted with weeds. If there was supposed to be a path, she could not spot it. Shrubs were ungainly because pruning had been skipped. Flowering plants had not been dead-headed and the brilliant blooms of autumn had taken on the colour of decay.

Maddy was briefly cross with Steve but then more so with herself. She had not been out here for months, except to marvel at it shrouded in snow, and she had avoided the place in autumn. Why? Because she had known what she would find: that the long hours Steve had been out of her sight had not been spent gardening; that he had lied about what he did and where he went; and that no matter what deals she struck with him, he deceived her and exploited her kindness.

She watched Jay's antics closely, hoping he would reveal how he had entered the courtyard. Perversely, he showed no interest in running off and it was a while before he focused on the shrubs at the end of the garden. There was a depression where feet had flattened grass. This was not the vestige of the old path but the beginning of a new one.

Seconds later she was thrusting through the shrubbery. An overgrown rose and a bowing philadelphus blocked her way but the dog guided her past them. She lifted branches aside and came to the wall. Its top courses were missing.

On tiptoe, she peered through the gap and saw down the field beyond. While she was considering the practicality of climbing through, she became aware that one of the big stones lay beside her. Maddy stepped up on to it and leaned into the gap. On the other side were the rest of the stones, tumbled against the wall. That, coupled with what she noticed in the fallow field, revealed the truth.

'My wall didn't collapse, it was deliberately pulled down to create an access.'

The stones had been arranged to provide three steps on the steeper side of the wall, and one large stone in the garden.

'He did it,' she said. 'No one else would have wanted to do, therefore he did.'

Then she grew afraid of blaming him out of hand because it was possible the wall had been breached by an intruder instead of by Steve seeking a way out.

'But who else? And why? How long has it been like this?'

Questions whirled but no answers suggested themselves. She lapsed into accusing Steve.

Maddy swung up onto the wall and stretched a leg down the other side until it met the topmost step. She balanced there while studying the field. Through it ran a streak of contrasting colour which marked the way he had come and gone.

Jay lolloped about the field, squashing swathes of grass and barking at her. It was odd to think the dog had known about the wall and the path and what lay ahead of her now, if she had the courage to explore.

'I'm scared,' she admitted. 'I want to do it but I'm scared. It's stupid because I can't say what I'm scared *of*.'

The sun appeared from behind a cloud and spread the fields with gold. Maddy felt in her pocket for the lead and called the dog to her. He cocked his head but was rooted.

She could not help laughing. He seemed to be thinking she had gone crazy, expecting him to be on a leash for a walk over the fields.

Calling him, she jumped down from the wall. He accelerated away.

'So much for you being my guard dog!' Really he did nothing for her dignity let alone her security.

Then she faced the new situation. Go home or rush after him?

She havered until he was at the other side of the field. Then she tore after him.

CHAPTER NINE

His hand reached out and touched the hem of the dead girl's skirt. The touch was electric. He shuddered awake, smothering a cry.

Recently he had been waking to the sound of his own anguish, coupled with the underlying dread that he had shouted words, revealing words that had been overheard and understood. He needed to be alone. He felt safe only when he held himself apart.

The nightmare faded and the reality, which was worse, replaced it. In the nightmare he did not know what was genuine and what was elaboration but in the real story he knew he was culpable. He did not know why it had happened to him, why he had done these things, and whether he could bear to think of the future. His past had been destroyed and, saving miracles, his future, too.

Unsteadily, he got to his feet, swung down from the hidden platform beneath the beams and went to the door of the barn. He stood just inside, concealed. He had lived most of his life concealed. It was afternoon but the sheep-cropped grass was stiff with rime that had resisted the feeble sun. A figure moved out of trees on the opposite hill but he did not want to stay and talk to her. Or listen, rather. It was usually a matter of listening. He hastened away.

His memories travelled with him. The figure on the hill had triggered thoughts of another woman in another copse, for a meeting he wished he had skipped. But wishes were wild creatures that whipped him in his waking hours and mocked him in his sleep.

He had not believed her because the coincidence of her recognising his name was beyond the bounds of probability. Not *impossible*, though, and it was, as she had pointed out, a small country with most of the population in one corner.

'I checked,' she said, when he denied his identity. 'I wouldn't be daft enough to accuse you without checking.'

He had not liked that 'accuse' although it was fairly used.

So he had checked, too, journeying up to London on the train to look up her original name among the records of births, marriages and deaths at St Catherine's House in Holborn. The paper trail suggested she was indeed who she claimed to be. She had already proved she was right about him.

Crucially, she had declared what was true and what false in his nightmares. Although he had sought to fend her off, to ignore her claims on him and what would one day be his, he had failed wretchedly.

'We have both survived in secrecy,' she had said, making them partners in an unkind venture.

But he could not do what she demanded. She refused to see that. It had ended disastrously.

He shied away from that memory and flipped back to St Catherine's House. Before leaving it he had digressed to inspect the records of his own family. However dramatic their lives, people were reduced to alphabetically listed names close-printed in books. He looked up one name, not his own, not even his own surname because it was a divided family of step-children.

He ran a finger over the printed name, wondering how it would have been if his mother had not remarried or had not acquired stepsons who seemed, to her own offspring, admirable and heroic. Questions hovered around this particular name but for days the woman had been insisting she had answers to them.

'And so do you,' she had said, 'except that you refuse to remember.'

He did, though. He remembered in his nightmares.

In the records office his hand had strayed towards another file, a file containing the name of her family. But he had wavered, suspecting he lacked the courage to open it at the significant page. A researcher muttered an 'Excuse me', leaned in front of him and took away the book of the dead. However startling their deaths, people were reduced to listed names.

He had turned away, wondering how many more deaths it would take before the story was brought to a conclusion. There was, he realised, a terrible possibility that it would require one more.

CHAPTER TEN

The trees were thinning. She was reaching the edge of the copse. Framed by the wintry branches was a valley of tentative green fields and champagne walls.

Beyond the ragged line of the trees was a stone barn. The land sloped away from it towards the river. She recognised features of the facing hill and the dark stain of Wychwood. In the heart of a familiar valley she had found an isolated spot.

She decided to venture as far as the barn, a traditional Cotswold structure under a roof of stone tiles. They were sturdy, these barns and lasted for centuries with a modicum of care. She could see only the sheltered aspect and was curious to learn how the rest had weathered. The wind which was prone to rampage along the valley might have ravaged the exposed walls and ripped holes in the roof. She hoped not.

Maddy was breaking cover when a man walked from the other side of the barn. She stood stock still. Had he glanced up he would have seen her jersey striking a discordant note. Luckily, he walked downhill and the lie of the land meant he was quickly out of sight.

She buttoned up her drab jacket with trembling hands. She knew him: the jutting chin as he appeared in profile beside the barn; the way his arms swung; the angle of his head. His clothes, too: jacket with fraying pockets; brown boots of a superior quality to the rest of what he wore; shirt with a plum collar. She had seen them frequently.

The path had led her across fields, over a bridle path, into the copse and right here to this barn and this man. Her temper rose and she wished she had pounced on him, tackled him about invading her property and spying.

But confrontation was too risky. If she were to rail at him she would not be able to control his reaction. Words might not satisfy him. Perhaps he was the man who had killed Beth.

Maddy quelled her anger. '*If he sees me, I'll say I'm looking for my dog. Unless I accuse him, he won't realise I've discovered he spies on me. And as long as he doesn't know, I'm not in danger.*'

The barn was intact and it was lived in. In the subdued light she made out a sleeping bag draped over a camp bed, an upright chair, and a table improvised from a board resting on drums. A lamp, a pottery mug and a book lay on the table. She was about to pick up the book to satisfy her curiosity about the title when she had the feeling she was not alone.

Maddy dashed out expecting to bump into him and have to apologise for intruding and ask after a runaway retriever. But she did not meet him in the doorway, neither was he walking up from the river.

She ran into the copse and home the way she had come, although the riverside path would have been quicker. She was afraid of him seeing her. Very much afraid. He was a predator who had already marked her out as his victim.

She wished she had not come. Her curiosity had outstripped her courage. One moment she had felt in charge and the next she was jumpy and running away. She was suffering the same uncontrolled anxiety as on the evening she walked the dog by the river and imagined assailants in every shadow, or when a man approached her car when she was looking for Felden Farm, or when she had convinced herself a man was spying on her in her kitchen. She was rational enough to see that although the anxiety was real, the lurkers were probably not. These episodes had only happened to her since the murder. Yet she could not prevent herself from being scared and running away.

Jay was waiting in the courtyard. She closed the gate

between garden and courtyard, and discovered it was impossible to lock it. In all her years at Meadow Cottage it had not been necessary.

'*Oh yes it has,*' she corrected herself. '*Only I wasn't aware of it.*'

She strode through the cottage and drove to the shop.

'I need a padlock,' she said to the schoolgirl who was serving.

This was the daughter of the owners. Anything more complicated than a pint of milk and she had to beg help. She begged it. Her father pushed aside the fly curtain of plastic strips and Maddy, averting her eyes from the dribbles of lunchtime soup down his shirt, repeated her request. Before he spoke she knew he did not stock locks. The downturn of the mouth was eloquent.

'You want an ironmonger's,' he said.

A woman's voice came from behind crates of fizzy drinks. 'Or a garden centre.' The sleeve of a fawn trench coat appeared, followed by the dog-walking widow from The Close. The animal had slunk into the shop and was licking a picture of meat on a pet food can.

'*He resembles an old yellow duster, with all the vigour washed out of it,*' Maddy thought.

She asked: 'Is there an ironmonger's in Chippy?' She could be there in a few minutes.

The shopkeeper was doubtful: 'Used to be. I'm not sure where you'd go now, mind.'

The widow still favoured a garden centre. 'They're sure to have them because they sell gates, do you see?'

Malcolm Winterson's voice chimed in. 'We're all security conscious since the Beth Welford murder, aren't we?'

The shopkeeper provided an example. 'People are saying they've given their kids orders to play in the gardens and nowhere else.'

His daughter offered another. 'Mum says Mrs Winterson switched the children's walk from Wychwood to the river.'

She looked to Malcolm Winterson for confirmation. It came in a nod.

'According to Jim, the postman,' said the widow, 'that weekend cottage by Mrs Spencer's has been broken into.'

She hoped she was first in the shop with this piece of news but it was not to be. Jim had been generally chatty that morning.

Winterson said: 'They drove down from London this morning and found a window forced. Broken glass but no theft. The police say it was probably kids.'

Maddy asked: 'How is Mrs Spencer?' And when she was answered by blank looks: 'I'll call on her on my way home.'

Mrs Spencer saw more lorries during the week than people and when weekenders visited their cottages flanking the lane, their plans did not include spending much time with an elderly neighbour.

Maddy set off brimming with good intentions but did not reach Mrs Spencer. Her car was waved to a stop by one friend and then another. The first asked whether she had any news of the murder inquiry. The second had gossip and sought help in deciding whether it was true. The third, Gilly, brought her riding school class to a standstill while she reported that Nesta was searching for Maddy.

'She was very anxious because no one knew where you were.'

Although she and Nesta had chatted over the washing-up that morning, Maddy was glad of an excuse to call at Park House again. She needed to talk. When it had been purely a matter of Steve not leaving, there had been nothing to say. But things had changed once the hole in the wall was discovered, and they had grown immeasurably worse when she recognised the man at the barn.

She wove around the pot-holes and parked outside the kitchen window. The room, the most frequently used one, was empty but she heard voices.

The door was flung open by Linsey whose ingratiating welcome was instantly replaced by a petulant scowl. Linsey flounced down the hall. Graham's voice started up again.

A conference was taking place in the flat. Outside the door

to it were piled blue towels, a china bowl with a primula in it, a green scarf, bed sheets, a bukhara rug . . .

Graham was facing Linsey who stood in the centre of the room, hands on hips, eyes blazing. Nesta appeared to be on sentry duty outside the bathroom.

Linsey was in full rant. Maddy caught 'intrusive, impertinent, intolerable', also 'disgusting, demeaning, despicable'.

Graham managed 'manipulative, meddlesome,' before Linsey hit back with 'disgraceful, detestable, interfering.'

'*Interfering!*' Graham echoed, astonished. '*You* are an interfering . . .'

Stuck for a word he was glad to have Maddy, unseen, supply: 'Magpie.'

He looked round and discovered her. 'Yes, magpie,' he said. 'Sneaking away with all the pretty things.' His fluttering fingers made a bird in flight.

'All *our* pretty things,' said Nesta who had not spoken until now.

Linsey began a speech about 'possessiveness, petty mindedness . . .' But no one was paying attention.

Maddy told Nesta: 'My spies in the village report that you were searching for me.'

'Where did you disappear to?'

Nesta cupped a hand to her ear as Maddy's reply coincided with Linsey soaring to a higher pitch. 'Where?'

Maddy shook her head, laughing. 'Trust me to choose a time like this.'

Nesta ended her shift outside the bathroom and stepped into the hall. She raised her eyes to heaven. 'She's crazy, of course. We knew it wouldn't be easy to chuck her out but who would have expected such ructions?'

'Why evict her now especially?'

Nesta flopped onto a chair. Maddy sat on the stairs.

Nesta said: 'We made a discovery. At least Graham did. He went to see a smallholder the other side of Charlbury, because we'd heard the man grows unusual vegetables.'

Maddy nodded encouragement.

'Well, the family turned out to be Mainders.' She waited

and when Maddy showed no recognition hurried on: 'Some of them used to live around here and a couple of the women worked at this house. Cleaning, helping in the garden and so on. Linsey had told us that was *her* family.'

This did not tally with the Linsey story as Maddy had previously heard it and she was not surprised when Nesta admitted: 'Oh, dear, it's so hard to remember what she actually said and what she allowed us to assume.'

'I recall that someone in your family claimed to remember her.'

'Yes, one of my cousins. But now she says the child was a beautiful little creature with jet black eyes and curls. *Not* Linsey.'

'So how did Linsey . . . ? Why here?'

A weary shrug. 'What made her come to our door? We've been trying to drag it out of her. Graham says she spotted us for the biggest fools in the village.'

'And what does *she* say?'

'That the lord sent her.'

'Hell.'

'Quite. Try reasoning with that Lord Buckshee, as Graham calls him.'

There was a hiatus. The argument had stopped. Maddy prayed the sound of silence was the sound of Linsey capitulating.

Then Graham appeared with towels, a rug and sheets in his arms. He dumped them at the foot of the stairs and was about to fetch more when the doorbell rang.

There was a flurry of flowing garments in the passage but Graham had the door open before Linsey arrived. A young man stood on the step. He wore shoulder-length hair, a shirt with a dark red collar, brown boots of decent leather . . . Maddy's blood turned to ice.

'*No!*' She heard the word escape her lips. No to letting him in, no to him having followed her there, no to him spying on her in her cottage . . .

Nesta clutched her. 'What on earth is it?'

Graham was telling the man: 'Linsey's just leaving.'

Before he could enlarge, Linsey dived through the space between them and drew her visitor into the hall.

Graham shouted at her. 'Don't you listen to anything that's said to you? You're to leave . . .'

Linsey laughed, covered her face with her hands, bobbed and pushed the young man towards the flat. She shut the door in Graham's face.

Storming into the hall he demanded: 'Did you see that?'

But a new mystery appeared before him. Maddy had fainted.

They took her into the dining room, the chilly room which smelled of soot as well as smoke because Graham had poked about in the chimney when he cleared the grate. They laid her on the carpet and flapped at her with a copy of *Country Life* although she was not hot, not even comfortably warm.

'Aren't we supposed to undo tight clothing?' suggested Graham.

'I don't think she's wearing any.' Nesta tweaked Maddy's woolly jumper. Baggy by any standards.

Maddy, who had come round but was incapable of fending off superfluous attention, plucked her jumper from Nesta's grasp.

Nesta spoke over her shoulder: 'Graham, would you fetch a glass of water?'

'*Please God,*' Maddy thought, '*don't let them chuck it in my face. Please.*'

Graham brought brandy. Nesta worried that it was impossible to put the tumbler to Maddy's mouth with spilling. She dipped a finger in the brandy and prepared to splodge it on Maddy's lips. Maddy got a hand to the glass.

It took a few muddled moments to convince the Collinses she was not ill but had eaten next to nothing and had had a fright. Her story came tumbling out, willy nilly.

A gap in the wall . . . a path over fields and through woods . . . a man spying on the house . . . Linsey's man at the barn . . . Jay, that wretched animal, had known all along . . . and Steve, somehow Steve was in it, too . . . what to do?

While the Collinses were stunned by her revelations,

Maddy rose and, the brandy having sped to her brain, crumpled onto the nearest chair.

'What can I do?' Maddy repeated. 'This is what I came to ask advice about.'

Nesta patted her hand. 'Oh you poor dear, and you found us brawling with that dreadful brat.'

'Never mind Linsey,' said Graham. 'I want to know about the boyfriend.'

'If that's what he is,' Nesta added.

'I want to know that, too,' said Graham.

Maddy drank again. Her tumbler seemed to have become a widow's cruse but never empty of brandy. She had missed Graham's replenishing.

'I can tell you several facts,' she said. 'He's a student at one of the Oxford colleges. He's been around here since their term began last Autumn. He lives rough. Mind you, having seen the barn I wouldn't say it was all that rough. Some houses on the . . .'

She was rambling, drawing comparisons with a tatty housing estate outside one of the county's less favoured towns. She felt drunk.

'Go on.' Nesta was avid for detail.

'Coffee,' said Maddy magisterially.

'Oh . . . er . . . right.' Graham was on his feet.

'I think,' Nesta to him *sotto voce*, 'I should take her upstairs. Shock, you know.'

He, inaccurately, interpreted that to mean 'women's trouble', and disappeared to the kitchen.

A few minutes later Maddy noticed she was on a bed but without any idea how she got there. Graham arrived with a tray bearing three mugs of coffee and, in a mute display, sought Nesta's permission to stay. In his experience, women's trouble usually led to exclusion.

Nesta wore her bewildered look, making plain she had no idea why his eyebrows were doing aerobics. 'Do sit down, darling, you're making us dizzy.'

He sat on the edge of the bed and told her: 'News from downstairs.'

'Hm?'

'Our free-loading tenant has invited her friend to move in with her. He's ferrying his worldly goods into our flat.'

'*Whaaat!*' Nesta sprang to her feet and was half-way across the room. 'Don't just sit there. We've got to stop them.'

'Nesta, wait.' He shot on to the landing after her.

'Wait for what? Until they've got squatters' rights? Or spawned offspring?'

She was edging to the stairs. He edged too, arguing about needing to work out a strategy, about fearing revenge and avoiding physical violence.

'Theirs or mine?' Nesta took the stairs at speed.

Graham hesitated long enough to groan before going in hot pursuit.

Maddy, reeling from one jolting scene to another, levered herself off the bed. '*I ought to be there in case they need me. To be a witness to what happens. Or something. God, I don't know.*'

She tugged her jumper down over her jeans and ran fingers through her hair, then she walked downstairs with considerable care. Nesta was remonstrating with Linsey through a locked door. A noisy *raga* erupted inside the flat and Nesta's arguments were obliterated by sitars.

Nesta retreated and began telling Maddy that Linsey had restolen everything. The doorbell rang. Graham, exhibiting extreme reluctance, went to the door. Would he be faced by Linsey's friends planning an *asram* under his roof? Or a van delivering the boyfriend's belongings?

Two police detectives were there. The Glaswegian sergeant flashed his identity card. 'Detective Sergeant Laing, Mr Collins.' Behind him Detective Constable Dodd wore a look of suppressed excitement.

'Come in.' He did not care that he looked smug.

Nesta shouted above the *raga*. 'Did you call the police?'

'No, it's what's called a happy coincidence.'

Laing said. 'A wee bit loud, wouldn't you say?'

'I would. Please feel free to order them to turn it off.'

He savoured Laing strolling to the flat, hammering the door

with his fist and announcing in a tone that brooked no refusal: 'Police. Open up.'

The door opened. Simultaneously the music died. Linsey filled the doorway, a cloud of incense billowing around her. She was poised for argument.

Laing said: 'Excuse me, miss. It's your friend here we want to talk to.'

The young man was escorted outside.

'Is this him, sir?' Laing was speaking to a figure at the wheel of a car parked next to the police car.

Presumably the answer was yes because Laing ordered the student into the police car. Linsey strutted about the drive muttering mantras. The other car drove away.

Constable Dodd satisfied the Collinses' curiosity. 'The owners of a cottage that was broken into think he did it. They say he hangs around, behaves strangely.'

Nesta jumped in. 'Maddy also has a problem with him.'

So Maddy explained she had been spied on and described the path to the barn. Linsey interrupted with a spirited defence. He was not a burglar and not a snooper, she said; he had heard The Truth and lived a pure life.

'Thank you, miss,' said Laing, and reached past her and opened the car door. Another moment and the police car was gone.

Linsey chanted in the middle of the drive. Graham rounded up the restolen goods. Nesta shifted the student's possessions into the hall.

Graham brought out the tape-player. 'Don't know whether this is his or whether Lord Buckshee granted it as a blessing to her.'

But no one was listening to him. Nesta had just remarked on the coincidence of the detectives being the pair who had interviewed Maddy. And it was dawning on her that they were still on the murder case, that the student was a suspect, and that for a brief span of time he had lived at Park House.

CHAPTER ELEVEN

Church bells woke Maddy on Sunday morning. Sunlight glinted beneath her curtain and horses' hooves clattered past. She had overslept having lain awake into the small hours fretting. The reassurances she and Nesta had given each other had faded like moonshine.

Word of the drama at Park House had spread through the village during Saturday. Peter Ribston had telephoned to confirm it. Gilly had described the youth's demeanour in the police car as it flashed by her skein of horses leaving the riding school. Gina Winterson had claimed he always looked shifty; and her husband added that people who burgled were capable of worse. The shopkeeper remembered a morning he suspected the youth of shoplifting. The widow from The Close claimed no one would rent him a flat in Oxford because he was an unreliable tenant. The farmer whose barn had been loaned without quibble proceeded to quibble.

The river of talk flowed on, rippling excitedly around the student's unknown past and his habit of taking cross-country shortcuts instead of sticking to thoroughfares where everyone could keep an eye on him. By evening, the weekenders who had pointed the finger at him were enjoying enhanced status in the pub. The episode had catapulted them to the forefront of village life. Never mind a broken window at an empty house, they had unmasked Beth Welford's murderer.

Maddy was not deceived for long. It had been comforting to believe the police had caught Beth's killer but none of the tittle-tattle mentioned evidence. Gossip inflamed by a community's urgency to find the killer in its midst did not count. The police might not have anything to connect him with the break-in at the cottage, either; and only the line of a path implicated him in snooping.

Her dog nosed open her door and rested his head on the duvet.

'In a minute,' she said.

Jay took the edge of the duvet in his teeth and delicately pulled. She gave in, got up.

Because she was late the central heating had been on for hours and the house was cosy. She sat at the kitchen table in her dressing gown reading the Sunday paper. While she was lazily wondering whether to pour a second cup of coffee, Nesta rang.

'Everything all right?'

'Fine, thanks, Nesta. You?'

'Yes. No more dramas.'

In the background Maddy heard Graham saying: 'Or farces.'

Nesta said: 'It's a lovely morning. Can we come and photograph your herbs?'

'Er . . . yes.'

'Graham needs the sun, you see. The forecast said it's going to be overcast later.'

The Collinses were watching over her. When they arrived, Graham dangled a padlock in front of her.

'Happened to have this lying around.'

It seemed new. There were no marks to show it had been screwed to anything or out in the weather. They trooped out to the garden and inspected the gap in the wall and the trace of a path over the field.

Graham said: 'I can lift the stones into place, if you like.'

But Nesta argued: 'The person who broke the wall would know Maddy has found out.'

He frowned. 'He does know. The police were talking to him yesterday.'

Nesta smothered a protest.

'*She knows,*' Maddy thought. '*She's been round the same course I have. There's no evidence it was the student and it's more likely it was Steve.*'

Graham said: 'It's your wall, Maddy. Your decision.'

'I'd like it mended.'

Now it was Nesta frowning at her.

Once he had taken a closer look at the damage, Graham climbed back into the garden and said that rather than balance the stones he would come next day and make a proper job of it.

He fixed the padlock and when that was done turned to photographing the herbs. Nesta pointed out various aspects of the salad burnet and the thyme that she particularly wanted him to illustrate; but she was careful not to touch in case she came up in bumps. Then she and Maddy went indoors, taking Jay who was fond of Graham and kept padding around him and casting unwanted shadows.

As Maddy made fresh coffee, Nesta was reminded to ask: 'Did you check the telephone number of the coffee bar?'

Maddy admitted she had forgotten.

Nesta said: 'Let's do it now.' She picked up the phone. 'What's the number?'

'You can press 3 in the memory and it will dial it automatically.'

'Three?' Nesta listened a moment before reporting an unanswered ringing tone.

Maddy was losing interest except for wondering what Nesta might say if Steve answered.

Nesta put the phone down. 'You must have misdialled when you got the unobtainable signal.'

'But . . .' She had a good memory for numbers and could keep a dozen in her head.

Nesta, skimming through the directory, recited a number as she keyed it in.

'That's what I called,' said Maddy.

'Unobtainable.'

'But how . . . ?'

'This memory thing . . .' Nesta scrutinised the telephone.

'I've never had to do this before. I'll get the instructions.'

She produced a booklet. 'Right. I press this.' She did. 'And this.' She did. 'And the number in the memory is displayed here.'

There was a tense moment while she held up the display panel for Nesta to read. Then, her voice tight, Maddy said: 'I don't know this number. I don't know where it is.'

Nesta said: 'Check the other numbers in the memory, to make sure it's working.'

They were accurate.

Maddy said: 'Steve changed his number to prevent me calling him at work. But I spoke to him on it twice. So where was he?'

'Perhaps you can find out from the telephone company where that number is.'

'Doubtful, they have so many rules to protect their customers.'

'In that case you'll have to get the truth out of Steve.'

Something was nagging at Maddy but she was loath to discuss it. Her reasons were mean as the Collinses cared deeply for her. But there it was: she was afraid to say anything that would increase their anxiety and she preferred to be on her own.

She used Jay's pestering as an excuse to change the subject. They went to see how Graham was getting on.

By lunchtime she had the house to herself. She had refused a drink at the pub with a couple of friends and had promised the Collinses she would head for Park House the moment she felt uncomfortable being alone. The format amused her. Nesta had given up all pretence of trusting Steve and made it obvious she felt Maddy might be all right in the house on her own but perhaps not when he was there.

Maddy checked her padlock, for the novelty of doing so,

and attached its key to the belt on her jeans. Then she settled down with the paper. Jay dozed by her feet.

Her mind strayed, though. It hovered around the discovery that Steve had tampered with her telephone. What else might he have done? Unwillingly she gave in to another bout of speculation. In the night she had struggled with the notion of him tearing a hole in her wall. He had had ample opportunity but why should he have done it? *The man had keys to her house*. He came and went as he chose. During the day she was out longer than he was and even if she had been inclined to do so, she could not have checked whether he was in the garden or had left. So why had he created a secret exit, a secret entry?

She knew of only two possible culprits: Steve and the student. According to the village he was called Everard or Everett, spelling variable. His first name was Jake or Jock. She elected to think of him as Everard, as that was the first rendering she had heard.

She posed the same question about him. What possible reason might he have had for breaking her wall? Snooping was unconvincing. Unless he had a fetish involving estate agents approaching forty, there were prettier women in accessible houses and easier to ogle.

And then there was Linsey's vociferous defence of him. Well, perhaps one would not take Linsey's word for much, not about her own identity or her rights to property, say; but her conviction that he could not be a criminal was passionate. Linsey knew Everard, which was not true of any of the people who spoke against him.

If his liberty had rested in Maddy's hands he would probably have resumed his life as a latterday scholar gypsy. But there was the path and the path led to him. It did not lead to Steve at a secret telephone number, it led to the barn where Everard camped.

She stiffened as another thought crowded in. '*What happens after that?*'

There was only one way to find out. '*Oh God, I don't know if I could face it.*'

A vague plan formed. If Everard were detained by the police next day she would see where the path ended up. She need not struggle across country again, the riverside path would take her most of the way. If he were free she could still go although she did not fancy meeting him. She had felt his eyes on her when she was prying in the barn, presumably *his* eyes because nobody else had been there.

Maddy stood up, tripping over Jay and making a commotion. They were both recovering their equilibrium when Patsy Kimball, the solicitor who had been a guest at the frightful dinner party, rang.

After polite preliminaries, especially apologies for disturbing Maddy on a Sunday, Patsy got to the point. 'My colleague Dallas who's representing Chris Welford had an anguished phone call from him yesterday. A man went to Church Cottage during the afternoon saying he was a potential buyer come to view it.'

'Oh, no.'

'He had details from your office.'

'He *stole* them.'

'I see. I couldn't imagine how it had come about. I persuaded Dallas to let me have a word with you. Chris seems poised to make a hell of a fuss.'

'Complain to my head office, I suppose?'

'To the press, to the police . . . You name it.'

'Patsy, are you simply warning me the storm's about to break or is there a way to avert it?'

'Face Chris? Grovel?'

A bitter laugh. 'Done it.' She explained.

Patsy was bemused. 'It's incredible he didn't know Beth was putting the place on the market.'

Taking a line from Steve, Maddy said: 'Tells you something you didn't know about the Welfords' relationship, doesn't it?'

There was an interesting pause before Patsy said: 'You've hit it, Maddy. I'd better get on to Dallas. Oh, before I go. Do many people know about it?'

Ironically: 'Why would I have broadcast it?'

'Good. 'Bye, Maddy.'

The nastiness of what had happened made Maddy feel sick. Beth had misled her, the young man had stolen from her, and Chris Welford, whose wife had been murdered, was being harassed. She was not proud, either, of her method of wriggling out of trouble at work. Thank heavens Patsy had grasped the point swiftly and not obliged her to stress that Chris would do well to keep quiet about anything which supplied a motive for murder.

She was watching a nature programme on television that evening when, out of the corner of her eye, she saw Jay's ears lift to alert. Then there was the rasp of a key in the lock.

Maddy followed the dog into the hall. Steve was kicking off his boots. They had left muddy patches on the flagstones.

'Sorry I didn't get back sooner,' he was saying, as casually as he might if he were an hour late instead of two whole days. 'Didn't mean to miss Nesta's dinner party but I don't suppose she minded.'

'Steve, you might have let me know you weren't coming. It was embarrassing.'

Another formula, she noticed. She had not been embarrassed. Various other things but not that.

'I'm sorry. I've said I'm sorry. OK?'

He sounded belligerent, not apologetic. They were both being dishonest.

He threw his jacket down on the bench and walked past her to the kitchen. Maddy saw a pale streak of yellowish mud on the jacket sleeve.

She trailed after him saying: 'Well, come on. Tell me where you've been?'

He weighed the kettle in his hand and decided there was enough water for a cup of tea.

He gave her a sidelong look. 'You wanted me out, remember?'

'Yes but not a disappearing act.'

'I went up to London. A friend of somebody I met in Oxford is setting up a business.' He paused to drop a teabag into the pot. 'A scientific magazine, actually. They need somebody to look over technical stuff for them. Write occasional features. That sort of thing.' He took his mug from its hook on the dresser.

'Freelance or staff?' Maddy found a safe question. She put no faith in the friend or the magazine or in Steve being anybody's technical editor but it would not do to suggest that.

'Freelance to start with. See how it goes.'

The kettle boiled and he poured water onto the bag. Maddy took the packet of milk from the fridge and stood it on the table.

'Tell me the rest,' she said. A nice open question, one that ought to draw information but avoided challenging him with the fact that an interview took an hour or so, not a weekend.

He slipped into his vaguest mood. 'Oh, you know.' He made drinking his tea an excuse not to go on.

She prompted. 'Did you stay in London?'

'Yes, I mooched around, went to a couple of exhibitions, the usual things you do in London.' More tea drinking.

'How did you get muddy?'

'I walked from the station.' He picked up the newspaper.

'All that way?' The station was in the next village.

Steve turned the pages. 'Hm? Yes.'

'It must have taken ages.'

'About forty-five minutes.' He became engrossed in reading.

She pictured him striking off across country with the light going. Tracks dwindled to footpaths, footpaths meandered through woods and fields, and at dusk they demanded special care. You could slip, get snagged on walls and shrubs. You could get lost. You could take hours.

She said: 'I expect you were the only passenger getting off there.'

126

Slowly he disengaged his mind from the newspaper and looked up at her. 'Yes.'

He was making her feel awkward for wanting a conversation, wanting information. She was undecided whether it was deliberate. His eyes rested on hers. He was waiting for her, weighing something in his mind. She had caught him in a blank moment between expressions, when his face was choosing how to look. What it would decide depended, apparently, on her.

All at once she grasped what was going on. She struggled to conceal the fact that she had made a discovery. A loud signature tune blared from the television, conveniently giving her a reason to leave the room. When she returned to the kitchen the tricky moment was over.

She feigned a headache and went to her room early. Jay brazenly joined her, having shattered the rule that he was not allowed upstairs. She looked down the long length of the village. Porch lights glowed. A cat prowled by a wall. Moonlight was silvering the road but it was too dark for walking without a torch and certainly not for blundering about on footpaths.

Steve was lying to her. Probably the only honest thing he had said was that he had walked across country. Mud was irrefutable. She doubted he had been to London. Two nights away meant luggage and he had not been carrying any.

Then there was the train. Or rather there was *not* a train. A flurry of commuter trains stopped at the station on weekdays but nothing on Sundays. He had spotted his mistake as soon as she asked whether he was the only passenger; and he had been assessing whether she was being sarcastic or whether he had got away with it.

A lamp snapped off in a window that would remain blank for a week. Car headlights appeared close to the weekenders' cottage. They grew bolder, patterning her wall. Before the vehicle had swung through the bends she drew her curtains.

Sighing, she dropped down on the bed. Jay nuzzled her and she absent-mindedly stroked his golden coat.

'*Why should I care that Steve's lying to me?*' she thought. '*He's always lied, about finding work and about adventures when he was a kid in Africa.*'

Some words of Nesta's floated into her mind. 'He's a sham.'

No argument. So he was. But what did any of it matter, now that he was going?

CHAPTER TWELVE

Maddy's heart quickened as she entered the small bedroom. Somewhere amidst the mess might be clues to the truths Steve denied her.

Already she felt guilty. It was unlike her to be underhand. She fought down the urge to retreat, stepped across a scattering of papers and shoes and dropped to her knees by the chest. With shaking hands she tugged at the bottom drawer.

It was heavier than she expected. It stuck, too, and she had to jiggle it open.

'Suppose I can't close it again? What if he realises I've done this?'

Two hours ago, waking to a grey damp morning, she realised her anger at his latest crop of lies was unabated. When she had heard him leave the house, it had hardened into a determination to help herself to the facts.

The drawer held music tapes, papers, and a jumble of oddments. She whisked through the papers but there was nothing of interest. With some difficulty, she closed it. The others contained clothes plus odds and ends. There were no clues to what he had been doing with his time.

A frisk through the pockets of clothes in a cupboard produced only innocuous till receipts.

Maddy contemplated the clutter, gauging whether she dared disturb it. She decided it was also doubtful that anything secret would have been left lying around.

LESLEY GRANT-ADAMSON

Kneeling again, she explored beneath the bed. What she saw took her by surprise. She had forgotten that, short of space, she had stowed a pair of folding steps under what had, at that time, been a spare bed. *'Why hasn't he asked me to put them elsewhere?'*

She dragged them out thinking that, if he caught her, fetching the steps was an excuse for being in his room. Then, as her eyes adjusted to the gloom, she noticed one of her storage boxes and reached for it.

At that instant there was a thump behind her and something landed on her legs. With a squeal she wriggled out from under the bed and rolled over. A stool had toppled, apparently nudged by her foot, and the clothes and books that had been dumped on it were now dumped on her. She scurried to set the stool upright and replace the mound. Her right hand was very dusty. She wiped it down her jeans.

Everything she did now was hasty. The mishap with the stool had shaken her control. She whimpered when a book slipped off the pile. 'Stay there. Please.'

It was not right, this new arrangement on the stool. Maddeningly, she could not remember exactly how it had looked. All she was sure of was that it was different and Steve was bound to notice.

'Leave it. Take the steps away.'

Fright being the spur, she dreamed up an excellent place to store them downstairs. Meanwhile, she hoisted them into her room and leaned them against the wall beside the door.

Then she went to Steve's room, anxious that the falling stool had dislodged other things. But catching sight of the time, she had to dash to the bathroom to wash her face and dusty hands. She had not left herself long to change into her suit, snatch breakfast and drive to work.

Minutes later, eating a biscuit and drinking coffee, she discovered that guilt had given way to dissatisfaction at her inefficiency. It seemed impossible she had found nothing of significance.

But what had she expected to find? Hardly a journal with an account of his days. Yet . . .

Something hovered just beyond her consciousness.

Frustrated by failure, she decided to check the one statement that *could* be checked. She picked up the telephone.

For a second she listened to a train in the background. Then the young man in the ticket office was speaking to her.

'Do trains stop there on Sundays?'

'Sorry. Nothing timetabled on Sundays.'

'But is there a chance that one which wasn't scheduled to . . . What I mean is, did a train stop there yesterday evening to let passengers alight?'

'No. Definitely not. The last one through was on Saturday. There was nothing else until this morning.'

She was glad to have the fact confirmed because it was the only lie she could nail. She spurned the rest of her coffee and hurried into the hall. Bending to take her good shoes out of the cupboard, she saw Steve's jacket on the bench. It lay where he had thrown it the previous evening, muddy sleeve uppermost.

Maddy snatched it up and felt in the pockets. A virtually indecipherable bus ticket. A wrapper from a chocolate bar. A pocket knife. A couple of paper handkerchiefs. Then she started on the inside pockets. Oddments of no interest. She laid the jacket on the bench and arranged the muddy sleeve on view.

'That's good,' he said, alarming her so that she screamed and jumped back against the wall. 'No one would ever know.'

He was in the sitting room doorway. She had watched him walk away from the cottage hours ago but never conjectured a secret return. Her head reeled. How long had he been there? How much did he know? About the bedroom? And the call to the station, too?

Shock made her inarticulate. She stared, hot and guilty.

'I suppose you've searched my room, too.'

Did that mean he knew it or not? She gulped, still bereft of words.

'Well, did you find whatever you were looking for?' He was sneering.

What kindled her aggression was his superiority. The missing words came rushing forth.

At the height of it, the postman arrived with a package too big for the rather small letterbox. Maddy, nearest, opened the door. The man's face told her she must be a strange sight: wild woman in a business suit.

'Good morning, Jim. How's the weather out there?' Another automatic response, a stupid formula.

'Still near freezing,' he said. Then: 'They're saying Everitt's been charged with the murder. Have you heard if that's right?'

'Sorry, no. I expect I'll be the last to be told, so don't rely on me, Jim.'

He started down the path but Maddy did not close the door between them.

'I have to go,' she said coldly to Steve. She fetched her bag and car keys, tossed her post on the passenger seat and drove off.

After a couple of miles she stopped in a field gateway. Her mind was racing over the morning's events and taking her concentration away from her driving. She needed a quiet minute or two to recover. Winding down the window, she took deep breaths of clean, sharp air.

It occurred to her that her fruitless search might yet achieve what her patience and persuasion had failed to do. It might get him out of her house. If so, it would be worth his sneering contempt while she had raged. She wondered where it might have ended if Jim had not brought the post. Maddy opened her mail, a disappointing selection of bills and advertising leaflets. The package was a sample of detergent. Turning the radio to heart-warming Mozart, she drove on.

Woodstock was shiny after a light shower. '*If only spring would come,*' she thought, '*instead of dithering in the wings, peeping around a curtain of cloud for a few hours here and there.*'

'Good morning, Maddy.'

A generously moustached man who owned a gift shop

walked up as she unlocked her office. 'Any news of Ken?' His face furrowed with concern. Ken was liked. Ken was missed.

'Not since Friday. I hope to hear from him this morning.' She imagined Ken resigned to a hospital bed until the doctor did his rounds or the bed was needed for an urgent case, whichever was the sooner.

'He could be off some time.' The moustache twisted in sympathy, for Ken and his hurt and for Maddy and her extra workload.

She remembered the man's wife had been an invalid for months after a spine-wrenching fall from a step-ladder.

'I'll tell him you asked after him,' she said, opening the door and glad to escape from the sparkling cold day.

She switched on a heater, skipped through the post and listened to a high-volume message from Mrs Morris.

'Maddy, love, I want to go over to the bungalow Monday afternoon to measure up for curtains. Can you can fix it with the Peglers for me?'

Maddy smiled. As far as she was concerned, Mrs Morris could have anything she asked for. She was buying a house and there were not enough people like her around. Curtain-measuring was a positive sign emphasising commitment. The visits that made Maddy's heart sink were the non-specific ones, those that, even if the visitor was unaware of it, were fault-finding excursions. Fault-finding led to backing out.

She walked to a shop a few doors down to buy milk and a bun as she had missed breakfast. A wind had blown up. It buffeted her relentlessly. When she returned, the answering machine was flashing.

'Ring me, Maddy, will you?' Ken said. He sounded rushed, leading her to imagine various kinds of hospital drama.

Before she had time, Cathy was on the line from Witney. What news of Ken? What news of the murder?

'According to Jim, the postman,' began Maddy, knowing

how Cathy relished detail and demanded sources, 'a university student who's been camping in a barn outside the village has been charged.'

'Gosh. Do you know him?'

'He's called something like Jake Everard. I often see him when I'm walking the dog.'

Cathy made a shivery sound. 'Oooooh. It makes you think, doesn't it?'

No. Until Cathy said that it had not entered Maddy's head that she might have been the victim instead of Beth.

'Mmm,' she said, covering up her lack of imagination. 'But I've been managing not to dwell on it.'

'Was it on the radio?'

'I didn't hear it.' Hardly, she had been too busy searching Steve's room and having a row with him.

'I'll see if I can catch it on the hourly bulletins.' Cathy kept her office radio tuned to the local station. She had once confided to Maddy that she wished she had become a journalist, having such a keen nose for news.

'Call me if you do,' Maddy said, ringing off. No need to have asked. Cathy would be relaying it before the words were out of the news-reader's mouth.

Maddy was poised to return Ken's call but Clive from her Oxford office got through first. Even his 'good morning' sounded a warning.

'I've had a Dallas Grenville on, a solicitor, complaining you've upset her client. She's representing the husband of that murdered girl. Welford, is it? Anyway, you're supposed to have sent a man to view his house which isn't even on the market.'

She groaned. 'I hoped I'd sorted this out.'

'How in the world did it happen?'

Maddy gave a resumé of the confusion, ending lamely: 'I should never have let him see the details. But at the time I was so involved with Mrs Morris . . .'

Clive helped her out. 'You weren't to know he'd pinch them.'

'Exactly.'

'Well, I'd better call Dallas Grenville and do a bit of grovelling.'

'Please don't volunteer me to grovel to Chris Welford. I made a hash of it last time. He isn't amenable, Clive.'

'No, I'm sure you needn't do that. Not now he's dragged his solicitor into it. Well, sorry to wreck your Monday morning with this.'

She gave an ironic smile. As Monday mornings went, this was high in her league of worst evers.

She went into the cloakroom to comb her hair after the battle with the wind. She touched her eyelashes with mascara, her lips with Rose Blush. As she was washing her hands, a vague recollection stirred. Hand-washing had revived it but she could get no further than that.

House buyers came and house vendors went. She reached Ken and learned he was to stay in hospital.

'God, I can't wait to get back, Maddy. You don't believe you enjoy work all that much until you're prevented from doing it.'

'*Or,*' she thought, '*wasting time driving around the countryside and keeping lunchtime rendezvous with young ladies beginning with S.*'

She wondered whether the current S. had visited him. 'Do your friends get over to Chippy to see you?'

'Yes, not that I can hear a thing they say with the two fellows in this ward rabbiting on. I've got a farm labourer and a man who's worked all his life in the furniture factory up the road. There's nothing Arnie hasn't told me about slurry or Brad hasn't told me about staves and struts and webbing and . . .'

'All right. I'll look in myself.'

'Be an angel, Maddy, and bring me a decent bottle of scotch to numb the pain.'

She bought it at lunchtime, then locked it in the boot of her car when she went to collect Mrs Morris. It was beyond the call of duty to take buyers on curtain-measuring excursions but Mrs Morris did not know that. Maddy made an exception, believing the session would run more smoothly if she were present. There had been a time when buyer and sellers had got on each other's nerves.

Mrs Morris lived in a hamlet on the edge of the wrong town. During her husband's lifetime it had been quite satisfactory, first because he worked at a local factory and then, in his retirement, because he enjoyed his garden and pottering around in his car. Mrs Morris did not drive and the steep staircase was increasingly difficult because of her bulk. Her only family lived a mile from Dunflirtin which was close to a different town.

Maddy's car began to climb the rise to the hamlet. She had made exceptionally good time and it was just after two. On other occasions she had been caught behind farm vehicles and had had to race to keep the appointment. She did not want to be early, though, so she stopped and switched on the radio.

'. . . with the murder of Jean Dellafield. Thames Valley police said a man would appear in court in Oxford later today.'

'*So it's true.*'

But she ran out of words, giving way to vague sensations. Relief, of course, that the culprit was under lock and key. Admiration for the police who had got their man. Disquiet because she had been at risk whenever she had bumped into Everard. Further disquiet at her lack of judgment in having believed him diffident and harmless. Mystification about his motive for killing Beth. Lingering uncertainty simply because it was too difficult to accept that a person she knew was a murderer. Realisation that she had been hoping the killer was a man without links to the village.

'*Everard has only a slight connection . . .*'

But it was no good squirming away from it. His connection was strong enough to make the difference between the killer being a stranger or a familiar face. By hovering on its edges, isolated and unobtrusive, Everard had intensified interest in himself. Nearly everyone who lived there would be able to claim they 'knew' him.

Her reactions to the dismal news occupied Maddy until she was with Mrs Morris, when conversation hinged on curtains. Nets or no nets? Pleated headings or pelmets? Tie backs or hooks? Ready-made or made-to-measure? Stitched-in linings or loose? Patterned fabric or plain? Various colours or one throughout the house?

Oh, yes, there was plenty to be said about curtains. Mrs Morris said most of it on the way to Dunflirtin. She had reached washable fabrics versus dry-clean, and was telling Maddy her brother Jack's opinion of their merits, when they pulled up outside the bungalow. A hush descended on the car. The first for miles.

A grateful Maddy tugged at the hand brake, a hazardous movement while her passenger's right thigh was hiding it from sight and depressing it. But Mrs Morris did not notice the embarrassing fumbling.

A soft moan escaped her. 'Oh . . .'

Maddy felt her go rigid, if one so large and loose could be said to do such a thing.

'What is it, Mrs Morris?' She abandoned her struggle with the brake and extracted her hand from beneath the woman's thigh.

Mrs Morris was transfixed. 'They've changed it.' She wailed like a child with an empty stocking on Christmas morning.

Maddy's eyes widened. Then she clenched them, shutting out the problem and hoping it would be gone when she peeped again. It was still there. She steeled herself to deal with it. Beside her, Mrs Morris was pushing the car door open and pouring out. The car bounced until this was done. Maddy pulled the hand-brake on properly.

They stood, one either side of the car, looking at the bungalow. There was, as Mr Pegler had promised, no evidence that the property had ever been called Dunflirtin. He had removed the name-plate, filled in the holes in the rendering and he had repainted the gateposts and the front garden wall. Yellow. The red brick bungalow sat there like a dollop of rhubarb in custard.

Mrs Morris wobbled around the car to Maddy. 'What's he done that for?'

'He was being kind,' said Maddy, who had herself meant to be kind when she encouraged him.

'*Kind?*' It was the sharpest tone ever heard from her. 'What's kind about daubing that yellow over my wall?'

'Shall we go in?' Maddy had seen a curtain – fancy pleated florals, no nets – move in the sitting room bay.

She took a step towards the house and discovered Mrs Morris was stuck fast, gazing without rapture at the yellow paint. Maddy went smartly to the gate, opened it, looked round. Mrs Morris's stricken face quashed the cajoling remark Maddy had ready. For the second time that Monday she waited for the bad news which was bearing down on her.

'I can't abide that yellow, Maddy, love. It would really get me down.'

Disheartened by the yellow paint affair, Maddy returned to her office in no mood to be nice to time-wasters. She had used up her day's store of diplomacy during the terrible episode when Mrs Morris told Mr Pegler he had spoiled the bungalow, and he had defended himself in a way that, under different circumstances, Maddy would have found admirable. As it was, she had been forced to placate everybody, including an offended neighbour who had the misfortune to drop in and cheerily ask Mrs Morris whether she didn't think the gateposts looked lovely.

Being 'got down', Mrs Morris measured only one window, rather cursorily, before choosing to go home. There was less chat on the homeward journey.

Maddy shut the office door as firmly as she might without slamming. She glared at her flashing answering machine, accused it of being the bearer of bad tidings and then ignored it. She had it fixed in her head that Mrs Morris had left a message saying she had changed her mind about buying the bungalow; and that Mr Pegler had rung to say he refused to sell to her. This was not unwarranted fantasy: they had come perilously close to saying these things to each other face to face.

It was the worst of days to be alone. Like everyone else, she liked Ken and she had more reason than most to miss him. She enjoyed the camaraderie, the joking squabbles, the saga of his love-life and the silly bets. Damn, she was going to lose the Dunflirtin bet.

She wondered how he might have advised her to handle the Church Cottage stolen details affair. Or Dallas Grenville's complaint to Clive. Or the yellow paint.

No! Not the yellow paint. She forbade herself to think about that. Ken, she would think about Ken. About how she was missing his comradeship. About how his natural gallantry would have led him to protect her from the wrath of Clive had it proved necessary, and from Chris Welford's when it did.

Perhaps she should stop thinking what a great chap Ken was and go and see him that day. Not to relive disasters by relating them but to take her gift and hear about life as a patient. She went to buy wrapping paper.

The afternoon was drawing on. She leaned into the wind as she crossed the street, heading for the stationer's. A few people were hurrying along, hunched into collars to cheat the cold. A woman pushed a baby that seemed frozen to its chair. An old man with rheumy eyes stopped to cough, leaning a leather-gloved hand against the wall of the chemist's. A young shop assistant in a thin overall darted from the baker's to a shoe shop two doors away. A young man stepped out of the gift shop owned by the man with the moustache and marched down the street towards Maddy.

She could not quite place him. Briefly his eyes rested on her and then he was swinging to his left, crossing the road, his face averted. Cars passed between them. A high delivery van pulled up and masked him.

In the stationer's she flicked through the rack of wrapping papers, seeking something Ken-like. Most of the designs were more Mrs Morris than Ken.

'*No! Don't think about her. No yellow paint, no Peglers, no Mrs Morris.*'

A tartan emerged from amongst the whimsy and Maddy seized on it. While she was carrying it to her office, she identified the young man. He was the one who had stolen the Church Cottage details. No wonder he had avoided meeting her.

The bright eye of the answering machine winked at her as she entered the office. 'Oh, all right. I suppose I can't ignore you for ever.' She jabbed buttons.

'Clive, Maddy. Can't catch Dallas Grenville today. I'll keep you posted. Bye.'

'This is Charles Watson about Felden Farm. Message for Maddy Knewton. Apologies about the mix-up last week. I'm around for the next couple of days so we could try again.' True to Felden form, the message was cut off before he had finished.

'It's Steve, Maddy. Can you ring me before you drive home? I've got a message for you.'

Next a man requested details of a house he had seen in the window over the weekend. This was followed by a plaintive message from a woman whose house nobody wanted.

The only puzzling message was Steve's. Did the fact that he had not said where he was mean he was at Meadow Cottage? Yes, she decided, because how else would he have been given a message for her? Ah, she was assuming it was a telephone message. Her life was so ruled by telephones that she was slow to remember messages could come by other means. In the village he might have spoken to someone in the street. Nesta or Graham. Patsy Kimball. Ribston. Lots of local people might have given him a message for her.

Huh. Oh, no they would not. He disliked and avoided most of them and they distrusted him. Anyone who wanted to tell her anything would pick up a telephone.

Perverse, she tapped out the number of the Oxford coffee bar. Unobtainable. She looked up a name in the business directory and spoke to a man in a shoemender's shop.

Maddy played her role against the grind of machinery.

'Sorry to trouble you but I'm trying to contact Dennis at the coffee bar next door. They seem to have a problem with their phone.'

'They've gone out of business, that's their problem.'

'Oh? When?'

'Last Christmas, I think. Hold on a minute.'

He shouted to a colleague. The grinding came to a halt. A voice called. He came back to Maddy. Grinding again.

'Yes, about a week before Christmas, it was. Went bust, shut up shop, end of story. Sorry.'

Before returning to his customers he indulged his curiosity. 'They don't owe you money, do they?'

'No, nothing like that.'

'You're luckier than some, then. People reckon they took off for Spain and the creditors are scratching.'

'Oh, dear. Well, thanks for your help.'

'Cheers.'

Next she tried, unsuccessfully, the strange number, the one in her telephone's memory. She rang the operator.

'If I tell you a number can you say what part of Oxford it's in?'

'What's the number?'

She read it out. The woman said it was in the city.

The key, Maddy felt, was to understand what Steve had hoped to achieve by swapping the number. *Had* achieved.

She was working it out aloud. 'He wanted me to believe he was employed at the coffee bar. If he simply wanted me to think he was working, he could have invented a new job and fooled me just as easily. For some reason, he wanted to keep the coffee bar idea alive. Why?'

She prowled to the cloakroom and back. No answer.

'Next point. When did he make the switch? That's easy. When the coffee bar closed down.'

But immediately a voice in her head argued. '*You don't know that. It could have been ages before. The shoemender told you when Dennis's business went bust, not when Steve stopped working there.*'

CHAPTER THIRTEEN

Ken was numbered among the walking wounded. Maddy's quaint fantasies about a brave little face jutting above snowy linen vanished. He was strolling down the corridor outside the ward when she arrived. His eyes rested on the promising bulge in her bag and his welcoming smile moved up a notch.

'They get you on your feet sharpish,' he said, pretending to resent being denied a lie-in of several days' duration.

His colour was good. She suspected he looked healthier and happier than she did. But then he spoiled it by wincing and fingering the strapping around his chest.

'Mind if we sit down? There are a few chairs in the ward.'

He turned delicately and they walked side by side to the ward, Ken promising: 'Clarice who does the teas will be along shortly. Life in here is measured by such petty routines, you know. Were you ever in hospital?'

'I'm strictly a visitor.'

He waggled a hand towards an armchair covered in bloated black plastic. 'That one's not too crippling to sit on, so I'm told. I could tell you all about its construction but I promise to restrain myself.'

He settled for a firm upright affair himself. 'My strapping doesn't allow sagging but *you* may lounge as much as you like.'

Maddy drew the armchair near to where he sat. The plastic was unpleasantly tacky. When she sat down the chair wheezed.

Ken grimaced. 'Sorry about the whoopee cushion effect. You'd think they'd have more compassion, wouldn't you? Fancy putting a joke chair in a ward where no one dare laugh for the pain?'

'How long have they given you?'

'Oh, it isn't fatal.'

Maddy laughed at his deliberate misunderstanding. 'I mean until they let you out!'

'That's better,' he said. 'The first decent smile since you got here. What's weighing you down? Not pressure of work, surely.'

'I hate hospitals. You don't know how privileged you are to have enticed me in here.'

'As long as it's not the office. I'd have to add guilt to my splendidly mixed emotions if you said you were bowing beneath the workload.'

'I've been missing you. There's no one to discuss anything with.'

He looked sceptical. 'The line from Witney is frequently busy, I seem to recall.'

'Not the same thing.'

'Well, no, you can hardly bicker with Cathy about the minutiae of our daily round. Talking of which . . .' Forgetting, he began to twist round, thought better of it, jerked another inch and then gave up. 'Is that Clarice's trolley I just heard?'

Maddy skipped to the doorway and scanned for a tea trolley. Her agility seemed out of place so she sauntered back. 'Tea's on the horizon.'

'Nab her when she gets here, will you? She's inclined to fly past.'

He appeared about to delve deeper into the trolley pusher's habits but Maddy headed him off. One thing she loathed about hospitals was the way the world shrank to utter tedium. There was too much disturbance to concentrate on serious reading but no stimulation. Quite intelligent people took to trolley-watching.

Maddy slid the tartan parcel onto his bed. 'With love from me, and the ardent wish that you get well soon.'

'If that's what I believe it to be . . .'

'Wouldn't bring you anything less, Ken.'

'Could you pop it in my cupboard? Before anyone sees it.'

'Is it banned?'

'No but it will be drained if my voluble companions from the worlds of farming and furniture-making glimpse it.'

Hiding the bottle on the bottom shelf, she asked: 'What are you going to do? Guzzle it under the bed-clothes?'

He winked. 'I'll find a way.'

It was a shade more exacting than trolley-watching.

She told him about the well-wishers who had telephoned or stopped her in the street. 'Your absence has left a gap in the life of Woodstock. I thought you ought to know that. They really can't do without you.'

'What about . . . I mean, has there been a call from . . . Well . . .'

A shake of the head. 'Hasn't she rung you here?' Sarah? Sally? Susan? Sandra? Why wouldn't he use her name and clear the matter up?

'I don't think she realises she can.'

Maddy was afraid he was going to ask her to be go-between but he was side-tracked because it was time for the news.

She obliged by pressing buttons until he was happy with the picture. They talked during the run-up. Trolley wheels squealed nearer. Two large, leathery, interchangeable men arrived ready for the dual ritual of Clarice's tea and the regional news.

The reading of the day's headlines coincided with Clarice's jolly arrival: 'Ah, so here we all are again! And how is everybody now? Doing fine? Good. Oh, and a visitor too. Tea for you? Good . . .'

The woman had a handsome African face – Ghanaian?

LESLEY GRANT-ADAMSON

Nigerian? – rolled-up shirt-sleeves and a brisk way of going
about her work. Clatter of mugs, clanking of urn, grating of
spoons.

Ken was invited to introduce Maddy to his ward-mates,
Brad the chair-maker and Arnie the farm labourer, and also
to Clarice. The men vied in the banality of their remarks to
Clarice. In the corner of the room the news-reader mouthed
the day's drama.

Clarice squeaked away down the corridor. Maddy heard
her repeating her greeting, word for word, in the next room.
'Ah, so here we all are again . . .'

For a second, Ken and his fellows had their attention on
the screen but then they simultaneously decided not to be
interested in a road planning saga. Conversation broke out.

Ken spoke to Maddy. 'Brad thinks . . .' He attempted to
tip his head in Brad's direction but his bonds did not allow
it. The gesture was transformed into a courtly obeisance
from the waist. '. . . the police have arrested a man for Beth
Welford's murder. Have you heard anything?'

Cocooned here, in the ersatz world of the hospital, the
outrage of Beth's killing seemed long ago and far away.
Maddy nodded: 'I heard it first from the postman and then
I caught a radio bulletin early this afternoon.'

Brad called over to her. 'You knew him, didn't you?'

She repeated what she had told Cathy: she saw him when
she walked the dog.

She was ready with her concise explanation that he was a
student called Everard who camped in a barn. But the road
saga was replaced by a photograph of Beth and she let the
news-reader tell it.

'The common-law husband of Jean Dellafield, whose
body was found in Wychwood forest last week, has been
charged with her murder. Christopher Raymond Welford
appeared in court in Oxford this afternoon. He was remanded
in custody for seven days.'

Beth was superseded by scenery: forest on hilltop; long
shot of village; church; close up of Church Cottage. The
camera lingered on Church Cottage.

146

As soon as the item finished, Maddy faced a welter of questions. Ken was crowing: 'What did I say about husbands, Maddy? They're usually the culprits.'

Brad said: 'It's a wonder it took the police so long.'

Arnie replied. 'Did you see him making that appeal after she was killed? Really cracked up. Amazing he'd got the gall to try it.'

Brad was nodding furiously. 'That's what I mean. If the police had leaned on him a bit then . . . The state he was in they'd have got it out of him.'

They continued arguing whether the police had blundered by not being tough enough.

Ken made one of his stiff bows in Maddy's direction. 'You OK, Maddy?'

Her hands flew to her cheeks. 'So stupid . . . All afternoon I've been convinced they meant Everard.'

'Who's he?'

She mumbled the thing about a student who lived in a barn. The room suddenly seemed terribly cold and she wrapped her arms around herself. Oh, she felt so foolish, so easily confused and deluded. Why shouldn't Chris Welford be the killer? Because she knew him; because he was Beth's husband, of sorts; because women put absolute trust in the men they allowed into their lives and it was a hurt to all of them when one was violated.

Ken spoke again. 'Drink, your tea.' He meant it would do her good, that she looked upset and needed distraction. He winked at her: 'If you don't, I won't be responsible for what Clarice will say when she comes for the empties.'

The threat of Clarice forced a weak smile from Maddy. With an unsteady hand she lifted the mug to her lips.

She had tricked herself by patching together the postman's rumour and some half heard words on the radio. For hours she had been ready to pass on her delusion as accurate information. Underlying her mistake, she saw now, was her suspicion that Everard had spied on her. Primed by suspicion, she had been willing to believe him guilty of the greatest wickedness.

In a flash her make-believe world had been destroyed. She felt silly, and hot with embarrassment to have come within a second of announcing what was totally untrue. The incident thrust her back to an afternoon when she was nine, a child making a categorical statement that revealed only the fractures in her thinking. She had never forgotten the ridicule. Yet the chief ridiculers had proved equally capable of harbouring delusions. Take her mother's unmovable belief that telephone calls to Australia could not, by laws of nature, be any good. Take her father's happy belief in a future everyone else knew he would not live to see.

She felt she was being unfair, and reminded herself that refusing to face up to a terrible situation was not necessarily a bad thing. What she had done was compound her suspicion about Everard, and that was a different matter from declining an invitation to be morbid. Between truth and delusion there lay a space for the positive self-protection her father was practising.

Her mind drifted back to the conversation in the room. Brad was turning down the sound of the television. Apparently there had been a consensus that the rest of the news was boring.

Arnie was saying: 'It's not a common name, Dellafield. You wouldn't think there'd be two people of that name murdered.'

'What do you know about the other one?' Ken asked, sliding in a question to suit Arnie who was pregnant with information.

'Quite a lot. I'm from Stratford, see, where it happened. It caused a stir because there were theatre folk involved. You know what the papers are like, if they can get a celebrity into a story they will.'

Brad sat on the edge of his bed and swung his slippered feet. 'Which actors were involved?'

But Arnie was disappointingly unspecific. 'Lots of them. They were at a party, see, after the play finished. And while they were drinking and carrying on, Pippa Dellafield was being killed a few hundred yards away. No wonder the police couldn't find anybody who'd heard anything suspicious. What with the music and all that racket . . .'

'They've got carrying voices, actors.' Nobody contested Brad's assertion.

'Go on about the case,' Ken prompted.

Maddy looked from one to the other, taking no more part in the scene than a woman in an audience. She felt incapable of becoming involved, her ability to assess character or absorb information being disastrously flawed.

Arnie was reciting the basic facts of the murder. 'The girl in the case was about nineteen, Pippa, a wild one. She got herself killed. Strangled. They found her in a field down by the Avon.'

'In Stratford, was it?' Brad liked to be precise.

Arnie had the address ready. 'On Ludds Farm. The body was found by a man walking his dog before going to work.'

'Means the dog found her,' murmured Brad.

Interruptions irritated Arnie who rushed on. 'Well, the police had an idea who was responsible, see, and they pulled him in. He was called Clark. Robert Clark. They charged him and the story in the town was he'd made a confession. But when it got to court the case was stopped and he was set free.'

Pressed for details, Arnie could not supply them.

Brad tried another avenue. 'Was this Clark the boy-friend?'

'Oh, there were a number of those.' Arnie gave a suggestive laugh. 'She was known to have enjoyed a good social life, which is how the detective in charge of the case put it. Brought a smile to a few faces around town, that did.'

Maddy was startled by the levity. The woman was dead, where was the joke? *'Another time I'd think of something to say to put a stop to this,'* she thought. But not now, not when she was accusing herself of endless stupidities.

Arnie said: 'Clark had been seen around with her.'

This time it was Ken who made a joke of it. 'Sounds as though half of Stratford was.'

Maddy flinched. Even kindly Ken seemed to have forgotten she knew Beth who was murdered and Chris who was charged with killing her. *Must* have forgotten, for him to be so insensitive to her feelings.

'*I've strayed into a male club. They don't have to think about feelings or about women except as the butt of jokes. Do groups of men always denigrate women? It's pathetic if they do but we never find out, do we?*'

Ken and Brad continued to nudge Arnie's memory but it was no use. Whatever Arnie might once have known about any relationship between Pippa and Robert Clark was lost to him. With each shake of the head, each shrug and each no, he was losing his audience.

He was unwilling to let them escape so easily.

He raised a finger. 'Now, then. The interesting part is what wasn't in the papers. It was known in the area that the police had a witness who could swing the case but they couldn't get him to give evidence.'

Brad, easing the bandage on his leg, said: 'Couldn't he have been subpoenaed? That's the word, isn't it? When you're forced to give evidence?'

'Yes,' Ken said, approving the definition.

'No,' Arnie said, taking up the main point. 'He couldn't. He was young. That was the trouble, see. The killing was watched by a kid.'

There was a general rumbling of distaste, that a child should see such a thing as murder.

'It came down to this,' said Arnie. 'One witness who could not be used and not enough evidence for a trial.'

Ken put another question. 'This was in, what, nineteen seventy-something?'

'Seventy-three.'

'So that lad,' Ken went on, 'say he was younger than ten in seventy-three, well, he'd be in his twenties at least now. Has anybody asked him about it since he grew up? He'd remember, wouldn't he, something as vivid as that?'

Brad saw an alternative. 'Or shut it out of his mind because of the trauma.'

Arnie hoped to explore the case a while longer. He had not yet mentioned that his uncle had worked as a part-time barman in a pub where one of the police on the case was a regular. The reality of the uncle gave his reminiscences credence, he was sure.

But before he could drop the uncle into conversation, Brad said: 'That was the very hot summer, seventy-three.'

A chorus put him right. 'No, the heatwave was seventy-six.'

After that they talked about the weather.

It began to rain as she drove away from the hospital into open country, a nasty sort of rain that the wind flung in stinging handfuls. A figure hurried ahead of her, cowering beneath a cape. There were no sheltering trees, nothing to shield it from unkind weather.

'This could be a Victorian scene or a much older one. A man wrapped in a cloak, his trousers plastered to his legs by the wind and the rain. Makes me think of a Hardy novel.'

But as she gained on the figure the impression changed. Instead of a cloak she saw a blanket. Instead of trousers, a long limp skirt.

Maddy overtook slowly and then waited for Linsey to catch up.

With the car door open and the rain gusting in, Linsey went through the performance of touching her face in absolution before she sullied herself by entering the car of an unbeliever. Maddy heard the Collinses' voices in unison in her head: *'I'd like to wring her neck.'*

Once Linsey was ensconced and the door shut, Maddy took a tissue from a box beneath the dashboard and wiped splashes from her face. She invited Linsey to do the same.

'The rain is good,' breathed Linsey, declining. 'The water comes from heaven.'

She sat there with the heavenly water trickling through

her hair and down her face, until it dripped off her chin and pooled on her lap. Maddy restarted the engine.

'You could do with an umbrella,' she said after an awkward pause.

'Ah no, it's best to be simple. To have few possessions. An umbrella is not necessary.'

Maddy restricted her response to a murmur that might have been either doubt or concurrence. She did not fancy debating the tenets of Linsey's faith all the way to the village. For a mile or two neither of them spoke.

Then Maddy decided to ask where Linsey wanted to be dropped off. It was just possible she had accepted she was not wanted at Park House and found another berth.

'Park House,' Linsey said.

Her eyes were glued to the road ahead. Nothing in her tone or demeanour gave a clue what tack her thoughts were on. She might be meditating on the pleasures of a good soaking or she might be planning her next raid on the Collinses' property. Anything. Knowing Linsey it could be absolutely spiritual or utterly practical. The two sides of her nature seemed to fight for precedence the whole while. No wonder Graham and Nesta found her hell to have around.

Linsey said: 'I was thinking, Maddy, about Chris Welford. You know he was charged today with Beth's murder?'

'Er . . . yes. I saw it on the news.'

'Well, I was thinking what a strange nature he must have.'

'Do you know him?'

'Yes. I used to clean their house. Sometimes he was there. Not too often because of his work but sometimes. It's strange, isn't it, how people conceal their natures? Their minds are like onions, layers and layers, and the more you peel away the more you learn. A bad thing can be buried deep inside. It can hide there until something happens and suddenly the layers are shed and the person does a bad thing. A very bad thing.'

Maddy bit her lip, resisting an inclination to laugh. *'Onions, indeed. Linsey hates onions. Look how she's eradicated them from the Collinses' kitchen.'*

Aloud she said: 'I'm absolutely shocked that he did it. I can't even come to terms with that, let alone find explanations.'

'Ah, the answer is in his nature. It lies deep inside him, Maddy. This is why you are surprised.'

Against her instinct, Maddy was drawn into arguing. 'But that's not enough of an answer. How can we ever hope to understand human beings if we settle for that sort of vagueness? If you could tell me he was jealous of Beth or unable to forgive Beth something she had done . . . Those are *real* reasons. Those are human emotions. Those things I can understand.'

Linsey was agitated, 'No, no, Maddy. Emotions are only the expression of what lies beneath the layers. The important thing is whether beneath the layers there's a good nature or a bad one. Look at Jake . . .'

'Who? Oh, yes Jake Everard. Well, what about him.'

But she guessed what Linsey was about to tell her.

'He has a good nature. He could not be guilty of any crime. He has an aura of honesty. How could the police or the cottage owner accuse him?'

'Because they were told he was at the scene of the crime,' said Maddy drily.

'No, no, he was *not* there.'

Because Linsey was adamant, Maddy pressed her.

'How can you be certain?'

'His nature . . .'

'No, come on, Linsey. What you actually mean is you were with him at the time, somewhere else. That's why you're so certain.'

There was sufficient hesitation to convince Maddy she was right. Then Linsey confirmed it. 'Yes, but . . .'

Maddy did not care what the 'but' might be, she was simply pleased to have undermined Linsey's onion-layer theory. A half mile further on, though, she decided she might care, after all.

'Were you and Jake at your temple?' The cult had one in Oxford.

'Not the one you mean. There's a little place we go to in the trees where we can be at peace with nature.'

Nature, again. Maddy winced.

'And where's that?'

Linsey flapped a hand. 'Over there. It's tranquil. We can see the valley but we're in another world.'

The long hedge came in sight. Maddy dropped her off at the bottom of the drive.

When she arrived home, there was a message from Nesta begging her help with Linsey who, she feared, was pursuing her scheme of moving Everard into the flat.

Nesta was especially flustered when Maddy rang. 'Oh dear, I'd forgotten all about it. I left it when I was thinking Everard was involved in Beth's death. But now that Chris . . . You *have* heard about Chris, haven't you? Oh dear, this is no way to break it to you if you haven't.'

'Nesta . . .' It was difficult to get a word in. 'Nesta, it's all right. I've heard about Chris. What's more I've just given Linsey a lift to your house.'

'Did she have Everard with her?'

'No but she told me about him. He has a mind like an onion.'

'A what?'

'An onion. Or maybe that was Chris.'

There was a puzzled silence down the line.

Jay, who had slumped on the kitchen floor beside Maddy's chair, plodded into the hall, tail swishing.

Maddy said: 'Nesta, Steve's just come in. I'll have to go.'

'We'll talk tomorrow. I'll ring you.'

As she set the telephone down, she listened for sounds of Steve. In the sitting room? Going up to his room? The house was silent. He moved very quietly. She had never put it into words before but it was a distinct trait.

She heard the fumbling sounds of a jacket being dropped onto the pine bench. A picture filled her mind: herself feeling in his pockets while he watched. She hated the picture and had forced herself not to dwell on it but here it was again, vivid and shaming and likely to be triggered each time she heard the familiar sound.

'Steve?' Maddy bobbed into the hall, a spurious smile on her face. She hoped he would follow her lead and pretend they had not had a row that morning.

'Hi.' She was surprised by his appearance. Instead of his usual pallor, his cheeks were flushed. But it was more than that. His eyes were intensely bright. Drink? Drugs?

Steve squeezed her arm in a pally gesture that said they were friends still if no longer lovers. He went into the kitchen, Maddy trailing behind him. She had the daft idea she was experiencing what her dog habitually felt: partial understanding but not enough, nothing like enough.

She said: 'Have you heard, they've charged Chris Welford?'

'Yes, I know. So much for the happy Welfords. I suppose the locals are now saying they aren't surprised.'

'Not yet, they're still just amazed.'

'Haven't you eaten, Maddy?' There were no food smells, no used pans.

'I've only been home a few minutes because I went to see Ken in hospital.'

'Oh? How was he?' He was scanning the shelves of the fridge.

'Obviously more damaged than they thought at first which is why they're keeping him in.'

'I thought you said broken ribs.' He took out a bottle of wine and held it up for her approval.

She nodded, lifted a corkscrew from a dresser hook and slid it across the table to him. 'His chest *is* strapped up. I didn't ask him for an inventory but there must be more.'

The cork was eased from the bottle. Immediately she was imagining Ken secretly sipping whisky beneath the sheets to deny Arnie and Brad a taste.

'I took Ken a bottle of whisky,' she began, a prelude to sharing the story with Steve.

But he spoke at the same time, offering her a shimmering glass of Chardonnay. 'Cheers.'

Maddy was distracted by his appearance. If it were caused

by drugs, would he be starting on a bottle of wine? If it were alcohol, why had it never had this effect before? She ruled out his intermittent fever because that made him sweaty, anxious, retiring and not remotely like this.

'Is something wrong?' He was staring, too.

Neither of them had tasted the wine. Their glasses were poised but they were studying each other.

With a half laugh, she moved the scene on. 'I'd better see what there is to eat.'

He stepped aside for her to inspect the fridge. Eggs and fillings for omelettes; bacon and sausages and breakfasty things; cheese. She bent down and opened the freezer. A lamb and lovage casserole, a gift from Nesta, came easily to hand. Maddy put it in the oven.

'I'll do some rice with it,' she said.

She raised her glass and drank. She thought: '*He's waiting for something. Maybe he expects me to trawl for details of his lost weekend. But why should he think I'm bothered about that when I want him to go for ever?*'

The telephone rang and he answered because he was closer.

'Hello? Yes, she's here.'

Maddy raised an enquiring eyebrow.

He held the mouthpiece against his sweater to prevent the caller hearing as he told her: 'Gina Winterson. Wants you at a crisis meeting.'

She flung an exasperated look to heaven before taking the phone but her voice was happy enough when she spoke. Rather like her professional self, in fact. 'Hello, Gina. You'd like a meeting?'

Gina's voice squeaked, making Jay prick up his ears and Steve go into a dumb show of a talkative woman. Maddy turned her back on both of them and gazed out into her courtyard. The only herbs in view were scraggy tufts miserable with cold. She worried that few of them would revive.

Maddy murmured interest to Gina and continued to concentrate on her herb garden.

Then Maddy began to resist. 'Surely the meeting ought to decide . . . Mmm . . . No, I really think it's better to wait and see what the meeting thinks . . .'

The squeaking started up again.

It was Maddy's turn to cut in. 'Look, you fix a time and I'll be there. OK?'

She ended the call rapidly before the woman dredged up fresh ways of changing her mind.

Steve was sitting at the table. The story came bubbling out of her. 'She's so brazen. She wants one or two villagers she thinks have local influence to go along with her ideas and to hell with what everyone else thinks. What's the point of a public meeting if it's only to announce what she and Malcolm have decided? Or worse, have actually done?'

He grimaced. 'Which of her campaigns was it about? Dodgy school buses? Unreliable library van? Pollution in Evenlode?'

'The lorries. She's all for issuing McQuade an ultimatum, and then telling the village. She says that if it's discussed at a meeting, people might decide not to go along with it.'

'And she wants to be able to say you supported it.'

'Yes. Peter Ribston has agreed and so has Patsy Kimball.'

'Who's she?'

'A solicitor who lives in one of those big old houses down Bridge Lane. Blonde. Always so well-groomed you can't believe she's real.'

He laughed, a ripple of good humour. It suited him, the rosy colour and the warmth of amusement. They used to laugh at one time. Oh, it seemed ages ago. Every week since things went wrong between them had been interminable. She no longer knew or cared why their relationship had soured, she merely regretted it and wanted him gone. If they could part while he was on this happier note, she thought, it would be better for both of them. She dared to hope it might be so.

She delved for crisps and biscuits to nibble with the wine while they waited for the lamb to thaw and the rice to cook. Before the food was ready she took two more calls.

Peter Ribston was first. They had not spoken since the fiasco after the dinner party. The episode had been so awful, she felt a rush of embarrassment when she recognised his voice.

'Maddy, Gina Winterson says you're supporting her plan to tackle McQuade. Look, I've turned her down. I don't want to seem disloyal or anything, and obviously you've got a different perspective on this, but to my mind it's pretty unfair of the Wintersons to grab hold of the issue and expect the village to tag after them.'

'Peter . . .'

'Anyway, that's what I told her. Just wanted to let you know my reasons for not coming onside.'

'Peter, I turned her down.'

'You did?'

'She rang about half an hour ago.'

'I had her on the phone this afternoon.'

'So by the time she rang me she'd known for hours that you weren't backing her. And yet . . .'

'Did she try to persuade you by saying I was on board?'

'Oh, yes. She tried that, all right.'

'Well, I'm damned.'

Maddy laughed. 'Good thing it didn't work. It makes me wonder, though, about the other person she claimed was in favour.'

'Who was that?'

'Did she mention any other names to you?'

'Only yours. Who was it, then.'

'Patsy Kimball.'

'Ring Patsy and ask her. I would. I mean, if you don't, I *shall*. It's not as though we don't all know each other, is it?'

'Actually, Peter, I'm convinced the Wintersons haven't grasped the extent to which people around here *do* know each other.'

She had an inkling this failure was about to cost the Wintersons all they had striven for. People disliked being bossed about, lied to and cheated. They also disliked being misrepresented. However worthy the cause, there was a limit to how much they would put up with.

He said: 'I wonder how many other people Gina's been after? In fact, I think I'll make a few telephone calls myself and do a spot of checking.'

'Oh, is it really worth going to that trouble?'

'Yes, if you're sitting here with your leg in a splint and there's nothing on telly.'

So they got around to the leg and Friday evening, after all. He said he was well but had to rest. He thanked her for returning the car so promptly, not that he was able to use it himself but he felt it was safer in The Close than parked in her part of the village. She wished him a speedy recovery.

'I heard,' said Steve, fending off a reiteration of the entire story.

Then Patsy Kimball came on.

'Tell me it isn't true, Maddy. Gina Winterson says you're behind a scheme to . . .'

'No, no. I promise it isn't true.' She recited what had happened.

'She can't do this, you know,' Patsy said firmly. 'I'm going to sort this out before it goes any further.'

'She won't be home now. She told me she was leaving for a meeting she's called in the pub, to do with the children's sponsored walks.'

'Fine. I've always wanted to cause a scene in a bar.'

Patsy hung up. The phone rang again at once. Patsy again.

'Sorry, I'm so steamed up I forgot the other thing. Chris Welford.'

'It's a shock.'

'We're all shocked because he's local and he's an acquaintance.'

They did not really have anything to say about Chris Welford. Neither did anybody in the village although they all felt the need to mention him, to let each other know the news had touched them.

Maddy was reminded of something from earlier that

evening. Because Patsy had talked about the case at the dinner party, she mentioned it to her. 'I heard some men talking about the Pippa Dellafield case this evening. Joking about it. Blaming the dead girl. Tell me it won't be like that with Beth.'

Patsy talked to her for a while, letting her know her revulsion was not an aberration and that if the time came she would not be the only woman who rose to defend Beth's reputation.

Maddy was gazing into the courtyard again. A reflected Steve was in the window beside her, sipping wine. When she came off the line she said to him: 'Sorry, you're having an evening of eavesdropping on my phone calls.'

It was intended as a quip, a facetious apology for being so taken up with other people and other matters that he got no attention. And, indeed, no supper.

But he did not find it funny. His face clouded, the good humour drained out of him.

He moved towards the door.

She cursed her clumsiness. 'No, don't go. It was only a joke.'

He shook his head, rejecting her apology. He looked fragile, pale.

The room was full of the aroma of food. That, she thought, would bring him back.

She tried to be cheerful. 'Supper's ready, now. I'm sorry it's taken so long.'

But her voice wavered and sounded as though she were pleading with him. *'Please don't lapse into the difficult Steve. Please don't make me feel responsible for this change in you. Please don't shut me out.'*

Steve said he did not feel hungry and he left the room. Once he was out of sight it was as though he had vanished. No footsteps on the stone flags, no click of a television in the sitting room, no creaking treads on the stairs.

Maddy spooned rice and lamb onto her plate and settled to a lonely supper. For all her anticipation, she barely noticed what she was eating. The meat was succulent despite its months in the freezer. The sauce, an invention of Nesta's, was richly satisfying. It was comforting cold-weather food but she was not comforted. Her thoughts circled around her stupidity in upsetting a delicate peace. With one ill-judged remark she had spoiled it.

By the time she was rounding off her meal with a banana, she had decided to look in on him when she went up to bed. She knew it would be a pathetic attempt to put matters right between them and that he, as so often before, would rebuff her.

First she had to let Jay into the courtyard and accompany him to the gate, which she needed to unlock for him to run in the garden. She did not venture through herself, notions of lurking men deterred her, but she stared through into the grassy space that flowed away to walls and fields and woods wrapped by the night. Fear touched her spine as she realised that a man could be spying on her.

Linsey, she thought, would claim Jake Everard had much too noble a nature to indulge in Peeping Tom activities, and maybe she was right. But there were other men in the village whose peeled onions might reveal less endearing characters.

Maddy looked up at the house. Lamplight showed through curtains in Steve's room. *'Once he's gone,'* she thought, *'I'd like to change those curtains.'* They were old hand-me-downs a friend had given her and she had hung them carefully so that bands of faded material were not apparent.

Her thoughts meandered from one subject to another, all inconsequential ones because she could not face the terrible and the frightening, such as Chris Welford as a murderer, and an unknown man as a prowler, and Steve . . .

The dog came and she locked the padlock, checked it twice and then followed him into the house. Her contest with the bolts on the kitchen door was marginally easier than when she had started shutting out evil.

'I'm getting the knack.'

And then she realised she need not do this, anyway,

because the threat of a killer on the loose had ended. She gave a self-mocking smile but left the bolts secured.

'No roaming killer, but a fear has been planted in my mind. I don't suppose I shall ever go back to the carefree days before Beth died. None of us will.'

When she went upstairs Steve's door was closed and she did not go in. Pushing her door wide, she crashed into the ladder. It impeded her closing the door on the inside. Jay insinuated himself through the gap while she was repositioning it.

'I suppose you think I haven't noticed you,' she said as he circled in a corner by the window and settled for the night.

She ran out of ideas about where in the room to put the steps overnight and left them buttressing the door. As she got into bed, the answer to a small query from early in the day came to her. Her hands had not become dusty from handling the steps but from touching her storage box beneath Steve's bed.

The rest did not clarify until she was on the verge of sleep. She snapped awake, saying to herself: 'My box has gathered dust because it hasn't been used, but the steps weren't dusty because they *have* been. I haven't touched them until today, therefore Steve has. But what on earth has he been doing with them?'

A few minutes later she had the answer to that, too.

CHAPTER FOURTEEN

Jay did his crazy dance around the hall when Maddy picked up his lead. The unexpectedness excited him especially. She had prepared to go to work as usual but suddenly she was offering him a walk. He paused in mid leap, exactly long enough for her to attach the lead to his collar.

Maddy laughed at his joyful confusion and wished she could be equally happy about their jaunt. Like much of her work, this morning's task of valuing Wren Cottage was tinged with sadness. Houses were sold because people died, divorced, grew too ill to run them or too poor to afford them. The sad stories lingered in the mind, not the growing families, young couples marrying, and the newly rich flaunting their wealth.

The Wren Cottage story was age and infirmity, and a step on the way to poverty. Doris Laverty had entered a nursing home in her eightieth summer and was being forced to sell up to pay the fees. Her niece, Heather, had arranged to meet Maddy at ten. Encouraged by a few shafts of sunshine slanting down the valley, Maddy had decided to couple the outing with walking the dog.

The first stretch of the journey was uneventful, except for the nuisance of cars flashing by too close. Then she began to meet people. Mrs Spencer was on the doorstep of her cottage on the corner of the lane leading to the haulage business. She beckoned Maddy into her front garden to say wasn't it terrible about Beth being killed by her own husband? Their conversation was drowned by a lorry clashing gears as it made the tight turn into the road. Maddy used the interruption as an excuse to leave.

Next she met the widow with the ailing retriever. Jay initiated the nosing ritual but the old dog lacked interest. His owner said what a blow it was to learn that Chris Welford was the murderer. She asked whether Maddy had heard any details.

The nearer Maddy drew to the heart of the village, the more frequently she was stopped. Gilly from the riding school said she had been commiserating with Chris Welford an hour before his arrest, and when she learned he was the killer she had had an attack of vomiting.

The shopkeeper's contribution was that the Welfords had not paid their paper bill for two months and he was worried whether he would ever see the money.

A youth cleaning windows called down that it was unbelievable Chris Welford was the Monster of Wychwood, the title bestowed by one of the tabloids. 'Whenever I done the Church Cottage windows, the place seemed very posh. Not what you'd think a monster would live in.'

Maddy doubted he was trying to be funny. She was anxious to get by but the lad came down his ladder, wrang out his chamois and blocked her path while he tried to impress her with what he had seen through the Welfords' windows. Jay, growing bored, raised a hind leg against the ladder and suddenly they were freed.

Near the village hall Maddy encountered the Wintersons. Gina was flushed. Both were frowning. In the background a detective was making a rude gesture. Spotting Maddy, he transformed it into head-scratching lest she thought it was directed at her. Her grin at his antics was interpreted by the Wintersons as a greeting.

'Maddy!' cried Gina, in a voice loud enough to greet tour groups at Tenerife. 'Isn't it appalling about Chris Welford?'

Her husband added: 'As I keep pointing out, Gina, he's been charged but he isn't convicted yet.'

Maddy asked whether the police were about to vacate the hall.

Malcolm said: 'We've been to ask them now you've got the killer, why can't you clear out and let the kids have their playroom back?'

Gina added: 'They say they intend to as soon as possible. Of course, they won't say when that might actually be. Don't like to tell you anything they don't have to, do they? Getting information is like sucking blood from a stone.'

Then he took it up. 'You'd think they'd make a point of being customer-friendly. There's so much crime these days, they need us if they're to tackle more than the tip of the iceberg.'

'Have you heard the latest, Maddy?' asked Gina. 'Flower theft.'

Maddy echoed. 'Flour theft?' She imagined bags of self-raising sneaked from the village shop.

'Yes, from gardens all round the village. Malcolm had a winter rose cut off the bush by our porch. Mrs Piercey had a primula taken from her back garden. And we heard today that old Mr Redgold has had all three flowers snipped off his daphne, within a day of them opening.'

Maddy was mystified. 'Who on earth could want one rose, one primula and three daphne blossoms?'

Gina said: 'We're going to insist on a meeting of Neighbourhood Watch. It's all very well people putting those little signs in their windows saying the system is operating in the area, but if nobody's bothering to keep a lookout for crime, what's the point?'

A figure came out of a lane and walked past saying hello.

Lowering her voice, Gina said: 'Nobody wants him around, either. You'd think he'd have the grace to leave, after what he did.'

'Everard? What's he done?'

'Broken into a cottage,' said Gina.

'A weekenders' place,' added Malcolm.

'No,' said Maddy, 'they decided he didn't do it.' She felt

odd to be defending him, having believed him a killer and a prowler.

Gina was undeterred. 'Oh, the police had to let him go. He's wandering around free as air. But the people who own the house know it was him.'

Malcolm backed her up. 'He's not wanted around here. Doesn't fit in. If you ask me, it's doubtful whether he's a student at all.'

Maddy summoned Jay and cut short the discussion. 'Sorry to rush but I'm on my way to meet someone.' Leaving, she threw a mischievous question over her shoulder. 'How was the sponsored walk meeting?'

Both their faces showed shameful recollection of Patsy Kimball's scathing attack which had interrupted proceedings.

But Maddy was gone, hidden from sight by a tree on the bend. She was laughing, quite loudly.

Jay trotted past Wren Cottage and she yelled to him. Heather heard her and came out of the house. She was a young-looking forty wearing jeans and a padded jacket, hair tied in a pony tail.

'I used to come here on holidays when I was a kid,' Heather said. 'After London, it was magical.'

'It's still magical.'

Maddy looked at the patchy blue sky, bravely greening fields, the glint of the river and the forest thrown like a cape over the shoulder of the hill. The cottage had been part of this scene for two hundred years.

It was long and low, somewhat like her own house but with several touches of distinction. The portico was grander, the carved drip-stones over the windows were fancier and the front garden bigger. It was taller with a small round window peeping like a watchful eye under the gable. Most importantly, it was a detached house in a lane where vehicles did not rush by on their way to more important places.

She was always pleased to handle the sale of a house she liked. Before she was through the door, she had good feelings about Wren Cottage.

In truth it was stuffy inside. Scuffed walls needed repainting. Painted woodwork needed cleaning. Soot lay in the hearth.

Heather stuck beside her, seeing the place with a stranger's eyes. 'Needs a bit of a clean-up.'

'Does this window open?' Maddy banged the frame until it gave.

Heather whizzed round the house flinging the others wide. A chilly draught blew through the rooms.

'When Auntie Doris was here,' said Heather, 'I only noticed her. She's a terrific personality, I didn't realise how shabby everything was getting. Do you know her?'

'I've seen her occasionally.' She had the vaguest recollection: a wisp of a woman who had shrunk inside good quality clothes; a mannish voice.

'Auntie was very active until she had the illness and then the fall. Oh God, it's a frightful prospect, isn't it? You see these things happening to other people and you start wondering whether you'll end up the same way.'

Maddy went through the rooms, listened to Heather, got the feel of the place, listened to Heather, spoke her notes into a tape-recorder, listened to Heather. Jay strolled in from the garden. Heather stroked him and told him the house used to be a cats' domain.

Cats. Maddy had already decided a history of cats would explain the lingering smell. She switched off her recorder and asked a few questions which Heather, not being the owner, was not confident of answering correctly.

'I'll find out. Auntie Doris's solicitor should have the answers.' She named a firm in Oxford.

They shivered around the garden, with Maddy noting mature fruit trees and a view which would add to the appeal if not to the price. Heather said she was very sad the house had to be sold.

'Auntie Doris always said it would come to me when she died or didn't want it any longer. We never dreamed it would have to be cashed in to pay for nursing care.'

Maddy, who had sold other houses for this reason, hated

being part of the misery, the bitterness. She murmured sympathetically and concentrated on professional matters.

Heather wondered aloud whether the plot of land might not be large enough for a second house to be built on it. 'Having outline planning permission would increase the value.'

Maddy described the planning authority's attitude to new houses in old gardens. She was delaying mentioning an asking price because Heather was bound to be disappointed. The sluggish market and the condition of the house were against a high price.

Eventually she, named a figure. 'I'm afraid it's probably lower than you were hoping.'

Glum, Heather shrugged. 'Hope hasn't got anything to do with this. Auntie Doris wasn't hoping to sell at all. Me, neither.'

'Of course, with planning permission . . .'

But Heather was not cheered. Her features contorted with distress. 'And the more Auntie Doris gets, the more they'll take off her. Unless she dies first. She said that herself. She's not a stupid old biddy who's lost track of things. Maybe that's the worst of it, Maddy, she knows exactly what's going on.'

She covered her face with a hand. Helpless, Maddy moved away, towards the house with its residue of cats and happiness.

After a few minutes, she and Jay began the walk home.

She swerved down a track beside a field, thinking it might be quicker as nobody would stop her to swap opinions about Chris Welford. Soon the track was running through a sparse wood. She heard the dog blundering about in the undergrowth ahead. Away on her left something stirred. She stopped, realising she had done a rather stupid thing in letting Jay go exploring. Even if he had any instinct to protect her, he was not available.

Then she remembered. '*There's no need to worry because the man who killed Beth has been caught.*'

But Beth's killer was not the only one. Women fell prey

to murderers all the time. Some killings were copycat crimes, committed by morally weak men aping reported crimes. Beth's murder had been widely reported. How many millions of people had watched television pictures of Wychwood, the village and Church Cottage?

Maddy shuddered and wrapped her arms around her. Over on the left something was moving. Something tall. Something threatening.

She gulped, forced her limbs into action and lunged forward. Stumbling, she tried to call Jay but her mouth was parched and her breath lacking. She could die without screaming. Beth had.

Terror was squeezing the strength out of her. *'I'm unable to run. Unable to scream.'*

Maddy tripped, threw out a hand to save herself, snatched at the scratchy trunk of a tree. Stinging pain and the sight of blood jolted her back to normality.

'Jay! *Jay!*' She was haring down the path he had taken.

At last she was answered by a bark. Not a yelp of concern but a bark. It came from her left. Maddy slithered to a halt. Her tape-recorder flew out of her pocket and landed in mud. Cursing, she rubbed it on her sleeve.

'Random,' she told herself. *'No one knows I'm here. It can't be anybody who's set out to find Maddy Knewton. It's an opportunist who doesn't care who he finds. And kills.'*

Panic whipped up her imagination until she fancied figures behind every tree, footsteps creeping from all directions. She was hot, sweating, primed for flight but unable to choose the least dangerous route.

From her left came thudding feet, undergrowth crushed by an urgent advance. She shrank behind a tree and knew she was not really hidden. A patch of jacket must be showing, one trousered leg or a boot. Not hidden at all. But what did it matter? Whoever was charging towards her knew she was there. They were coming for her.

Heart pounding she gripped the bole of the tree with both hands and dared to look round it. Her impression was that the wood was alive. Everything that might be jiggling and juddering was. And setting the whole thing in motion was a golden bundle of energy.

Maddy began an hysterical laugh that lasted long after the dog had bounded all over her. When the wild laughter died, she talked nonsense to him. 'You saw who it was, didn't you? That's why you barked.'

He resented being put on a lead for the rest of the way and tried tweaking it out of her hands. They came to a headland at the edge of the trees. It gave an overview of the strung out village and, surprisingly, she could see her cottage. The back of the house and the rear boundary wall were clear, although not the courtyard or much of the garden. Nearer, she recognised the side elevation of Park House and was astonished to see Nesta tossing grain to her hens. Nesta's red hair was distinct.

Maddy looked at the church tower and, crouching beside it, Church Cottage which had no garden but a field running up close.

'*From here . . .*' She left the thought without expression, not clear what she meant except that there were remarkable possibilities. With binoculars one could spy on most of the village.

'*And from here . . .*'

The idea niggled at her, pestered her, demanded to be discovered and considered.

Then it hit her that she was remembering Linsey. Linsey had waggled her hand towards this side of the village when she had been describing, or rather avoiding describing, the spot where she and Everard faded into the trees and contemplated nature.

'*Nature be damned. They spy on us.*'

Jay tired of nuzzling at objects within the lead's length and tugged at her jacket with careful teeth to coax her on.

She did his bidding but the idea of Linsey and Everard spying stayed with her, all the way down the sloping hill and across the stepping stones in the snow-flooded river.

She stopped, to catch her breath and let Jay satisfy himself that he did not enjoy drinking icy water. A path ran up the facing hill. Over the rise lay Everard's barn. But where was the continuation of the path she had followed from her garden? The land between the barn and the river was so heavily trampled none was visible.

Curiosity led her to the barn. Was Everard continuing to live there after his brush with the law? Had the farmer evicted him or the villagers chased him out?

His belongings were there – table, chair, lamp, sleeping-bag, books – but he was absent. She imagined what it must have been like living there through an extremely bad winter. No wonder he was in favour of Linsey's attempts to move him into Park House.

Maddy climbed the steep path to the copse and paused to scan the valley. The trees she had walked through, on the hill opposite, drew her eye and she could almost swear a face was staring back at her.

She jerked Jay's lead and they ran all the way to her garden. Even allowing for the scare, their journey had been quick. Not as quick as striding along tarmac but there had been no pauses for chit-chat. She had not even seen anybody whereas if she had walked through the village . . .

'That's it,' she thought, coming to her padlocked gate. *'I was looking for complicated reasons for Steve making another access instead of using the front door. But he just wanted to come and go unseen.'*

She rattled the gate, then began working out the shortest route to the house now that her security measures had locked them out in the garden.

CHAPTER FIFTEEN

It was the padlock that led to the final row. If Steve had not been in the cottage when she walked in . . . if he had not smirked when she mentioned trespassing in neighbours' gardens . . . if he had not made her suspect he had seen her at the locked gate but chosen not to let her in . . . But perhaps it would have blown up that day all the same. The way his moods swung, it was impossible to say.

She drove off to Woodstock angry, late, trying to switch her mind from domestic disaster to professional matters. Heather Laverty might telephone with the information Maddy sought. And Heather might have made up her mind whether or not to apply for planning permission.

Then there was Felicity Fisher who was not keen on a flat in Netherlands but might be attracted to one in a former factory. That, though, would mean a sale through the Witney office with Cathy collecting the commission. The woman had insisted she was only interested in Maddy's area but it might be time to put her determination to the test.

And then there was the former hotel that Ken had valued on the day of his accident. Before Maddy spoke to the owner she needed details from a colleague, Diane, about a similar property Rigmaroles' Oxford office had recently handled. Diane had been off sick.

It was a bad day to be preoccupied by Steve.

'He promised he'd go as soon as the killer was caught

*but he hasn't. I suppose he's waiting for me to point it out.
Then there'll be another scene . . .'*

She sighed, slowing as she caught up with traffic. Steve
was no longer a minor problem she dealt with at home. He
was encroaching on the whole of her life. For all the wrong
reasons, she could not get the man out of her head.

Several people waved to her as she drove into the town.
While she was walking from the car park, a woman
rearranging a dress-shop window paused, pins jutting from
her lips, to mime a greeting.

'Ken,' Maddy thought, *'would be doffing his hat and all
I do is wave. Perhaps I should develop a quirky response,
too.'*

She unlocked the office, sniffed the milk, decided it would
do for another day and put the kettle on. Without thinking
how late it was, she was going through her usual routine.

Clive from Oxford had left a message to say he did not
expect to hear from Dallas Grenville now that her client had
been charged with killing his wife. 'In the scale of things,
your letting a piece of paper fall into the wrong hands doesn't
amount to much, does it?'

*'No, Chris Welford and his lawyers certainly do have
weightier matters on hand.'*

The man who owned the hotel urged her to ring him. He
provided his mobile number.

'I'll have to stall unless Diane has returned to work.'

Felicity Fisher confirmed she was not interested in living
at Netherlands. 'It's a super flat but sadly it's not for me. If
you hear of something similar, Maddy, but in a friendlier
location, do let me know, won't you?'

'A factory by a river.'

Mrs Morris bemoaned the yellow wall outside Dunflirtin.
'Have you been able to do anything about it yet, Maddy,
love?'

'Such as repaint it myself, you mean?'

Patsy Kimball said: 'Our conversation about the Pippa
Dellafield case made me curious, Maddy, and I've looked
it up. If you want to know any more, try me.'

'Interesting. I'll call her this evening.'

Graham Collins was last in line. 'About your wall, Maddy. I'll make a start on it this afternoon.'

'Oh, good. I didn't like to chase him up.'

A couple in their twenties came to pore over the photographed houses in the window. They looked too young, too indecisive and pinched with cold. The woman had a red beret and a red nose. The man was very fair with the sort of skin that appears blue when the temperature drops.

'They ought to come in and browse in comfort but they won't.'

If Ken had been there she would have bet him they would not come inside. Whichever of them lost a bet had to wash the coffee cups. Maddy won more often than Ken but he was a lousy washer-up so she had to redo it.

Patsy rang. Maddy said she had only just played the tape.

'I was late because I went to value Wren Cottage.'

'Mrs Laverty's house?'

'Yes. She's in a nursing home.'

The eyes of the woman in the red beret skipped from one photograph to the next, seeking a dream, failing to spot it and moving swiftly on in hope. The man was ponderous, probably reading prices as well as scanning pictures.

Patsy said: 'What shape is it in?'

'Not bad. Needs redecorating, of course, plus some updating.'

'It could be a gem, though. And it's in a lovely location.'

'Hang on, you sound more like an estate agent than I do.'

Patsy said: 'Maddy, I've discovered I have to go to Woodstock early this afternoon. Are you free for a pub lunch?'

'One o'clock at the Dragon?'

The red beret came to a halt in front of the photographs on the left of the window. A hand plucked the man closer. The hand gestured. At Barn Cottage? At Providence Cottage? At Sheppy Farm Cottage? All those in that section of the window display were charming but expensive. Maddy was not ready to cancel her bet.

Patsy approved the Dragon. 'I'll report on the Dellafield case. Or cases, rather.'

'I'm intrigued.'

The couple were in a huddle in front of Barn, Providence and Sheppy. Then the woman rested her hand on his arm again. Steering him away down the street or only the two paces to the door? Maddy's confidence wobbled.

Patsy said: 'Oh, by the way, I left the same message at home for you because I wasn't sure where you'd be.'

Out in the street the uncertainty continued. The woman dodged round behind the man and reappeared on his right, further from the door. Abruptly, he opened the door and ushered her inside.

'Sorry,' said Maddy when she rushed into the Dragon to find Patsy eating. 'People came streaming through my door. Every time it seemed safe to leave, another one arrived.'

Amusement danced in Patsy's grey eyes. 'I saw you ensconced as I drove past. Calm down and decide what you'd like to drink.'

Maddy thrust tangled hair away from her face and marvelled, as usual, at Patsy's unruffled elegance. It was impossible to imagine *her* having, either literally or metaphorically, a hair out of place. The sums Patsy spent on clothes and hairdressers did not entirely explain it. In fact, Maddy recognised a chain store blouse beneath the lawyerly suit.

'Attitude is what makes the difference. But where does one acquire poise like Patsy's?'

Aloud she said: 'Ginger beer, please.'

'I read that's become one of the most popular pub drinks.' Patsy took a sip of white wine. The corners of her mouth turned down and she muttered: 'At least you know what you're getting which is more than can be said for pub wine.'

A youth appeared and took Maddy's order for ginger beer and the vegetarian lasagne. Patsy asked him for a mineral water and used it to dilute the wine.

They had not lunched together before. Neither would have claimed they were friends. Occasionally they met at village events or in someone's house for an evening. Their professional lives did not overlap and Maddy had not sold Patsy her rather splendid house.

Beth's death was bringing them together. Obliquely, Patsy said so when she began to talk about the effect the murder was having on village life.

'I'm amazed at the way it's fracturing friendships and altering people. Neighbours who've always rubbed along together are now divided by loyalty to Beth or to Chris. Have you heard them in the shop?'

'Yes, and the gaggle around the postbox.'

'They seem to believe they're under an obligation to pick sides. For every regretful remark that's made about Beth, there's a counter-remark suggesting she was asking for it. And, of course, they don't actually know a thing. That's one of the most disturbing aspects, that knowledge isn't required, merely a willingness to chatter.'

They traded examples. Then Patsy said: 'In future the village will divide its history into BM, before the murder, and AM, after it.'

Maddy suggested that, in a cockeyed way, it was better than the terrible event going unmarked. 'People are saying we're going through a rotten patch and the passage of time will heal, but I'd feel it was wrong if things went back exactly as they were. It would mean Beth and what happened to her were unimportant and we were capable of forgetting her.'

'I won't be able to carry on as though it never happened. It's made me wary. No doubt that will grow less intense but the effect is bound to be long-term.'

Maddy was nodding. 'You'd think that knowing Beth's death was a domestic murder would alter that because whatever went wrong concerned one close relationship. But it doesn't. It undermines our own marriages and love affairs because, if it could happen to Beth and Chris who were outwardly a happy couple . . .' She ended with a shudder.

Patsy weighed her words before replying. 'You were asking me whether Beth's name was likely to be blackened. From what I've heard around the office, Chris Welford is denying he killed her and is trying to establish an alibi. If anyone savages Beth's reputation, it won't be him.'

'Because doing so would suggest he had a motive?'

'Precisely. And for the same reason it's possible it would suit the prosecution to blacken her.'

She looked at the pub clock. At the table below it a young man in horn-rimmed glasses had a notebook out and was interviewing the man who owned the dry cleaners. Patsy said: 'Oh dear, I haven't much time and I want to tell you about the other case.'

'Yes, please.'

'Well, Pippa Dellafield wasn't the victim of a domestic murder and it wasn't established that the man who was charged knew her. The defence denied it. They adopted the tactic of making it appear she had known lots of other men.'

'I've heard her called wild and fun-loving.'

'Her family and friends objected to that description but as she had an illegitimate child she was an easy target. The defence claimed she was living in a commune, a word with overtones of free love and laxity. It was a misnomer. She was actually sharing a farmhouse with friends. The owners were abroad and their daughter invited friends to live there with her, for company and to look after the place.'

'Students, people of Pippa's age?'

'Yes. It was exactly what they needed, a cheap roof over their heads and congenial company. Naturally, what the neighbours noticed was parties and pot.'

'Killjoys.'

'Unfortunately, it went down in local history that the girl in the case was a ne'er-do-well with loose morals who lived in a hippy commune.'

'And therefore deserved everything she got.'

'Which included rape. That's another crucial difference

between the cases. Beth was strangled but not sexually assaulted.'

She picked up her bag. 'I have a meeting in ten minutes and it'll take me two to walk there.'

She laid an envelope on the table beside Maddy's plate. 'Photocopies of newspaper cuttings. I'll have them when you've finished. No hurry.'

And she left.

Tilting the envelope, Maddy slid three cuttings into her hand. One was a feature written about the case long after it was over. The others were a news story about the murder hunt while it was in progress and a report of one day's hearing in the Crown Court. She ran her eye over them. She was too busy to read them later and while she was driving home she realised they were lying on her desk.

The nearer she got to home, the worse her anxiety about Steve. All the irritations of the morning resurfaced. She was convinced he had deliberately left her on the wrong side of the locked gate, and his sly look proved he believed she deserved it.

After a few miles of this, she pulled up by a forest track and got out of the car to clear her head. She was afraid of indulging in further delusions, reading more into his actions than was to be found there. Her stupidity about Everard had left her especially cautious.

'*It's not like me to be this twitchy,*' she thought. '*I've put up with Steve for months, so how come I'm letting it get to me now? I must keep calm and be determined. Chris Welford has been charged with the murder and the moment that happened Steve's last chance was used up. He has to go, and he has to go tomorrow.*'

She loitered near the car, not tempted to stride down the track beneath the arch of low denuded branches, although she would have felt better for a walk.

'*If I hurry it won't be too late to take Jay for a short walk. He'll need one as much as I do.*'

But when she parked outside Meadow Cottage daylight had gone and the prospect of going to the river or into the forest was simply frightening. Patsy's fear had reinforced her own.

Steve was out. Maddy unlocked the gate for the dog to go into the garden. She wondered whether Graham had finished repairs but as she was not carrying a torch, she could not check.

Indoors again she discovered a message from him saying he could not do it that day because a magazine had given him an urgent commission to photograph a restaurant in Burford. Two people had rung with snippets of gossip about the murder. Then Gina Winterson announced that if Maddy wanted to attend a crisis meeting about the lorries, she should be at the Winterson house at eight sharp the following evening. Gina had put a heavy emphasis on the 'if'. Maddy resolved not to go.

She began to prepare supper. Part way through slicing an onion she paused, thinking there was something she could check on while Steve was out of the house.

'If I lock the front door, I'll hear him arrive and he won't be able to walk in on me.'

Flinging down the knife she ran upstairs, grabbed the steps from their temporary resting place against her bedroom wall, and carried them onto the landing. She pushed open the hinged panel that was the access to her roof, reached an arm into the void and clicked a light switch. Ancient oak beams appeared. She wriggled up into the loft.

The floor was boarded to make it safe for walking and to protect the insulating material laid by the previous owner. Maddy had rarely been up there. Twice, perhaps? She was not a woman who owned a huge amount and needed an attic to store her excess. When a builder had needed to check the roof and an electrician had been repairing ceiling lights in the bedrooms, she had gone up with them for the novelty of seeing her beautiful beamed roof.

She glanced wildly round the large empty space. Dust on the floor had been disturbed.

'My house has low ceilings. This is the only place inside the house for which a step-ladder's needed. But what could

Steve have been doing up here? There's nothing up here so he didn't store anything.'

The word leaped out at her. *'No, if he'd* stored *anything I'd see a box or whatever contained it. But if he hid it . . .'*

Maddy pictured a packet poked out of sight high on a beam. She quartered the roof in search of it. When her neck grew stiff and she had to break off to ease it, she realised she was looking at the other possibility. The floor. Beneath the boarding were granules of insulating material. A scattering of them had trickled over the floor where two boards met. The thrill of discovery sent a tremor through her body.

'I've found it. I've found Steve's hiding place.'

Immediately she was on her knees and trying to raise the edge of one of the boards. Fixed. Then the other one. It lifted easily. Underneath, in a hollow scooped in the granules, was a plastic supermarket bag wrapped around something solid.

She touched the bag. For a moment she resisted pulling it out. Here were the answers but did she truly want to face them?

She plucked the bag out, dropped the board into place, letting it fall more noisily than intended. The thud reverberated in her head.

Then she was remembering the scene in the hall when she searched his jacket while he watched. Her dread that he was about to make another untimely return was so fierce she felt it as physical pain. It damaged her breathing, making it jaggedly nervous.

Maddy crouched beside the bag, scared to open it. She already knew the unimportant things. It weighed less than a pound and contained three items. It bore the name of a supermarket in Chipping Norton. It was smooth and fairly new, rather than old and rough to the touch. It was Steve's, dammit, and it held his secrets.

She was desperate to know what they were and she felt entitled to. It was her house, he had invaded her life and hidden these clues to his real nature in her loft. She had the moral right to open the bag.

'Nature. Onion layers. Linsey. Steve.'

Underlying her hesitation was the suspicion that secrets which needed to be hidden so thoroughly were unlikely to tell her anything good about the hider.

She fingered the plastic again. Flying thoughts settled on one central concern: she *had* to look in the bag because having come this far she could not retreat. Even if it were possible to convince herself she ought to rebury it unopened among the cosseting granules, she could not relinquish her knowledge of it. To know it existed but not to know what it held would be absurd.

Maddy carried it towards the electric bulb. She angled it to let light fall on the contents. There were two video tapes and a slim wad of papers secured with a rubber band. She examined the tapes. Unlabelled.

As she felt for the papers, a noise reached her. Her nerves were taut and she had probably imagined it, but the longer she stayed the greater the danger of Steve discovering her.

'No, he can't. He can't get into the house.'

This was not totally reassuring. She scrambled to get out of the loft, slipping the handles of the bag over one arm, putting a foot on the top step and creeping backwards down to the landing.

'If he realises I've locked him out, he'll be suspicious and might check his hiding place.'

Jumping down the last two steps, Maddy dashed into her bedroom and buried the bag out of sight beneath her duvet. Then she folded the steps and carried them down to the ground floor. She manoeuvred them into the cupboard under the stairs.

Jay buffeted her as she backed out of the cupboard. She patted him and from the corner of her eye saw a figure in the kitchen doorway.

'Steve! I didn't know you were here.'

'You locked me out.' He looked mean. She saw he had intended to frighten her.

'Did I?' Too flustered to think of the best way to handle the situation, she automatically denied it was deliberate.

'Very effectively. A padlocked gate in the garden, the kitchen door bolted and the front door locked.'

Her cheeks burned, partly with embarrassment at being caught in a lie but equally in anger at his temerity. How dare he accuse her when he was not supposed to be living there, anyway? She concentrated on her anger and let her voice rise.

Seizing on the flaw in what he had said, she demanded sarcastically: 'If it was effective, how did you get in? I'm impressed that you managed it in the face of all those locks and bolts.'

'I forced the sitting room window.'

'You did *what?*'

'I came in through the window.'

Her head spun in the direction of the sitting room.

He said: 'Go on, take a look. The catch is broken.'

She stayed where she was. 'You forced your way into my house.'

'It's cold out there. I wasn't going to hang around in the cold because you decided to lock me out.'

The thing to cling to was his refusal to leave, not her wish to have her own home to herself. She faced him boldly. 'Steve, you promised to leave when Beth's killer was caught. He's been caught and you haven't gone.'

He rested an arm on the door frame and looked down on her. 'So you've given up pretending you didn't know you locked me out, and you're admitting you did it to enforce your silly little deadline.'

She hated him for his superciliousness, for his constant urge to put her in the wrong. She had frequently let him get away with it rather than have a scene. But he had used up all his excuses for staying and she was hellbent on getting him out.

'Stick to the point,' she warned herself. *'Don't let him slope away into arguing about my behaviour when what's at issue is his.'*

Exasperated, she said aloud: 'I don't want you in my house and you don't like being here, so what on earth is the point of refusing to budge?'

'You're pathetic, always fussing about your property. *Your* house, *your* furniture, *your* things . . .'

'Don't forget *my* window you've damaged and *my* wall you've pulled down.'

'You're exaggerating. I made a stile, that's all. I take it that's what inspired the padlock? Or rather, the fact that you couldn't bear the idea of me coming and going without you and the whole of this nosy village knowing about it.'

She was quick with her answer but her voice was low and taunting. 'Going where, Steve? Not to the coffee bar because that went bust last Christmas.'

He looked smug, guarding his secrets. 'I didn't want to work in a coffee bar. You wouldn't either but you expected me to. Forever asking about the bloody coffee bar, weren't you?'

'You didn't have to lie about it.'

'Oh, but I did. You demanded it, Maddy. You virtually made it a condition for staying here.'

His words threw an unflattering light on her steady encouragement to him to keep the job while seeking a better one.

She made another attempt to get at facts. 'What were you doing when you were pretending to be at work in Oxford?'

He shrugged. 'Breaking windows? Wrecking walls? Who cares? You know I wasn't slogging away as a waiter, that's all that matters.'

'That telephone number. You changed the one on the memory of my telephone.'

'*My* telephone. There you go again. You don't care how you treat me, you only care about your possessions.'

'Wrong, Steve. But you wouldn't want to understand. My house and the other things I've earned give me my independence. Without that I wouldn't have much of a life.'

He immediately proved what she had said about not

wanting to understand. His sneering infuriated her but she took perverse satisfaction from having her accusation confirmed.

He said: 'What life? You're an estate agent. You're nothing special, Maddy.'

She let the silence stretch before she asked: 'And what are you, Steve?'

Answers crowded her mind. A liar, a cheat, a layabout, a spiteful, greedy and indolent man who had deceived her and denigrated her. Caution held the words in check. Men were bigger, stronger, their reactions were physical. Once a row passed beyond the boundary of words, women got hurt. She clenched her jaw and waited to see what possible answer he could offer.

He seemed to think he had found one. 'I'm somebody who doesn't sell out. I'm more independent than you'll ever be because I don't let myself be sucked into the system. I'd hate to be like you, selling crummy houses to people who don't need them and can't afford them. Talking to them about attractive views and well-appointed bathrooms and . . . well, you know the crap better than I do.'

He was preposterous and she burst out laughing. Jay gave a sharp bark and ran in worried circles.

Maddy said: 'You know I didn't choose this job. I didn't have your education or any of your opportunities. I discovered what I could do and I try to do it well. You've never heard me make any solemn claims about it.'

Steve was shaking his head dismissively. 'People will never admit it when they've had an easy life.'

But she shot back: 'You make yours unnecessarily hard. You've got nobody else to blame.'

Without allowing him time to respond she issued her ultimatum. 'Your time has run out, Steve. Get your things and get out now.'

He ignored her.

Sarcastic again she said: 'Your possessions might not matter much to you but they matter far less to me. If you don't take them away now I shall put them out for the dustbinmen. They come tomorrow morning, in case you need reminding.'

She did not know what to do next because he stayed in the kitchen doorway, unconcerned, as though she were a difficult child having a tantrum and he were a sensible parent waiting for it to blow over.

After a second, she went into the sitting room and used the telephone.

Nesta answered. 'Hello.'

'Hello, I'd like to book a taxi for this evening please.'

'Hey? Maddy, you're through to . . .'

'Yes, it's to take one passenger and his luggage into Oxford.'

'Oh. I see. Yes, um . . . how can I help?'

'I'd like you to come as soon as you can. My address is Meadow Cottage . . .'

While she recited the rest of it Nesta chimed in. 'We'll be over right away. Are you all right, Maddy?'

'Yes.'

'Do you really want the taxi?'

'Yes, please.'

'I'll fix it. See you shortly.'

Maddy hung up. She told Steve: 'I've ordered you a taxi. It will be here within half an hour and it will take you into Oxford. If you want to take anything you own, you'd better start packing.'

He raised a hand in a placatory gesture but, for once, she was prepared for this. 'There's nothing you can say, Steve. Better spend the time packing.'

As she could not get past him into the kitchen, she retreated to the hall. But she could not hang around there until the Collinses rode to the rescue. Besides, she realised she needed to go to the bathroom quite urgently. Emotional upsets always had that effect on her bladder. Suspecting it was tactically the wrong thing to do, Maddy went upstairs.

After she had finished in the bathroom she lingered there, noticing her face had turned pale, except for heightened blotches of red on her cheeks, and her eyes were brilliant.

She had seen this effect on Steve's face on Monday evening, excited emotions betrayed by a physical change that could not be disguised. He had not been upset, though. On the contrary, he had been unusually happy. So what had happened to affect him like that? It was the day she visited Ken in hospital, gave Linsey a lift in the rain and learned about onion layers. The day Mrs Morris discovered the yellow paint at Dunflirtin. Above all, it was the day Chris Welford was charged with murder.

Maddy crossed the landing to her room. The door of Steve's bedroom was closed, as it had been earlier. She cocked an ear. The house was silent. It so often was. He had the knack of moving about without making a noise. Where was he now?

Furtively, she looked around her room. Once she was satisfied he was not in there, she closed the door and lifted the corner of the duvet. The bag lay there, apparently as she had left it.

She wondered whether there was any virtue in finding another hiding place but decided not. Car headlights were aimed at her from a quarter of a mile away. The bedroom wall was chequered.

Maddy backed to the bed and sat there, to watch what she trusted was the advance of the Collinses. The lights swung sharply east and went out of sight. Depending on speed, the vehicle would pass the cottage in a minute. If the Collinses were in it, it would slow as it came in sight again.

She had an intuition that Steve had sat here many a time watching for her return, so he could dodge out through the garden and reappear later, pretending to have been working at the coffee bar. There was no proof except for the occasional depression on the duvet right where she was sitting.

Previously, she had blamed the dog for resting his head where she slept. The notion of Jay moping for her had been pleasing but now it was obvious the other answer was more probable. A dog had plenty of bed to choose from for his purpose. A man looking through the window could perch only on this spot.

The car shot by at speed. She straightened the duvet and went downstairs. She did not see Steve. Maddy checked the window catch in the sitting room. Broken.

The bolts on the back door were undone. In the courtyard a shape moved. She opened the door and called Jay. He loped away from her.

Cursing softly, Maddy looked for the key to the padlock. She was still searching when the doorbell rang. Nesta and Graham jostled into the hall, side by side.

While Graham swept straight on into the house, Nesta clutched her in a mothering, smothering embrace. 'Maddy. Maddy. Are you all right? Are you sure?'

Maddy unclinched herself. 'There was a row but I'm fine. I'm furious but I haven't been hurt.' She felt a responsibility to calm Nesta down.

'You don't look all right,' Nesta persisted. 'You're over excited. Positively febrile.'

Maddy clapped a hand to her face. It felt scorched. She realised Nesta was seeing what she herself remembered in the mirror: the pallor setting off the patchy redness and the brilliant gleam of her eyes.

Nesta steered her to the bench, shoving Steve's jacket aside for her to sit. 'You look at the end of your emotional tether. I'd say you've been through hell.'

Anxious not to overplay it, Maddy switched the subject. 'Sorry about the peculiar phone call. I don't know the taxi number and, as Steve was blocking the entrance to the kitchen where I keep the directory, I had to dream up an alternative.'

Graham returned to the hall. 'Where is he?'

'Gone. He went while I was upstairs. The back door was unlocked when I came down, the dog was in the courtyard and the key to the padlock is missing.'

Graham was nonplussed. He had come prepared for battle and there was no one to fight.

Nesta said rapidly: 'Perhaps he's gone permanently.'

Graham and Maddy vied to see who could look the more sceptical.

Then Nesta said: 'Graham, why don't we find him?'

Maddy added: 'Before the taxi comes.'

Graham threw up his hands. 'Hey, wait a minute. We can't manhandle him or abduct him. We've only got the power of persuasion, remember.'

Maddy feared a digression. 'If it's possible I want the Steve problem resolved tonight. Because if it isn't, it means he's won. Also, I'd face the hassle again. I can't take any more.'

'I don't know how you've endured so long,' said Nesta.

Making an effort to be practical, Maddy said: 'We can flash a torch around outside to see whether we can work out where he's gone. But before we do that we should check his bedroom and nail up the sitting room window.'

She explained about the window. Graham offered to do it but she asked him to check Steve's room instead. When he came down, she was pounding nails to hold the two sections of the frame together.

Nesta produced a torch. 'One of us ought to stay indoors in case he comes in.'

Maddy nodded. 'And because the taxi should be here any time.'

The Collinses exchanged looks. Graham said: 'Actually, we didn't call a taxi.'

'Oh?'

Nesta explained. 'We decided it might complicate matters to have a stranger here if Steve seemed to be leaving under duress.'

Graham enlarged. 'We decided it was preferable to drop him in Oxford ourselves. If he goes off in a taxi, he could countermand the instructions once it pulls away.'

Maddy, frowning, had to agree. She sighed. 'Anyway, it's academic as I've lost him.'

To the Collinses' consternation she began to giggle. Nesta put an arm around her. Graham, with unobtrusive caution, removed the hammer from her hands.

Maddy said, gulping air: 'Sorry, it's just struck me that it's hilarious to be worrying how to find him when what I want most in this world is for him to go.'

Briefly, they joined in her laughter. Then Nesta said: 'The fact is, you need him to go on your terms and not his.'

And they began to talk about the row that evening and the man's pig-headedness. As they talked, they locked the house and crossed the courtyard.

The gate stood open and the padlock had been removed. Graham began to apologise for not having mended the wall but Maddy cut him off.

'He would have climbed over it or pushed it down.'

She hoped she had not sounded curt but her mind was not really on Graham and the wall. An unpleasant thought was troubling her.

After a few yards she asked: 'You haven't seen Jay, have you?'

CHAPTER SIXTEEN

Graham slept on her sofa. She tried very hard to dissuade
him but the Collinses were convinced Steve would enter
the cottage during the night.

'Nesta will have Linsey for company,' he said.

'I think Jake Everard might be there, too,' Nesta added.

Another time Maddy would have teased them about the
way Linsey and Everard had been elevated from undesir-
ables to assets.

Before she went up to her room, Graham rifled her
cupboard for whisky and presented her with a tot. 'A
bedtime drink, to help you sleep.'

Immediately she was under the duvet she swallowed the
whisky, with a grateful toast to Graham and Nesta. Then
she slid down, ready for sleep.

Her right foot discovered the supermarket carrier bag.
Maddy shot bolt upright and flung aside the duvet.

She tipped the video tapes and the wad of papers onto
her bedside table. Yawning, but too curious not to take
a glance, she worked the rubber band off the papers and
unfolded them. For a second she was completely confused
because they were photocopies of newspaper cuttings and
the name in the caption below the photograph of a skinny
dark-haired girl was Pippa Dellafield.

Her thoughts flew to Patsy Kimball and she searched for
a way in which she could have muddled the two sets of

papers. But no, the ones from the carrier bag were not identical. There were eight items instead of three. They were not the same but they were about the same thing. The same murder.

'*It isn't a coincidence. It can't be. Play the tapes. No, I can't, not while Graham's trying to sleep in the same room as the television. Oh God, I can't think. I'm just too tired.*'

She put the papers and tapes into the carrier, pushed it beneath her mattress, smoothed the valance and climbed into bed. A minute later, she was in dreamless sleep.

Graham roused her with a cup of tea. 'Seven o'clock and all's well.'

She had slept undisturbed and was surprised the night had flown. He laughed at her stretching and yawning and coming to terms with the day.

'Everything was fine, Maddy. I didn't have to repel boarders.'

'I don't think I'd have heard if you had. I slept right through.'

'Breakfast in half an hour.'

'Oh, I don't usually bother much.'

'I daresay but your new lodger is a cook, remember?'

She laughed, causing tea to splash in the saucer. 'Knowing you, Graham, you'll want to photograph it before I'm permitted to eat it.'

But she was silently begging she would not have to cope with one of the Collinses' innovative dishes. Where breakfast was concerned, she was unbudgingly conservative.

It turned out to be conventional. '*I should have known, of course, because there was hardly anything in the fridge. Must have clipped his wings a bit.*'

Aloud she declared it the best bacon and egg breakfast she had eaten for ages.

'What next?' asked Graham, sitting opposite and watching her keenly.

'I couldn't eat another thing.'

'No, I meant what happens today? If you go to work,

Steve might come back. Or are you going to look for him? Or what?'

'Oh dear, I haven't thought.'

'Well, I think you need a plan.'

She chewed her lower lip. 'You're right, of course. *He's* sure to have one, isn't he?'

A liar, a deceiver, a conniving fellow, a schemer . . . Naturally he had a plan.

Graham raised the teapot, offering a refill. 'And if you don't have a plan of your own, you'll find yourself following his.'

'Which is what's been going on here for ages, you mean. Yes, you're right. Don't ask me why it took me so long to see it because I don't know.' She held out her cup.

Pouring he said: 'Because you're too nice, Maddy. Too friendly, too kind, too helpful and too easily taken advantage of.'

She wagged a corrective finger. 'You missed out too stupid.'

He conceded with a nod. 'Could be.'

Then they stopped joking and worked out priorities. First they ruled out skipping work while Ken was in hospital and she had a busy day lined up. Next they decided he would summon a locksmith and have locks fitted on her windows and additional ones on her doors. Also, a new padlock would be fixed to the garden gate. Meanwhile, Graham would spread word that the dog had run off.

'Finding Jay will be a cinch, Maddy, because the entire village will enjoy hunting for him. But as for finding Steve . . .'

The doorbell rang. Maddy made a rapid deviation to check through the sitting room window before she risked opening up. Jim, the postman, stood on the path.

'Good morning, Maddy. Another one that won't go through your letterbox.'

The problem was a magazine. Steve's name was on the label. Without thinking she said: 'I'll take it but he isn't here now.'

Luckily the remark was ambiguous and not obviously a tidbit of news for him to disseminate. The phrasing could equally well suggest Steve was out for a walk as that he had stopped living there.

Flipping through a bundle of letters, Jim said: 'Taken to walking the dog for you, has he?'

But there was no doubt what this meant.

'Where did you see them, Jim?'

He gestured with a fistful of letters. 'Up the hill.'

There was a catch in her voice as she asked: 'Going into the forest?'

'Yes. I had to call at the Dawsons' house, way up the top. You know it?'

She said she did.

'I recognised the retriever first. "I'm sure that's Maddy's dog," I said, and I looked for you. But it was him I saw.'

He handed her two letters which she did not even glance at. 'Jim, can you say exactly which way they were going?'

'Been gone a long while, have they?'

She dredged up a smile. 'Much longer than I ever manage.'

'Well, let's see now. I was dropping down the hill from the Dawsons' and the dog ran in the road after I'd gone, say, three hundred yards. You know where there's that big tree and the lane swings wide because of it? Jay – he's called Jay, isn't he?—'

She agreed he was.

'He was running left to right, but he changed his mind and then I saw . . .'

She provided the missing name. 'Steve.'

'Yes, Steve, well I saw him calling the dog. They were going up the hill but not on the road, walking through the trees.'

'How long ago was this?'

'Must be twenty minutes now.'

He studied her face. 'Everything all right, is it, Maddy?'

She produced another smile. 'As long as they don't get lost.'

When she had waved Jim off, Graham told her he had overheard the conversation.

'Well, Maddy, we know where to start looking.'

A faint nausea was flowing through her. 'Yes but apart from snatching Jay and bringing him home, what do we do when we find them?'

There was a pause while they pondered that.

Graham got up from the table. 'Time I reported to Nesta.'

The idea that he was about to leave for Park House brought a flutter of worry but he meant only to telephone. Maddy cleared the table while he told a sleepy Nesta, woken by his call, everything that had happened since she drove home the previous night.

Maddy went upstairs and drew the carrier bag out from beneath her mattress. She had virtually made up her mind to seek Graham's opinion of the contents and to play the tapes there and then. A niggling reservation held her back.

'Am I tempted to ask him because he's here or because he's a man? Because I've had a few scares and I'm lapsing into being a frail female? If I really only want another opinion, why not Nesta's? Or Patsy's? Patsy knows about the Dellafield cases.'

Maddy threw the bag down on the bed. *'That's better. The more I lean on Graham or any other man in this spot of bother, the harder it will be to reassert my independence afterwards.'*

'Maddy?' Graham was calling from the foot of the stairs. 'Any decision yet about going in hot pursuit?'

'I'm still tussling with it,' she lied.

'And your time's running out. Woodstock calls you. I'd better mooch around the forest on my own.'

'I wish I didn't feel so useless but Woodstock really is important today.'

He brushed her apology aside. 'I ought to be able to coax the dog home, although I don't know there's anything I can do about Steve.'

She clutched at her hair. 'Oh God, it's so complicated. We need *you* here to repel boarders and organise locks, but also in the forest fetching Jay. We need *me* in Woodstock but here, too, while you're in the forest, and yet I'm also required in the forest because Jay's more likely to respond to my voice than anyone else's . . .'

'No, wait a minute. I've thought through most of that. Nesta's coming here to look after the cottage and let the locksmith in. That way you needn't worry about this place being unprotected.'

'There's still the question of . . .'

'Hold on. If you drive up after me you can spend a few minutes calling the dog before going on to Woodstock the long way. How's that?'

She beamed. 'Brilliant.'

'So get your coat and be ready to scoot off when Nesta drives up.'

Maddy threw her overcoat over her arm and paused, wondering what to do with the supermarket bag.

'Better not leave it here in case Steve comes.'

She accepted he would want to claim it one day. Only his timing was in doubt.

Thrusting it into her leather bag, on top of her mobile telephone and all the accoutrement of her working day, Maddy hurried downstairs.

She cleared Ken's desk and spread out the photo-copied pages. She kept them separate: Patsy Kimball's three on the left hand side of the desk, the eight from Steve's bag occupying the rest.

She read Patsy's first, starting with the shortest. This was the account of a day's hearing in Warwick Crown Court while Robert Clark was on trial for the murder of Pippa Dellafield. Her friend, Trudi Hartman, was giving evidence for the prosecution.

Pippa, she said, had been a happy girl who doted on her child and took her studies at a local college seriously. During the two years Pippa shared the farmhouse, they had become very close friends.

'She had boyfriends but no one special,' she said. 'She complained once that a man called Bob was pestering her. I took her to mean Robert Clark. He used to hang around.'

'Are you saying he was a frequent visitor to Ludds Farm?'

'No, he wasn't hanging out there, he was hanging around.'

Once the prosecuting counsel and his witness had sorted out the difference between hanging out and hanging around, he got her to say that Clark was known in the area and she had never been in any doubt that he was the Bob to whom Pippa referred.

Cross-examined, she clung to her story but there were damaging exchanges with Mitchell Sleathe, counsel for the defence.

'Miss Hartman, you have told the court that you and the victim became very close friends during the time she lived with you. That was how long?'

'Two years.'

'Yes, two years. How well did you know her before that?'

'I didn't know Pippa before.'

'How did she come into your life?'

'She arrived at the house looking for somewhere to live.'

'Arrived at the house? Out of the blue?'

'Yes.'

'That's not a normal way of seeking accommodation, is it?'

'Word must have gone round that I was sharing my parents' house with friends . . .'

'But she wasn't a friend. Was she a friend of a friend, perhaps?'

'No.'

'Very well. Where had she lived before she arrived on your doorstep?'

'I don't know.'

'Miss Hartman, you have turned your parents' home into a commune, haven't you? You have already told the court that between fifteen and twenty young people have been living there at any given time since your parents went abroad. I put it to you that you knew no more about Pippa Dellafield than you did about most of the others who, to adopt the description given by an earlier witness, "drifted through".'

'That isn't true. We were friends.'

'I suggest to you that you knew nothing of her life before she went to the farmhouse, except that it had produced an illegitimate child, and nothing about the men she consorted with while she was living with you . . .'

'No, I . . .'

'And nothing whatsoever to suggest that she and Robert Clark ever met.'

'This isn't . . .'

'The plain fact is you didn't actually know much about her, did you, Miss Hartman?'

Maddy finished reading and swivelled in Ken's chair to gaze out of the window while she pictured the courtroom scene. Trudi Hartman had been made to look an irresponsible girl who made the family home into a crash pad for feckless, drug-taking youngsters as soon as her parents' backs were turned. Maddy assumed a jury of sensible property owners. Clark's defence counsel had known how to play on their prejudices, how to shake any confidence they might initially have had in Trudi Hartman.

Wind-nipped faces hurried by. Maddy shivered, because of the frosty day that held no promise of spring and because of Trudi discredited.

'*She was brave*,' Maddy thought, '*going into court with her scanty story and knowing the defence would try to make a liar of her.*'

A woman with a shopping trolley stopped to look at houses in the window. Maddy turned back to Patsy's cuttings.

They confirmed what the first one had suggested: that Trudi Hartman was the only witness to claim Robert Clark had any connection with Pippa Dellafield. As the author of the long feature wrote: 'By concentrating on her lifestyle, Mr Sleathe raised doubts about her value as a witness.'

What had made the case worth writing about long after the event was that it had not been brought to a judicial conclusion. The trial was stopped and a retrial ordered. But no retrial took place. No one else was charged. In fact, no one else had even been accused in the court of local opinion.

Like all good stories, the case contained more than one mystery. Apart from the chief one, about the identity of Pippa Dellafield's killer, there was the mystery of the unnamed witness. The nub of it was that the police believed someone watched the murder but they could not use his evidence in court.

Maddy stumbled over the wording. It had grown awkward because the writer was being meticulous in referring to the mystery witness as 'the person' or 'they' instead of 'he' or 'she' which presumably risked identifying someone.

The cuttings in Steve's collection were shorter, all but two being extracts of longer items. Without the lengthy feature Patsy had chosen she would have found the other pieces unintelligible.

She reached the conclusion the two selections had been made for different purposes. Patsy's aim was clear. She had wanted to give a picture of the case to someone who knew next to nothing of it, and to illustrate how women's reputations had been made an issue.

Whoever had compiled Steve's batch had focused on the mystery witness. But because it *was* a mystery, they were obscure. A cautious comment by a police officer was practically impenetrable. A neighbour was equally cryptic: 'He hardly went anywhere without him. He followed him everywhere.' Who was 'he', who was 'him'?

The one cutting that did not refer to the mystery witness contained a statement from Clark's solicitor to the effect that his client had no plans to return to the Stratford area, and he could not say when his client would be reunited with his family.

Maddy felt thwarted. 'Unless the video tapes spell everything out for me, I shall remain stumped.'

She would have to wait for evening for a chance to view them.

It was a relief when the telephone began to ring and she became embroiled in the Dunflirtin yellow paint fiasco; and Graham Collins calling to say the locksmith had finished at her cottage but the search for her dog continued; and Heather providing information Maddy had requested about Wren Cottage; and so on and so forth.

She worked through without a lunch break, determined to keep busy and steer her mind away from unsatisfactory court cases and mystery witnesses. And, equally, to stop herself fretting about Jay and Steve, and what Steve might have done and what he might yet do.

During the afternoon she telephoned Felicity Fisher with news of the factory conversion on the riverbank; chased up a tardy solicitor who had dragged the purchase of an old vicarage out to three months; and slotted in a call to Ken.

'*Another* bottle? What are you doing with the stuff? Drinking it?'

'Don't be harsh, Maddy. There are three of us in here, remember.'

'Ah, so you didn't manage to keep it to yourself.'

'They sniffed it out, damn them. And all I get in return is fruit drops and lectures on chair-making.'

She laughed off the rest of his self-pity. 'All right, I'll see what I can do.'

But it was his turn to laugh. It had all been a tease. 'Save your pennies, my sweet. I'm away home tomorrow, God willing.'

'Well, *I'm* willing, especially if it saves me the price of a bottle of scotch.'

'Dare I ask whether everything is going well?'

'No problems,' she said, editing out the Dunflirtin business, her dog being abducted and her former lover giving her more grief than a girl would have believed possible.

'Er . . . Maddy . . .'

'No, sorry, she didn't ring.'

'Oh, well. Never mind.'

He bet her he would be at his desk before Friday. She took the wager reluctantly.

'But, Ken, they're sure to tell you to rest.'

'That wouldn't preclude a little gentle estate agenting, now would it?'

When she came off the phone, still smiling because he always made her smile, she noticed shutters sliding down in shops opposite, window lights going out, all the signals of the working day being brought to an end.

She stepped gingerly from the car and stood by it, her hand on the door. Keys dangled from the ignition for a quick escape. Being by the forest made her nervous.

'Jay.' The word became visible, her breath a pall of steam.

'Jay. Here, Jay. Come on, Jay.'

She waited, desperate for an answering scuffle in the undergrowth and the dog to come bounding towards her. She did not care if he was muddy, matted, smelly from rolling in fox scent. She did not mind how much grooming and patching up he required, she just wanted him back. She called.

Maddy looked at the straggling ranks of trees beside the road, at the uninviting darkness of the forest and the empty lane. She shouted again. A few minutes later, when the darkness had deepened towards night, she drove away.

Graham's message had included the instruction to call at Park House to collect her new keys and stay for supper. She was torn about the supper invitation. Although it would be good to have company while she was feeling vulnerable, she needed to be at home in case Jay returned. Also, she wanted to play Steve's video tapes.

'Do you have a video recorder?' she asked once she was settled in the Collinses' kitchen with a tumbler of red wine to hand and a flame-haired, pink-faced Nesta scuttling around in a scarlet apron.

'We hardly use it,' Graham said in a confessional tone. 'The fact is we're not much good at setting it to record anything.'

'I don't want to do that, only to play a couple of tapes.'

'I think we can manage that.' He put on a voice heavy with mystery. 'Come with me . . .'

With a sinking heart she realised they were heading for the ghastly dining room, scene of the smoky dinner party and the room where she had been laid out in a faint.

He ushered her in with theatrical courtesy. It occurred to her she had been cocooned by false gaiety ever since she arrived.

'Oh God, what bad news are they keeping from me? How long until they spit it out? After I've had a drink? After they've got a decent meal down me?'

He came to a stop in the middle of the room and swore. 'That thieving bitch.'

Striding to Linsey's flat, he pounded the locked door. 'Hey, Magpie. I want my video recorder.'

Maddy said: 'Isn't there a spare key? You can't have given Linsey the only one, surely.'

'The words "Linsey" and "give" do not crop up in the same sentences, Maddy. I thought you knew that.'

'Sorry.'

In the kitchen Nesta paused, spoon at her lips and cabbage-scented steam rising into her hair.

Graham told her: 'Lord Buckshee has inspired the Magpie to nick the video.'

Cabbagey liquid dribbled off the spoon. 'No!'

'And the door's locked.'

Nesta dropped the spoon into the pan and opened a drawer. Instead of reaching into it, she felt beneath. When she withdrew her hand, she held a key attached to a strip of sticky tape.

Seeing Maddy's expression, she explained. 'I got the idea

from a spy film. Linsey helps herself so I've had to hide things.'

As Graham unlocked the door of the flat, incense oozed into the house and a shrine leapt into view. The Collinses' new bowl was before the shrine and filled with daphne blossoms, their new blue towels glowed from the bathroom and their video recorder sat on a table beside a television set they had never seen before.

Graham spoke for them all. 'Who has she stolen that from?'

Nesta took control. 'Let's grab our stuff while we have the chance.' She instructed Maddy. 'Get the towels, will you? And that rug in front of the shrine. It's supposed to be my bedside rug, not that you'd ever know it.'

Graham said: 'It'll pong of joss sticks, Nesta.'

'I don't care. It's mine. Get it, Maddy.'

Maddy did as she was bid.

'One feels so stupid,' Graham objected as he eased the video recorder through the doorway. 'This keeps on happening.'

Nesta, scurrying from the kitchen, having squirreled away her booty, said: 'Maddy, you can bring that lot.'

The sweep of her arm encompassed a range of possibilities. All the things on top of the chest? Pictures on the wall? No, not those, they were oriental gods. For all she knew, they were Lord Buckshee himself. Ah, this was more like it: video tapes. Maddy checked a label. *Alfredo Smarty's Television Cookery Course*. That was very much a Collins interest. Perhaps one or other had been a guest on the programme. Maddy bundled up the tapes and tottered to the dining room.

She risked a small joke. 'You should have asked the locksmith to fix extra locks on your house.'

Graham gave her a jaundiced look. 'Most people are trying to keep the bad guys out. We've got one *in situ*.'

She shuffled tapes into a semblance of order and stacked them beside the recorder. The Collinses did not aspire to specially designed stands or shelves.

Nesta returned to her cabbagey sauce and Maddy fetched a tape from her bag. She would have preferred to watch alone but Graham, saying he preferred to keep out of Nesta's path for a few minutes, sat down on a chair beside her.

As the picture appeared, Maddy gasped.

Graham said: 'What the hell is this?'

After that they watched in stupefied silence.

Beth Welford was in the sitting room at Church Cottage. She was wearing her familiar patterned jumper. Maddy knew the room, knew she was sitting on the sofa rather than the matching chair because of the mirror on the wall behind it. Beth was uncharacteristically serious. People in home videos usually posed happily but this was different.

'I'm making this recording,' Beth said, 'in case anything goes wrong. It's a sort of insurance. I want to put down everything I know and this way there's no doubt that it's me saying it. I'm putting a copy of it in a safe deposit box in a bank.'

There was a break while she collected her thoughts. Then she began again, her voice steady although her right hand was shaking.

'I've lived with this as long as I can remember. All my life. It changed my life from whatever it might have been into something different. Sorry, I'm not saying it right. I've got to try and remember I'm not only talking to one person who knows, but I might be talking to heaps of other people who, if they don't hear it from me, won't hear it at all. And it's not . . . Well, it's a hard thing to do. All of it, I mean.'

There was a painful pause. Then she grabbed the wavering right hand and held it still and started to speak again.

'Anyway, I've decided to set it down so this is it. My mother was called Pippa Dellafield and she was murdered on farmland near Stratford-on-Avon when I was three. The man who killed her was put on trial but the judge died and the trial was stopped. The man was called Robert Clark. His brother saw what happened. To begin with, the brother said he was there but then he said he'd made it up. Oh, I forgot to say the brother was eight.'

Another gap, a deep breath before she rushed on: 'If the brother had told the truth, Robert Clark would have gone to prison. My life would have been different. I could have kept my own name instead of having it changed to Harries. They did that because Dellafield had become a bad name after the nasty things that were said about my mother in court and in the papers.

'This is the bombshell bit: I saw it. The brother wasn't the only witness. I was there too.'

She gripped her hands more tightly. Her words tumbled out.

'I saw him. I saw what he did. He was in the trees. He came down when it was over, and he went and stood by my mother's body. He knelt down and touched her dress. I remember that. I saw it. And I know who he was. It's not something you forget, and it's not something you forgive.'

At that point the tape lapsed into flashes on a black ground. Graham let it run through to the end. Neither he or Maddy spoke.

Eventually he ejected the tape and examined it, searching for a label. He held it up and looked quizzically at her.

She shook her head. Before she could speak he said: 'Well, *I* know what this is. It's dynamite.'

CHAPTER SEVENTEEN

'I knew you weren't telling us everything.' Nesta stood in the dining room doorway, the smell of cabbage wafting around her.

Her words were an accusation. Graham, who had shared his wife's sense of exclusion, was intent on soothing. 'Hard to know how much to tell, I should have thought.'

They had played the video tape through again. Having protested that she could not spare the time, Nesta had insisted on staying in the doorway as if that would make the process quicker. What she saw had left her flustered, cross with every-one in a mysterious world she could not hope to understand.

'I've been *so* worried about you, Maddy. You know I have. He's always been . . .'

Graham warned her off. 'Nesta . . .'

Ignoring him she ploughed on. 'He was never right for you, and then there was all that nonsense about him refusing to move out.'

He chipped in again. 'Nesta, I don't think . . .'

Maddy said: 'I didn't want to exaggerate the situation or exacerbate it.' The other tape seemed to have fallen out of her bag in the car and she was waiting for a break in the conversation so that she could fetch it.

'I know, *I know*,' Nesta was saying. 'You argued you could deal with him. You thought you were in control. You told me that. Whenever I brought the subject up, that's what you said.

And now *this*. Now you waltz in here with a tape that suggests he had something to do with Beth.'

'Hold on a minute,' said Graham. 'We don't know that Steve has any connection with the things Maddy found in her loft.'

Nesta rolled her eyes. 'Oh, really!'

Maddy added: 'Who else could have put them there?'

He said: 'We're making assumptions. Because the most likely explanation is that Steve hid them, we're saying that therefore they're his and he's the person Beth addresses in the tape.'

'They're reasonable assumptions,' Maddy said, wishing they were not.

'But that doesn't make them true. Look, you saw Linsey's room earlier. It would have been a reasonable assumption that the contents were either hers or things we'd given her permission to use. And what about the alien television set? As she'd stolen our video recorder, it would have been . . .'

Nesta, tiring of the lecture, finished the sentence for him. '. . . a reasonable assumption that it was ours, too.'

'Well, there you are.' The tape finished rewinding and he extracted it from the machine.

Maddy said: 'What we assume doesn't matter. The police will have to work it out.'

She was opening the door, saying she was going to fetch something from her car. Rather than dramatically announcing a second tape, she chose to be vague.

Outside she delayed, having recovered the tape from beneath the passenger seat. Seeing the recorded Beth had shaken her profoundly and she was relishing a few minutes to herself, away from Graham being sensible and Nesta edging ever closer to saying I told you so. Well, fair enough. Nesta *had* told her. And the warnings had not been heeded, and . . .

She sighed. Everything had gone wrong. All her hopes and happy anticipations had been proved naive and stupid. Her life at Meadow Cottage was not the carefree one she needed. Steve had been a nightmare, worse than her marriage or The

Disaster with John. And Ken was right about village life; it was less congenial than she pretended.

She had invested a lot of emotional energy, as well as more money than she could comfortably afford, to make a life in the village, and the life she was leading was not good enough. Things fell short. Everything she did was inadequate, everything she owned was substandard. The same mistakes came round and round with the seasons, and she seemed unable to avoid them.

Maddy recognised what she was doing, what she repeatedly did and which landed her in most of her trouble. She was skirting the painful issues and dealing with the peripheral bits that seemed manageable. Despite the astounding revelations in the tape, she was indulging in mental arguments about her friend's right to crow over her. The crowing and her own lack of judgment did not matter a jot. The important thing, the one she was refusing to confront, was the hideous inference that Steve had, in Nesta's words, something to do with Beth.

Graham came out. 'You OK, Maddy?'

She gritted her teeth before adopting a nicer mood and saying yes, she was just coming, she had been waylaid by looking at the stars, weren't they wonderful tonight?

He came to her. 'Look, don't let Nesta upset you. She doesn't mean to be unkind.'

'I'm not upset. And she has every right. She loathed Steve from the beginning and she told me why.'

He checked that Nesta was not at the kitchen window before saying: 'Actually, the truth is *she's* upset today.'

'Oh?'

'You remember Glenys, the magazine editor who came to dinner?'

'Of course. What's happened to her?'

'She's lost her job. We had a letter today saying thanks for a lovely evening and all that stuff, and then telling us we won't be doing any other work for her because she's been given the boot.'

'Oh, I am sorry. That's very bad luck.'

'What rankles is that we think she was expecting it.'

'She knew before she came here?'

'It rather looks like it.'

They walked to the house together, Maddy thinking: *'So that was the bad news they were hiding. Trust me to assume it was something to do with me instead of them.'*

As they entered the ring of light from the hall, Maddy held up the tape, a silent announcement that there might be further shocks in store.

Graham slipped it into the recorder. Nesta came properly into the room and sat beside Maddy. Beth appeared on the screen, sitting on the same sofa. Maddy registered that she was wearing the same sweater, the one with brown and yellow abstract patterns. Only her demeanour differed. The diffidence was gone, the trembling hand steady and the voice strong.

Beth said: 'I hoped we could have sorted this out before now but you seem to think you can walk away from it, the way you walked away from my mother's body and walked away from the truth. You've spent nearly all your life walking away from the truth, haven't you? And because of it you've wrecked mine. Well, I'm not going to allow it to go on any longer.

'People say nothing can compensate for a death but that isn't the whole truth. What's worse than having someone important to you killed is having it lied about. Because of you, my mother didn't get justice but I want it for her now and I want it for me. By doing what I want, you'll have to face up to what you did to us, you and Robert Clark. Maybe he hasn't got a conscience but I believe you have. You can get what I want and you can get it from him. Although it can't buy back my mother's life or my childhood, it will be a compensation of sorts. I'm putting a copy of each of my tapes in a safe deposit box at a bank.'

The picture ended. Maddy said: 'That was much more direct. She was addressing the person she referred to as the brother in the first tape. And her manner was different.'

Graham said: 'Threatening.'

Nesta said: 'Blackmail.'

'Assumptions again,' Graham cautioned.

The women rounded on him.

'Oh come on, darling. Whatever else did it sound like?'

'Graham, it *was*. "Compensation". "Do what I want"'.

Nesta said: 'She was blackmailing somebody and Steve was in on it with her. She gave him a copy of her demands.'

Graham rewound the tape. 'You'll be saying next that Steve was the blackmail victim. Well, he can't be Robert Clark's brother because his name is Linton.'

'I've already thought of that,' Nesta said.

Maddy told them: 'It's time we handed these to the police. Here we are with two chunks of evidence while Chris Welford is languishing in jail.'

But she suggested there was no point in contacting the police that evening. 'They'll be busy breaking up pub fights in Chippy or chasing naughty drivers, plus everything else they do under cover of darkness. Morning will be quite soon enough.'

'Why don't you leave them here?'

'Yes,' said Nesta. 'There's no sense in taking them home, is there?'

Maddy was quick to agree. The thought of having them in the cottage made her shudder. She imagined herself being drawn to replay them, alone and fearful that Steve might choose that very night to return to the house and claim his secrets from the loft.

A shiver ran through her. It took a moment for her to realise she was in the chilliest room she ever went into and this accounted for two thirds of the coldness gnawing her bones. The other third was fear, misery and the knowledge that matters would not improve yet and she would be forced to hang on until they did. Life, one day, would be worth living. But not just yet.

'Cold?' asked Nesta.

'Thinking about Beth, that's all.'

That's all. That's everything.

Nesta, who was bothered about the supper which was keeping warm in a low oven, led them off to the kitchen.

While she clattered plates onto the table, Graham sloshed red wine into tumblers. Maddy ejected a cat from a chair. She did not think Nesta's vegetarian braise with cabbage sauce smelled enticing but she was ravenous and prepared to love it.

'Could this be Linsey's influence?' she wondered, as she helped herself from the crock Nesta set in front of them.

'In a way it is,' Nesta confessed.

Graham winked at Maddy. 'I expect that means she had to cope without onions and garlic. Or any of the other veg Lord Buckshee confines to the lower orders and Linsey consigns to our dustbin.'

Nesta tried to cheat him of further fun at her expense by changing the subject. 'We ought to get a pig, you know. Then hardly anything would be chucked in the dustbin.'

'Except the pig,' retorted Graham. 'Have you heard Linsey on the subject of unclean beasts?'

The question was meant for Maddy who waited for him to expound. But somewhere in the house a door banged. Footsteps approached the kitchen. Linsey posed there, bowed, touched her face in self-absolution for the sin of breathing the same air as unbelievers. She launched into her complaint.

'You have invaded my space. You have removed possessions from my home. You have . . .'

Graham sprang to his feet. 'And you have gone too far. If you're not out of my sight this instant, I'll . . .'

Her chin shot up. 'Persecute me? I bring The Truth to your house and you persecute me.'

Disdainful, she flounced away. Somewhere in the house a door banged again.

Nesta tugged at Graham's sleeve, trying to draw him back to his seat. He jerked free and went to close the kitchen door.

'That silly cow doesn't know the meaning of truth,' he said. 'She's brainwashed into believing it's the property of that wacky cult, and nobody else is allowed an opinion. Do you realise she . . .'

'Yes, darling. Don't get so het up.'

'Well, she gets me on the raw.' He sank onto his chair.

Nesta said: 'So we've noticed. Eat up before it gets cold.'

Maddy said: 'This is actually rather good.' And immediately wished she had kept the surprise out of her voice.

Acknowledging the compliment with a smile, Nesta explained Linsey's oblique influence. 'I was fed up with the smell of Indian spices around the house and it set me thinking how limited her ingredients are. She insists they're extremely nutritious and very cheap . . .'

Graham had heard enough. 'They're only cheap because they're cultivated by impoverished peasants. If the farmers got paid the same as the ones who grew your cabbage, the price would be . . .'

But Nesta also had heard enough. She guided the crock towards him. 'A little more, darling?'

He shook his head. 'And if you include the cost of . . .'

'Maddy, do help yourself.'

Maddy lifted another spoonful onto her plate. She was trying to decide whether it was tactful to avoid mentioning Glenys and the lost magazine work or to sympathise. Before she resolved it, Nesta asked her opinion of the cabbage sauce.

'It's entirely my own invention. Do you think it would be worth including in a book of vegetarian recipes?'

Maddy took a mouthful to allow herself time to work out an answer.

Graham had decided. 'No. It's palatable enough but ask yourself this: who would voluntarily try cabbage sauce? Recipes in books need to have instant appeal, Nesta, and cabbage doesn't qualify.'

Looking slightly bruised, Nesta waited for Maddy's vote.

'Perhaps you could leave out any mention of cabbage.'

Nesta was horrified. 'Leave out the cabbage?'

'No, just leave out the *word* when you name the dish.'

Nesta's expression changed to interested discovery. 'Brassica sauce. Hmm. It sounds Italian, doesn't it? And you know how dotty people are about Italian dishes.'

Maddy recalled previous conversations. 'But I thought

your idea was to get people to appreciate home produce rather than hop from one exotic foreign taste to another.'

A sigh. 'Yes, I do seriously believe it's folly to treat food as a branch of the fashion industry. But we need to make our living writing about food.' She gave Graham a sidelong glance. 'Maddy, we heard today that Glenys has lost her job, which means we've lost ours, too.'

Graham expounded. 'Her replacement has brought with her a string of French and Italian housewives.' He paused to allow Maddy's face to register high on the incredulity scale. 'Yes, amateurs. A staff writer will interview one or other of them each month and write a column based on the chat.'

Maddy said she did not see how it could be any good.

'No,' he said, 'but it *will* be cheap. Not much more than the cost of the phone calls.'

'What about photographs?'

He snorted. 'Equally cunning. A small portrait of the housewife and a drawing of a . . . a *cabbage* or whatever's in the recipe.'

He broke off as Nesta staggered to the table with a heavy brown bowl of creamy rice and almonds beneath a caramelised crust. She jabbed a spoon into it and the scent of almonds wiped away all trace of cabbage.

'I suppose,' she said provocatively, 'one of you will now tell me rice pudding also has a bad reputation.'

Soon after supper Maddy took possession of her new keys and went home. In the hall she kicked off her outdoor shoes. They were not the most comfortable footwear she owned and she had worn them all day. A sudden welling up of anxiety brought her thoughts to a halt. Muscles in her neck and shoulders clenched. The tension became a pain in her head, down her spine and in the fists she was powerless to relax. The spasm was swift, unexpected, and she did not understand the cause.

'I was only thinking about my shoes.'

Her chest hurt. She forced air into her lungs. *'I must be going crazy. To be scared out of my wits and not know why.'*

She took a faltering step forward, her stockinged feet dragging over the flagstones.

And then she knew. The flagstones were exceptionally cold because an icy draught was blowing down the passage from the kitchen.

It took an effort of will to walk down that passage. As she went, she flicked on electric lights in the hall, on the stairs and in the sitting room. Finally, her hand touched the one on the wall a few inches inside the kitchen. The back door, with its new lock and its two old bolts, was secure but the casement window was open.

Maddy rushed to close it, swung it too fast and made it bang against the frame and rebound. Her movements were panicky. She realised she must slow down if she were to achieve anything apart from noise and frustration.

Two of the small panes were broken. Glass had been knocked out of them. Shards lay on the window-sill and on the floor where she stood.

'My feet must be cut. They ought to hurt but I can't feel them.'

Before she backed away she looked around for the key to the window lock. It lay on the floor beneath the window. She bent to pick it up but then hesitated.

'I'm doing what Graham doesn't like. I'm making assumptions. About Steve again. But it might not have been Steve. Someone else could have done this and his fingerprints might be on the key. I won't touch it or the window, either. I'll call the police.'

She stepped away from the window, raised one foot after the other and checked for seeping blood on her soles. The left foot was the worse.

Maddy lifted the telephone.

Just before the police left there was an uncomfortable moment during which they appeared to think she was about to offer more information. When she said nothing, except her thank yous and her goodbyes, they looked a mite dissatisfied.

She imagined them discussing her once they were driving away, weighing up what she had told them and deciding it was not the whole truth.

She had explained that it was quite possible the person who broke in was the man who had been living with her and whose keys were redundant because the locks had been changed that day. 'But,' she had said, 'he hasn't taken any of his property and he hasn't left a note, therefore I can't be certain it was him.'

Maddy had withheld all mention of Beth's tapes because they could have no connection with her broken window and they were not to hand. Better to stick to the plan worked out with Graham and Nesta and report the matter to the appropriate police in the morning, she thought. All this seemed reasonable until the moment when two expectant faces read secrecy in hers.

After she had shut the door on them and locked herself in for the night, she made another tour of the house. She was checking, in particular, the position of her window keys. One of the policemen had said that, judging by the damage, her kitchen key had been left on the inside sill. A bottom pane had been broken for the intruder to get at it and then the other one smashed for him to reach the lock.

Once she had convinced herself that the cardboard blocking the gaps in the window would not blow off in the night, and that every lock and bolt was fastened, and the keys were hidden from the sight of anyone looking into the house, she went up to bed.

But she was edgy. Every murmur from her fridge, every glow of light from a vehicle on the road, every cry of a wild creature in the fields made her jittery. She prowled the house again.

In the back bedroom, Steve's mess was exactly as she remembered it. For a few minutes she chased the idea that the step-ladder had been taken from the stair cupboard and replaced in a slightly different position. But she had no justification for believing that and persuaded herself it was one worry she could safely reject. She reassured herself on another point, too.

'Steve doesn't know I've discovered the bag or that I know anything about the Pippa Dellafield murder.'

She laid plans for the morning. First she would leave

a telephone message for her colleagues at Rigmaroles in Oxford to say she would be late for work. Then she would drive over to Park House and ring the police from there to report the Beth tapes.

'I wonder whether they'll play them straightaway or take them away unseen. If they want to question me after they've viewed them, and they've taken them to Oxford, I might have to go there, too.'

She yawned. *'Or perhaps they'll interview me in the incident room here. I don't think the Wintersons have succeeded in evicting them yet.'*

Maddy gave a self-deprecating smile as she caught the drift of this speculation. As usual, her thoughts were circling the inessentials. Yet the heart of the matter was too appalling to confront, especially when she was alone in a house whose expensive new security measures had been breached.

The subject, though, was too powerful to dismiss and it bubbled below the surface of her consciousness. Although Graham resisted making assumptions, she had done a calculation that reinforced them. Whoever Beth was addressing had been a boy of eight when Pippa Dellafield was killed. He would now be a man of thirty-one. Steve Linton was thirty-one.

Even better than the Collinses, Maddy knew how reticent he was about his upbringing. This had not troubled her because she took the view that, to a considerable degree, people made their own lives. She felt it unreasonable to burden them with a name and a baggage of history belonging to a family they rejected. If they had suffered at the hands of their family, then they should be allowed to leave that in the past. Blessed with a happy childhood of her own, she was sympathetic rather than suspicious when other people were cagey.

The tapes cast a new light on Steve's reticence. Oh, he told stories about elaborate adventures when he was growing up but he did not tell the ordinary things. She had given up believing his stories. There was only his fever to convince her he had ever been to Africa. Unlike Graham, she did not assume the difference in names was conclusive. Steve might have changed his name rather than be identified as the brother of a notorious man. On the other hand, families were very muddled these days. By brother, Beth might have meant a half-brother or a step-brother, in which case Steve need not have changed his name because it would never have been Clark.

She pulled herself up. *'Don't be deluded a second time. Things fit together but it doesn't mean you've got the full picture.'*

She remembered Jay and decided to play through the tape on her answering machine in case she had missed a call reporting his whereabouts. Familiar voices repeated old news. But as the tape finished, she noticed something was wrong. She had not cleared the tape for days but the earlier messages had gone. She played it again. A cold sweat dampened her forehead.

'Steve knows,' she thought. *'He wiped the batch that included Patsy's message about the Dellafield case. He didn't guess she'd leave an identical one on my office machine. He doesn't realise how much I know, but he knows I was learning about the case.'*

The implications were frightening. Putting the worst possible interpretation on the situation, Beth's death could be the result of blackmail because of the Dellafield murder and Steve the man who killed her. Maddy's instinct was to call the police again but what could she say that would not make her seem an hysterical woman failing to cope with a smashed window? She relived the challenging moment when they had sensed she was holding back. It was enough to deter her.

Maddy walked around the house, wakeful and perturbed and impatient for dawn. Daylight was hours away.

The new day promised company and authoritative people to take charge of the troubles that beset her. It was a day she longed for and yet one she dreaded. Doubts which haunted her would be passed on to the police but, whatever the result, nothing good could come of it. Whether or not Steve proved guilty of a crime, the village would fashion her into a notorious dupe. Either she had been gulled by a killer and a deceiver, or else she had jumped to conclusions suggested by the tapes and had brought down suspicion on an innocent man. She would not get off free.

CHAPTER EIGHTEEN

The Collinses were having a full scale row. Maddy could hear them as she cut the engine.

'Steve called them temperamental cooks. Steve called Nesta a witch.'

She gritted her teeth, noticed this was becoming a habit and wondered briefly if she would ever return to being her happy-go-lucky self. Pessimism, born of tiredness and anxiety, made it seem improbable.

The front door of Park House opened at a touch. Nesta, near the foot of the stairs, was an unkempt virago. Graham, in the centre of the hall with his back to Maddy, had taken up a recalcitrant stance. He was booming a denial of whatever Nesta was accusing him.

Maddy shouted into the hubbub. 'Good morning.'

Nesta subsided, sweeping a hand over her face and turning away to study the blank wall beside her instead of meeting Maddy's eye.

Graham looked over his shoulder. 'Oh. You're here.'

He made her fear she was unreasonably early and she stole a glance at their long-case clock. But no, it was nearly nine.

Now that the racket had ended there was a depressing silence. Then Nesta sighed and came down the last two stairs. Maddy guessed she had retreated up there while Graham advanced on her.

Without looking at him for approval, Nesta said quickly: 'There's been a disaster, Maddy. The tapes are missing.'

Her words hung between them. No one reacted.

Maddy was not taking it in fully. They had exhausted the subject themselves and were waiting for her to ask questions. Her voice a broken whisper, she managed: 'How?'

This time Nesta looked boldly at her husband. Graham cleared his throat before he was able to explain.

'We left them . . . I mean *I* left them in the dining room last night.'

Maddy frowned.

He said: 'I know we should have taken them up to our bedroom and guarded them with our lives, the way we told you we would. But the fact is, I left them in the dining room.'

'Was the house broken into?'

This, he appeared to think, was a silly digression. 'No, of course not.' He jabbed a finger in the direction of the flat. 'It's a bloody Magpie job.'

Maddy could not see what all the fuss was about because property gravitated to and from Linsey's flat the whole time. 'Well, in that case let's go and get them.'

She started in the direction of the flat but Nesta touched her arm. 'It isn't that easy, Maddy. Linsey's in there and she won't hand them over. She's got hold of a mobile telephone from somewhere and is threatening to call the police if we break in. Someone's told her the law is on her side and we're afraid she might be right.'

Maddy said: 'If those tapes belong to anyone here, which is doubtful, then they belong to me. I'll fetch them.'

And when they simply stood there, limp and defeated, she became tetchy although all she said was: 'Look, please can we have some coffee? I came over here as fast as I could and I haven't touched a thing. I've been up all night . . .'

Nesta recovered first. 'Oh, you poor thing. We're being thoroughly inhospitable.' She led the way to the kitchen and put water on to boil.

'Literally awake all night?' Graham queried. He had always suspected it to be a figure of speech

'Literally. And it's hardly surprising.'

Maddy recounted the story of the broken window, the police visit and her realisation that Steve knew she was gathering information about the Dellafield murder.

As soon as she finished, Graham said: 'Get on to the police immediately, Maddy. They can wrench the tapes off Linsey.'

Nesta demurred. 'We're going to look fools if we have to ask them to do that. You try getting them, Maddy.'

Graham argued: 'The police need to know of their existence, that's the crucial thing. Then it's up to them to recover them.'

Maddy said it would be best for her to make a token attempt at least. 'If I succeed, all well and good. If not, then we send the police in.'

She tapped on the door. 'Linsey? It's Maddy here. You've taken my video tapes and I need them right away.'

No answer.

'Linsey?' A faint droning came from the other side.

'Linsey, I know you can hear me. Open the door, please.'

The droning grew fractionally louder. Linsey was chanting.

Maddy wheedled.

Words of the mantra became audible. *'Om . . . rama . . . naya supatha . . . om . . . rama . . .'*

Maddy grew threatening. 'Either you hand them to me straight away or I'll ask the police to get them.'

A blare of sitar and tamboura overlaid the mantra. Each time Maddy called through the door, the volume rose.

She retired, irked because this was precisely what Linsey knew she would be forced to do.

She reported to the Collinses who were taking refuge in the kitchen, Graham preparing a mash of cabbage, potato peelings and meal for the hens, and Nesta scraping at rice dried on a bowl.

'No good,' Maddy admitted.

'So we hear.' Nesta was sardonic.

'I'm afraid all I've achieved is Indian music.'

Nesta shifted the last grain of rice and rinsed the bowl.

Maddy followed Graham and the saucepan of chicken feed out of the back door. The smallest of the speckled Marans, who had become fixated on him when she was a chick, came pell-mell. Scratching in the dust, the others took longer to catch on and then ran after her in a stiff-legged hue and cry.

'I could try the window,' Maddy suggested.

'Break it, you mean? Oh, thanks. Just what we need.' Hens eddied about his feet. He strode through them and led them away from the house.

Not in the mood for his irony, Maddy walked round the house without replying. Although Linsey had drawn the curtains, they were an old pair not made for that window and they did not overlap. Through the gap she saw Linsey squatting before the shrine, swaying from side to side, eyes glazed and lips moving in the mind-numbing repetition of the mantra.

Incense curled from a vase. Nesta's new bowl overflowed with the pink flowers of a daphne. Maddy recognised the bedside rug Linsey was using as a prayer mat. She saw stacks of video tapes arranged before the shrine, apparently being offered up to the picture of the man Graham had dubbed Lord Buckshee. And she saw something else that made her even crosser.

She touched the window-frame firmly. It moved under her pressure. Maddy sought out Graham, who had finished pouring mash into an old enamel bowl from which the chickens fed and was fending off the smallest hen, more or less delicately, with his foot.

'Graham, I think I can get through the window.'

He flicked the persistent hen aside with his toe. 'This does mean a broken window, then.'

'No, but it means I need to borrow something from the kitchen.' She headed for the house, making him follow.

He and Nesta watched bewildered as Maddy hunted through the disorder in the kitchen.

'These should do it,' she said, holding up a stout knife and a steak hammer.

Nesta echoed Graham's misgivings. 'You'll get glass everywhere.'

They were having to raise their voices above the level of the *raga*.

'I promise I won't.' With gestures she demonstrated how she would do it. 'I'll slip the knife between the frames, next to the catch. And I'll use the hammer to force the knife across to move the catch.'

Graham looked sceptical despite admitting: 'I can see how it might work in theory.'

Nesta was even less convinced. 'Have you done it before, Maddy?'

Impatient to get on with it, Maddy was on her way out of the kitchen. 'No, but I'm sure it works.'

Graham, stepping aside to let her through, said ironically: 'I suppose it's one of the tricks of your trade.'

'Oh no, I don't break into houses for a living. This is something Steve taught me.' She faltered as she saw the dismay on their faces.

He said: 'If that's the case, why did he have to break the catch on your sitting room window? It's a sash, the same as ours.'

Nesta offered an answer. 'He didn't have to. He chose to. He was being bloody-minded because she'd locked the gate to the garden.'

This, Maddy suspected, was true but she was loath to squander time discussing it when she had Linsey to tackle. She went outside.

Finding Graham and Nesta on her heels, she redirected him to stand outside the door of the flat. 'Please, Graham. It's important she doesn't escape.'

The window catch opened smoothly. As she pushed up the lower half of the window, the noise came belting out. Hens who had congregated to peck her shoelaces and to bring Nesta up in a rash, scattered in jerky fright. Nesta clapped hands over her ears.

Using an upturned bucket as a stool, Maddy swung herself up on to the sill. She was thinking it was typical of life's inconsistency that in the midst of the blackest drama she should be caught up in absurdity. The hilarious and the horrifying were paired again.

Linsey was too far gone in her self-induced daze to notice. She sat cross-legged, her upper body weaving, long hair flapping and her mouth working at the words of the mantra. Her eyes were open but glazed.

Maddy pushed one of the curtains aside. She expected Linsey to respond but Linsey was deafened. Dazed. Drugged?

It flashed through Maddy's mind that people who were drugged could be unpredictably savage. For the first time she doubted the wisdom of getting into a situation from which there was no easy way out. If Linsey were startled and she attacked, Maddy might not make it through the window in safety. And she had no hope of fleeing through the door because she had been adamant that Graham was to resist it being opened. Up until now, her premise had been that Linsey was the one who might try to escape through the house.

The noise was causing her a headache, a thump, thump, thump in the temples. Could she dash past the swaying devotee and pull the plug out of the wall before Linsey sprang to her feet?

She felt a tug on her blouse. Nesta was apprehensive. 'What's happening?'

Maddy leaned towards her to speak, lost her balance, struggled to regain it and cast a fearful glance into the room. The *raga* pounded on, the body undulated, the trance was intact.

'She's in a trance,' Maddy said.

'Oh. Will you go in?'

'Yes but I don't know what might happen when she comes round. You won't leave me, will you.'

Nesta gave her a don't-be-silly look. 'Of course not.'

Maddy swung her other leg over the sill and eased herself to the floor. Her left foot made contact first but whatever she had landed on was unstable and shot from under her. Cooking pans went bowling over the carpet.

The commotion of the collapsing bench and the falling pans was masked by the maximum decibel *raga*. Linsey would have continued unaware had one of the pans not rolled into her.

The trance was broken. All hell was let loose.

Linsey was transformed from chanting acolyte into aggressive fanatic. Maddy was pushed up against the window. Anger came to her aid. She forced the crazed woman to back off by shrieking at her. To be retaliating restored a scrap of her self-respect, just to see Linsey cowering was a reward.

Linsey, though, was stooping to snatch up one of the pans. It was a wok, a thin steel bowl on the end of a long handle. Linsey raised it high. She charged, the pan swinging in an arc that threatened to connect with Maddy's head.

'She'll kill me.'

Maddy flung herself out of the way and dived for the window.

Nesta was frantic, being unable to help Maddy either in the room or in getting out of it. Suddenly, a man rounded the end of the house. Jim, the postman.

'Stay here,' Nesta begged him, and she ran to Graham.

Maddy had a memorable view of Jim's open jaw and the metallic fillings in his molars. The moment seemed to last. It ended when Graham grabbed Linsey from behind. None too tenderly he escorted her into the bathroom and trapped her there. That done, he switched off the music. Maddy dropped down into the room again.

It took several long moments for them to adjust to the quietness. Jim, leaning through the window and gesturing with a handful of buff envelopes, demanded his curiosity be satisfied. 'Is she often like that? Why do you have her around if she causes you trouble?'

Maddy, in a wave of hysteria, wondered whether he meant her or Linsey.

'Listen,' said Nesta.

Graham retorted: 'I can't listen. My hearing's been damaged by half an hour of musical torture.'

Jim said: 'Half an hour? Was she doing it that long? I could hear it by the shop. Indian, wasn't it?'

'Listen, *please*,' said Nesta. After they granted her a second's silence, her face assumed an expression of annoyed triumph. 'Water.'

Jim made a joke about Linsey taking a shower to cool her temper down. He was dejected when no one smiled. The Collinses looked as though he had brought them a letter bearing very bad news.

Nesta asked: 'How much water does the tank contain?'

Graham brightened: 'The water in the flat comes straight off the main.' He ran to turn off the water supply.

Jim poked the buff envelopes at Nesta and asked her to sign for the one which was a registered letter. Then he was on his way, leaving her chagrined that Park House had provided him with a wonderful tale to tell on the remainder of his round.

Maddy gathered up all the video tapes in Linsey's domain. There were a number of unmarked ones. In the dining room she slipped these one after the other into the recorder.

Nesta was removing Collins property from the flat. Graham tired of helping her and joined Maddy.

'Got them?'

'No. I'll take another look in the flat.'

Linsey was chanting in the bathroom. No one cared. There was no sound of running water. Everyone was pleased about that.

Systematically, Graham and Maddy searched the room. They moved the bed and raised the mattress. They checked whether the fitted carpet could be lifted which it could not. They took everything out of the drawers and looked inside everything that had an inside. There were no video tapes.

Nesta, garnering stolen bits and pieces, asked: 'Have you played all the tapes that have labels on? I was thinking that if I needed to conceal a tape I might put a misleading label on it.'

Maddy hurried away to play labelled tapes.

Graham arrived when she was on the third which was, as promised, a play recorded from their television set.

She said: 'Graham, I'm going to ring the police now. We're running round in circles trying to do what's better done by them. They won't thank us if we botch it.'

'I've done that by losing the tapes.' He looked as abject and foolish as he felt.

'No, you're hardly responsible for somebody else being a thief.'

'If I'd only taken them up to the bedroom . . .'

'Like Nesta's bedside rug, you mean?'

'Oh, I hadn't thought of that.'

'Linsey took it from Nesta's side while she slept. Do you think she would have left the tapes if she'd wanted them?'

His face puckered in a frown but before he could explore the thought, Maddy was on the telephone and summoning the police.

While they waited for them to come, Graham shared his reservations. 'How did the Magpie know about the Beth tapes?'

The question floored her. She put another tape into the recorder and waited for him to continue.

'Maddy, we've been assuming Linsey took all the tapes in the dining room because you'd previously removed all those in the flat. As we didn't know of the existence of the Beth tapes until yesterday evening, how could she have known and singled them out to hide separately?'

The screen was showing the titles of a cookery programme. Maddy clicked the button.

He said: 'We're crediting her with knowledge she can't have had. If any of us had known about the tapes earlier and talked about them, there would have been a chance of her finding out. But the way it was, she can't have done.'

'Tell the police that, too.'

Maddy pushed another tape into the machine. The label said it was a Hollywood musical. It was. She took up the next one.

While she waited to see whether the screen really would fill with opera, she stood up and yawned. Graham, taking pity on her weariness, stopped evolving brainteasers and went to make strong coffee.

An overture played over the titles of *Tosca*. She reached for the eject button. Her other hand fiddled the next tape into the slot. The label claimed it was a disaster movie.

Waiting, Maddy slid a hand into her pocket. Her fingers stroked one of the things she had removed from the flat. She had not mentioned it to the Collinses and she decided, for the present, not to.

The police said there would be no further questions until the missing tapes were recovered. Maddy set off for work.

Life at Park House had become so fraught that it was solace to be in the office. In her absence, telephone calls had been redirected to Witney. Cathy reported that a Ms Fisher had asked to be shown around a factory conversion on the river bank.

'Funny woman, she asked whether the neighbours keep dogs.'

'Oh, she's not the funniest I've had.'

'And your Mr Pegler rang to say he was putting his foot down on the yellow paint. Sounded messy to me. Do you understand it?'

'All too well.' She encapsulated the story of Dunflirtin and enjoyed it when Cathy giggled. It was, after all, the only sane response.

Maddy said: 'There's nothing on my answering machine. Did you clear the messages?'

'There were only two. A stalling one from a solicitor you'd accused of stalling. And Heather wants you to meet her at Wren Cottage this evening.'

Maddy winced. After her sleepless night, the last thing she wanted was an evening appointment.

'What time?' she asked.

'Not too late. Seven.'

'I'll ring her and confirm.'

'No, the message said you won't able to contact her during the day, just turn up if you can.'

Then, with business out of the way, Cathy asked: 'What's the gossip in the village now?'

Maddy grew vague but Cathy would not be put off. 'Come on, I've been riding shotgun for you all morning. You owe me a bit of tittle-tattle.'

'All right. How's this? My dog's missing.'

'Jay? The one John gave you.' Cathy had met and admired John.

'Yes, that one.' She teased the story out to let Cathy think she was being fed a tantalising tale. But it was difficult to achieve this without referring to Steve, and although she succeeded in avoiding his name Cathy mentioned it.

'Your dog went for a walk with Steve and didn't come home? What's Steve got to say about that?'

'Well . . .' Stupidly, she hesitated and that was enough to fire Cathy's imagination.

'Oh! Steve's run off too, has he?'

'No. No, it isn't like that.'

But it was and Cathy had been sharp enough to recognise it. She had met Steve once and not cared for him, or maybe her view had been influenced by Ken.

Maddy was thinking about him when Ken rang, cheerfully announcing that he was at home and feeling fit for work the following day.

Suspicious, she quizzed him about the doctor's precise instructions. To her it looked rather like Ken attempting to win one of their bets but he insisted the doctor had sanctioned a return to work. All she could do was wish him well and look forward to having his company again.

She was lowering the receiver when he shouted her name. 'Maddy? I nearly forgot. Have you seen the story about Church Cottage in the evening paper?'

Her heart sank. 'No. Can you read it to me?'

'Wish I could but it's been purloined by a demon chairmaker. Brad barely gave me time to scan it. I wouldn't mind except that I paid for it!'

229

His petulance made her laugh. 'Tell me the worst. Am I in it?'

He could not say and she was kept in suspense until she had run to the newsagent's and back. No, her name did not appear. A photograph of the cottage was alongside an update of the police enquiry. The story included her own descriptions of the property but did not mention that they had been stolen from an estate agent's office.

On the facing page she recognised the culprit, the young man in horn-rimmed glasses who had tricked her. He stared out from a by-line picture on another article. Maddy folded the paper and filed it in case rumours reached head office that the good name of Rigmaroles had been sullied.

Late in the afternoon Nesta called to say the tapes had not been found. 'Linsey was grilled by the police but denies knowledge of them.'

'Do they believe her?'

'Graham's told them *he* wouldn't.'

She described the scene where Linsey turned mystical rather than answer simple questions about her identity and her reasons for being in the Collinses' house. Maddy was sorry she had missed it, especially the moment when one of the officers reminisced about the time he arrested Linsey's guru for a breach of the peace.

'We've decided you ought to stay here for a while,' said Nesta and rushed on with a resumé of the discussion she and Graham had been having.

Maddy shook her head with a sad smile. Did Nesta really believe Park House was a sanctuary?

'That's kind of you,' she said, 'but I can't hide whenever anything unpleasant happens.'

'Why ever not? *I* would.'

'Because I have to go home eventually. Unless I sell up and flee, and that takes time.'

Nesta sounded nervous of the answer when she asked: 'You're not thinking of moving, are you?'

'No. I haven't the choice, anyway.'

'We'd miss you terribly, Maddy.'

'Oh, you'd manage.'

'With Peter Ribston? With the Wintersons? Maddy, you can't leave us to them.'

'I've told you, I'm not planning to go. After all, it's not as though . . .'

But she did not want to finish the sentence. She broke off, leaving Nesta to press her for the rest.

'It's nothing,' Maddy said. 'It doesn't matter.'

Nesta was disgruntled, knowing that when people said something did not matter, it did. But Maddy was not tempted to share her growing fear that all her troubles might end shortly with Steve's arrest. He had ever been a sensitive subject, because of the vehemence with which Nesta blamed him for everything unsatisfactory in Maddy's life. And an ungrateful Maddy was already finding Nesta's protectiveness wearing.

Her shift to sharing Nesta's opinion had not made discussion easier. She assumed Nesta did not mean to gloat at the way the scales had fallen from her eyes, but Maddy felt she did. Later, she supposed, when the whole matter was resolved and they both understood what had been the truth, what had been suspicion and what had been merely irrelevant, they would be able to talk about it sensibly. Maddy had vowed to avoid it until then.

A smart middle-aged woman came into the office and hovered while she rapidly ended Nesta's call.

'Come for supper, anyway,' Nesta ordered finally.

Maddy accepted, hardly knowing she was doing so because her attention was on her visitor.

The woman put an expensive leather bag down on the corner of the desk. Maddy summed her up as a professional who could, in all probability, afford to live wherever she chose. She jotted down her requirements and opened the filing cabinet.

'There's also a house on the hill below Wychwood,' she said as she handed over a slim sheaf of papers. 'If you don't mind carrying out a fair bit of modernisation, you might be interested in it.'

In reply she got a cheeky grin. 'Is that agent-speak for "it's falling down"?'

Maddy laughed. 'No, it's the honest truth.'

'In that case, I'm interested.'

She gave her those details, too.

When she was alone again, Maddy prepared to lock up. She almost left without her mobile telephone, spotting it on the desk when she already had the door open.

'I'm hopelessly tired,' she said in a voice that was little short of a sob. 'Oh God, I just want to sleep.'

But her momentary idea of driving home and sinking onto her bed was chased away by the recollection that she had accepted Nesta's invitation.

Telephone and cancel?

She decided to delay a decision until she was home. Whether or not she ate at Park House, she wanted to go to the cottage first. She felt protective about her home. What Steve had accused her of was true: she did care about her things and she hated it when they were abused.

The cold in the grey stone streets came like a slap in the face. She pulled up her coat collar and swathed her scarf tightly, then scurried towards the car park. Shopkeepers were putting out rubbish for next day's collection, locking doors and drawing down blinds. OPEN signs were being twisted round to become CLOSED signs. Another unseasonably bitter day was coming to an end.

Ice had formed on puddles in the car park. Maddy stepped around them, then found what she hated: a frozen film on her windscreen. When she had finished scraping, the exit was blocked by a van whose driver was doing the same thing.

Too weary to be impatient, she did not attempt to move but sat in the car with the engine running and the heater straining to produce a little heat. She toyed with the radio but the reception was too poor to listen to music and she could not face a news programme. Maddy picked up her telephone.

Ring Nesta and cancel?

No. She turned off the engine and tapped out the number

for her cottage. Her recorded voice spoke to her. She disconnected. She had not really expected Steve to answer.

Ring Nesta and say she preferred to go to bed?

Instead she tapped a different number. Steve answered. He answered the way he had done on the previous occasions she had got a response from the substitute coffee bar number.

'Hello?' Not his name, nothing but a cautious hello.

'It's Maddy.'

A slight pause before he spoke again, in a voice without warmth. 'What do you want?'

'All the things you can't give me, all the things you won't.'

Aloud she said: 'Steve, where are you?'

'Tell me what you want.'

'I want to know where you are and where Jay is.' Her tired voice sounded as unemotional as his.

'I haven't got him.'

'What's happened to him?'

She was doing it again, picking at the manageable bits. Massive questions were in abeyance while she fussed about her dog. And yet it was unthinkable that she should accuse him of a serious crime. She knew he was not an innocent man, she knew it bone deep. But she was afraid of putting her trust in delusions. No, she could fairly ask what he had done with her dog and whether he had broken into her house but she could not frame a question about blackmail or murder.

For a minute or two, while he was brushing off questions about Jay, she expected him to start winding up the conversation. This made her determined to keep him talking because it was probably the last conversation they would ever have. What he did not tell her now, she might never learn.

She made an effort to instil some passion in her voice, to make herself sound like the friendly Maddy he had once wanted to live with.

'Steve, you know how fond I am of Jay. Please tell me where he is.'

But the response was barely an improvement.

'I thought he'd run home.'

'Look, I know you took him up the hill to the forest. The postman saw you. But where did you take him after that?'

He shunted the matter aside. 'I thought he'd go home.'

Battling to keep exasperation out of her voice, she posed another question: 'Why didn't you keep him with you?'

He ignored that one entirely.

'Steve? Are you still there?'

'Yes.'

'I wish you'd tell me where you are. And where my dog is.'

His reply took her by surprise. 'Who have you got with you?'

'With me? Nobody's with me. I'm sitting in the car park in Woodstock, if you want to know.'

He considered before saying he did not believe her.

She gave a cluck of annoyance. Then: 'I'm going to reclaim my spare bedroom at the weekend. If you want anything of yours, you'd better fetch it.'

'There's nothing I want.'

'You've got until Saturday morning. After that it goes.'

Silence.

She said: 'Was it you who broke my window yesterday?'

'No.'

She took pleasure in saying she did not believe him.

He said: 'Will you be at the cottage this evening?'

'Yes.' She guessed he was about to weaken and say he wanted to salvage his possessions. She added inconsequentially: 'I won't be there all evening, I have to go out.'

He said: 'You'd better go then.' The phone went dead.

Maddy shuddered.

'He sounded inhuman, like a creature who'd never cared for anyone and never could. How on earth could I have . . .'

She drove out of Woodstock, past the long stone wall of the Blenheim estate and up the wide road towards the airfield, planning to take the route that skirted the forest. It would do no harm to shout for Jay again.

When she was several miles out of the town her telephone rang. Nesta playing mother hen, she supposed. Maddy swerved into a layby and stopped.

Steve said: 'I've been thinking.' Not his name, not hello.

'About Jay?' Her fears for the dog were at the forefront of her mind, so that is what she said.

'Not about that bloody animal. There are other things, you know. Important ones.'

She resisted making the scathing retort that was on the tip of her tongue. 'I'm listening, Steve.'

'I've been thinking. There's a lot of stuff I didn't tell you.'

Her eyes widened. She hoped she did not sound too excited as she asked: 'Such as?'

'Sometimes . . . sometimes when you've had a bad experience it makes you wary. You think what's the point because nothing you can do would ever make a difference. It's as though a big hand has reached out and changed the programme on the television and, whatever you do, you can never seize the control to turn it back. One minute you're a normal kid and then . . . Well, the picture changes.'

She was undecided whether he was drunk or having one of his feverish spells. When she started to speak, he interrupted.

'That's what I couldn't tell you. So I told you other stuff. Stories. Not true ones, although you didn't know that.'

'Wrong, Steve. I distrusted most of what you told me.'

'At the end.'

'No. Long before that. There were outright lies and there were confabulations. What I never understood was why you bothered. Did you think it made you interesting? Or had you forgotten what the truth was, anyway?'

He refused to believe she had seen through him. 'If you knew, why didn't you do anything about it?'

'I did. I stopped taking anything you said at face value and then I asked you to leave.'

Her bluntness rattled him. He was no keener on hearing the truth than telling it.

'I'm trying to explain, Maddy. Do you want to hear this or what?'

'Yes. Go on.'

But she got more of the same. He rambled, wrapping weak ideas in fancy imagery. The theme appeared to be that a childhood disaster could wreck a life, that it could not be outgrown or shaken off, that it haunted the child and destroyed the man.

Maddy was growing increasingly perplexed. He had not said anything that connected his meandering monologue with the Dellafield case or with Beth's murder. Had she been ignorant of those, he would have made no sense whatsoever.

From time to time, he interrupted his story to ask: 'Do you know what I'm saying?' 'Do you understand?' 'Do you see?'

The questions were cues for her to indicate she was still on the line.

Soon he was talking about people from the past reviving the worst of one's living nightmares. At least, that is what she surmised he was getting at. Weird images coupled with obliqueness made it hazy indeed. Too weary to analyse, Maddy let the story wash over her.

Then, shockingly, plain words sprang out.

'She wanted money,' he said. 'Too much of it. She wanted to be the only victim.'

Maddy sat bolt upright and clamped the telephone to her ear. Had she imagined that? Had she snatched a split second's sleep and supplied the words herself?

Before she could be certain, Steve dropped in another of his questions.

'You do understand what I'm talking about, don't you?'

She tried to speak but her mouth was dry. Instead of blundering on, he waited for her. She moistened her lips.

'Yes.'

It was a real question, not a prompt. She realised at last that they had all been real.

236

CHAPTER NINETEEN

The maddening dreams were with him by day and by night. They were guilt. They were fear. They banished his other thoughts.

His hand reached out and touched the hem of a woman's skirt as she lay in a field by a river. It drew from the hands of a woman in a forest the gloves that had flailed at him. Endlessly the hands repeated their performance, acting out curiosity and caution.

He had told himself lies to stop them but the lies had not worked. He had plotted escapes and disappearances but doubted they would do any good. His demons danced before his eyes and would travel wherever he went. He did not know how long he could bear to go on living like this.

Two women had died. He had been growing increasingly fearful that another death would become necessary.

His telephone call this afternoon to Maddy had left him numb. She knew, then. He had hoped it might not be so but she had told him she knew.

For days he had swung between assuming her ignorance or crediting her with jigsawing together the truth. He had decided to tackle her but lurched from one scheme to another and finally picked up the telephone.

His main schemes were to snatch her car and run away, or to buy her silence or persuade her that her deductions were wrong. Yes, he was sure that if he could persuade her to tell him what she believed and why, he could successfully refute it. And yet, after all, he was not so sure. She had heard too many of his stories. She had ceased to trust him.

There was a problem about offering her money. She was not supposed to know he received sums from his step-brother, insignificant trickles but the promise of a huge reward for continuing loyalty. Beth, to his astonishment, had learned about the transfers and guessed at the deal. To bribe Maddy, he would have to tell her the source of the money, and it would be tantamount to conceding guilt. The guilt of covering up for Robert Clark who killed Pippa Dellafield, and the guilt of silencing Beth.

He did not know what to do. He did not wish Maddy harm but she had learned enough to destroy him, if she chose. If only he could persuade her she was wrong! But she had been altered by the death of Beth, was suspicious and nervous all the time. For all his practice in deception, he could not think of anything to say this time to sway her. He had tried it with Beth, who had also known too much, and it had ended in flaring anger and his hands on her throat. He did not know how to deal with Maddy.

It was useless reflecting how easily he had gulled her previously into believing, for instance, that his life had been adventures abroad when it had been drifting through England living on handouts that were tacitly bribes. He wondered whether he might have turned his back on the childhood drama if it had not been for that income, the monthly reminder and the continuing shame. He had thought about it often since Beth confronted him on tape and then in a series of angry encounters,

Sucked too young into his predicament, he was ignorant of the implications. What began as pocket money of mysterious origin that tantalised his school friends, became a fetter chaining him to the past. Beth had found out and now Maddy had too. His head throbbed from worrying what to do. There must be a way out, there must. He did not want any more deaths, any more lives destroyed. And yet the power to decide seemed not to lie in his hands. Maddy held it. Everything depended on her. Perhaps if he talked to her, away from her pestering telephone and those buzzing Collinses . . . Perhaps he could convince her . . .

He continued to veer from one idea to another, none of them properly thought through because the hands intervened. The pictures played over and over in his memory.

CHAPTER TWENTY

'Did you go home first?' Nesta asked, welcoming her into the kitchen.

'I planned to but I changed my mind.'

Graham said: 'Did you yell in the forest for Jay?'

'I changed my mind about that, too.'

They were being kind and helpful but her mind was screaming with one thought only: *'Steve confessed he killed Beth'*.

She had to drag herself back from believing it. *'He's a liar. He's a deceiver. He's not a man I trust.'*

Anyway, the 'confession' had been utterly bizarre. Only someone with prior suspicions could have jumped to the conclusion that he was admitting to murder, or indeed to anything but an unhappy childhood.

He had not even gone as far as admitting breaking into Meadow Cottage. No, she must not yield to the temptation of telling the Collinses he had confessed to killing Beth. *'Better not mention him at all.'*

Graham reported Linsey's latest act of retribution, carried out in the name of Lord Buckshee.

'She shooed our chickens out into the road and told them they were no longer prisoners'

'Oh, no! Did you round them all up?'

'Not all. The little speckled hen got squashed by the school bus. And the others frightened the wits out of one

241

of Gilly's mares who took off through the village with a small girl on board.'

'Was she hurt?'

'Cried a lot but not actually injured.'

Nesta said: 'There was a brave lad cleaning windows and he did the heroic thing and stopped the horse. Gilly's been up here after Linsey's blood.'

Maddy was disappointed to hear Gilly had not caught her.

'The Magpie,' said Graham, 'seems to have flown the coop. We're hoping it's permanent.

Their other local news centred on the Wintersons' plummeting status as word of Patsy Kimball's verbal attack on them in the pub gained currency. Elaborate versions, involving language Maddy was sure had never sullied Patsy's lips, were being carried along on the tide of gossip.

When that subject was exhausted, the Collinses questioned Maddy about Steve. She caved in and told them about the telephone calls.

Nesta was quick to condemn but Graham said: 'It depends what interpretation you put on his words.'

'No matter,' said Nesta. 'Maddy must tell the police.'

'Not this evening, though,' Maddy said. 'I'm exhausted and I haven't finished work yet. Mrs Laverty's niece has asked me to meet her at Wren Cottage at seven.'

'In that case,' said Graham, 'we've just got time to inject a reviving shot of caffeine into you.'

He offered to drive her to her meeting. 'You might fall asleep at the wheel.'

She raised the cup of espresso. 'Not with this inside me.'

A shadowy man hurrying through the churchyard was the only person Maddy saw on her journey to Wren Cottage. Lights were on in the rooms above the shop. A dog was barking in the window of the converted barn. The pub looked as though it were shut for all time. Wood smoke coiled above houses where families were fugitives from the weather.

She was mildly cursing Heather for demanding this meeting. What was there to discuss that could not be done on the telephone or in daylight? Her queries had been answered and Heather had approved a draft of the particulars.

The village faded away. She entered the lane leading to the cottage. In the crisp clear evening the house stood out plainly, a long, low building with its back to the hill.

'No lights. She can't be there yet.'

Her heart sank. No lights, no car outside, no sign of Heather.

'Ten minutes,' she decided. *'That's all I'm allowing her.'*

She parked in the lane and walked up to the house, thinking there was a slight chance that a light at the rear of the house might not be visible. The kitchen was at the rear.

The front door was locked. Heather had promised to have a spare key cut for Maddy but had not yet handed it over.

'Perhaps that's why she's sent for me, to give me the key.'

She tried the back door. It was unlocked but there were no lights on.

'Heather?'

'Ten minutes. Then I'll leave.'

She flicked a light switch. The power was off. Maddy hunted for the main switch but could not remember where she had seen it on her inspection of the house. She had a feeling it was high up on the wall in the lobby off the kitchen.

She was puzzled. Heather had definitely told her she would be leaving the power on because she wanted the night storage heaters to keep the chill out of the air during the winter. Maddy remembered being pleased by that because it was easier to interest buyers in a cosy house than a sad, damp one.

The heater in the kitchen was warm to her touch. She opened the fridge. A sheen of ice covered the element. In the freezer compartment stood a tray of ice cubes. Obviously, the power could not have been off for long. The heaters must have consumed electricity the previous night, and a fridge without power would not have retained the cold for many hours in a heated room.

'A power cut? But there were lights in the village.'

The main switch was not in the lobby. She went through the lobby to the passage that led to the rest of the house. The natural light was too weak to penetrate the passage and she fumbled without success.

'I'll fetch my torch from the car. No, I won't. She's had her ten minutes. I'll go.'

But immediately she grew doubtful.

'Supposing it's an electrical fault? If the place burns down tonight I'll look worse than a fool. I can't walk away and leave it.'

She had noticed the stump of a candle in a saucer on the kitchen window-sill. She lit it. Holding her notebook close to the flame, to enable her to read the number, she telephoned Heather.

After a few failed attempts she abandoned that and called Cathy to see whether she had misunderstood the arrangement. Cathy's children bickered in the background as Maddy explained the client had not shown up and there was a problem with the power supply.

Cathy, with three-quarters of her attention on the squabble, said: 'Haven't you got her number with you?'

'I said she doesn't answer.'

'Maybe she isn't home from wherever she went. He did say she'd be unavailable during the day.

Maddy's mind filled with apprehension. 'He? I understood there was a message from Heather.'

'No, a man called on her behalf.' She repeated the rest of the message as before.

Terse, Maddy said: 'I'll talk to you later.'

'What? Hey, don't go. What's wrong?'

'You've helped a man lure me to a lonely cottage.'

'No!'

'I'm getting out of here. *Now.*'

'But the electrical fault.'

'I've discovered there isn't one.'

Maddy scrabbled her notebook and telephone into her shoulder bag, blew out the candle and prepared to run.

But a key had been turned in the lock on the back door. She could not get out that way. She whirled round. A figure filled the lobby doorway.

Maddy dropped her bag in fright. In the half light her eyes flickered over the kitchen in search of a weapon.

'Where's the cutlery drawer? The pans? Anything, any-thing at all.'

Kitchens were full of potential weapons, why couldn't she find one? Trembling, she gripped the top of a wooden chair. The chair took up the rhythm of her fear, its legs tamping the tiled floor.

The figure in the doorway gave a triumphant laugh. A woman's laugh.

'Linsey?' Astonished, Maddy was tentative.

'I wish you hadn't come, Maddy.' But Linsey's tone conveyed no regret.

'What are you doing here? Why have you locked me in?'

Linsey was a vague shape in a darkened doorway but Maddy recognised the gesture when the woman swung her loose hair and began bobbing and bowing. She could have identified her from that alone.

'Maddy, Maddy, you ask the wrong questions.'

'That's not an answer. Explain what you're up to this time, Linsey.'

Taking a step into the kitchen, Linsey said: 'Don't you want to know why the police let me go?'

Maddy took a blind shot at it. 'It was to allow them to check up on your true identity.'

This appeared to be close because Linsey tossed her head in defiance.

Maddy followed up with: 'This is my client's house, Linsey. Now hand over the key and we'll both leave.'

A mocking laugh. 'Your client can't live here. What's the sense in a house standing empty?'

'That's none of your business.'

'The lord says every human being is worth a home.'

'Fine, but he doesn't own this one and neither do you. Give me the key.'

She advanced as she spoke. Linsey blocked the doorway, arms akimbo.

'Anyway,' Linsey said, 'this house isn't as empty as you think.'

But she did not tantalise Maddy with the thought, instead she went on a mystical tack, enthusing about the spirituality of the insects in the skirting boards and the birds in the roof.

'It's a big roof, Maddy, a nice one. You don't know that, though, do you? You didn't go up there, you and your client's greedy niece.'

On the verge of retorting that the key to the attic had been missing, Maddy spotted where this was leading. She was not being accused of laxity, she was being told someone was camping up there.

'Everard?'

Linsey dismissed the suggestion with a snigger. 'He has a room by the temple in Oxford now.'

'Who, then?'

'Everard isn't the only one who's been chucked out.'

Maddy's spirits sank. 'Steve?'

'It's very nice up there. Not closed in like your loft. There's a window in the pointed bit.'

Automatically, Maddy provided the term. 'The gable end.'

She was disgusted with herself. She had noticed the little round window high up under the roof but she had not persisted in getting access to the spacious room that was bound to be up there.

She thought: *'At least I know where he's been hiding. Cross country it isn't much distance from my cottage. I know because I've walked it.'*

To Linsey she said: 'Is my dog here, too?'

'No. It's a good room. I've got the key. We can go up.'

Maddy shook her head. Oh no, she was not falling for that. Linsey might shut her in there and leave her. To Steve? Or to be found weeks later, dead of hunger and cold like a wild creature in the forest?

'No thanks, Linsey. Please give me the back door key.'

Lunging at her, Maddy hoped to grab it or startle the woman into offering it up. Linsey squirmed away.

Maddy thought: *'From the way she did that, it seems the key is in a pocket on her left. But where do I find a pocket in amongst all those flowing garments?'*

She said: 'This has gone on long enough, Linsey. We're leaving now. The key, please.'

'You can't leave until we say.'

'We?' She heard an echo of her conversation with Cathy: 'He?'

The answer, she feared, was the same.

Linsey tried to cover the slip by quoting the lord's theory about the nature of time. 'It's always changing, you know. When you're contented it's quick, when you're stressed it's slow.'

'Never mind about that. I want to leave and you're preventing me.'

'It's for your own good.'

'What on earth do you mean?'

'If I let you out now you'll go home and it's too soon.'

Maddy insisted on knowing what she was talking about.

Linsey's explanation was that if she returned home she would interrupt Steve in the act of clearing his possessions out of her house.

'Nonsense,' Maddy retorted. 'I spoke to him this afternoon and invited him to collect them.'

This was news to Linsey who dealt with her surprise by accusing Maddy of lying.

Maddy ignored the remark, asking: 'Does Steve use a telephone here?'

'A mobile.'

Prodding, Maddy elicited that calls were redirected to it from an Oxford number. This appeared to be enough to explain the substituted number for the coffee bar although the only detail she squeezed from Linsey was that the telephone was in a house that was temporarily unoccupied.

Now that she understood why Linsey was holding her, or rather *why Linsey believed* she was doing so, Maddy asked how much longer she was supposed to be detained there.

'Time!' Linsey cried. 'You always ask the wrong questions, Maddy.'

'All right, tell me a good question. Tell me one you're prepared to answer.' Quickly she added: 'But I don't want any of your mystical stuff, mind.'

Another toss of the head. 'You're so arrogant, Maddy. I offer you The Truth but you're too proud to listen.'

Waspish, Maddy said: 'You don't know the truth, Linsey, and you're afraid to face questions.'

'You have offended the lord, Maddy. You desecrated my shrine. I made it beautiful for him and you spoiled it.'

'You used my Indian scarf to decorate it and I took it back. It was stolen when my house was broken into the other evening.'

'Steve gave it to me.'

'It wasn't his to give. You knew that. You'd seen me wearing it.'

'But you took things of his, his tapes. When he went to fetch them, they had gone. He thought they might be in Park House, and he was right. I had to get them back for him.'

Maddy took no pleasure in hearing it confirmed that Steve was the one who broke in through the kitchen window and Linsey had stolen the Beth tapes from the Collinses. But at least she knew who had them now. Steve. Unless he had destroyed them.

Linsey was quoting religion to defend her actions. 'The lord says . . .'

Maddy butted in. 'I dare say, but what did Steve say? Did he tell you he was coming here this evening? Or is he taking his goods and chattels and sloping off?'

'These are the wrong . . .'

'No, Linsey, they aren't the wrong questions but you

don't have the answers. He hasn't been honest with you, has he?'

'He's a good person. Look how he helped me, telling me about the flat in Park House. I was brought up in a home, there's never been anyone to help me, but he did. You only ever look on the surface, Maddy, but a personality has many layers.'

'I remember: onion layers.'

'Perhaps he has done things that are not so good but underneath . . .'

'He's a decent sort of onion. Fine. I used to think so too.'

And it was then, when they were embroiled in onion layers, that Linsey blurted out facts.

In pursuit of The Truth, she said, Steve had whiled away time with her and Everard in the woods and the barn. During the worst weather they had commandeered empty houses, including the weekenders' cottage next to Mrs Spencer's. The criminality and impudence escaping her, she painted an edenic picture.

Maddy, by contrast, was confident Steve had used Linsey for companionship and free meals rather than as a conduit for truths. Her own fragmented memories gave credence to Linsey's story of his secret life. Having edged away from ordinary people in the village, he had gravitated towards the oddities.

Linsey launched a challenge. 'You're going to deny it, Maddy, I know you are. You want to deny it. You don't like to think of Steve accepting The Truth.'

'No, wait a minute.'

But Linsey brandished her irrefutable proof. 'He believes, Maddy. I can prove it. He was spreading the word, that's how sure he is that he's heard The Truth.'

Maddy was incredulous. 'Spreading the word!' Grammar deserting her, she demanded: 'Who to?'

Linsey's excitement peaked. 'To Beth Welford. They used to meet among the trees to talk about it. And he was so modest, Maddy, he didn't tell me until I came upon them one afternoon. Afterwards he explained she wanted to learn about the clean way to live, thinking good thoughts and eating the right food. He was sharing with her everything I'd shared with him. That's what the lord says we should do, Maddy. Help one another towards the light, that's what we must do.'

Maddy's head was reeling. The stupid woman had known all this and told no one? It seemed impossible. Well, impossible for anyone except Linsey.

Linsey was gabbling. 'That's why he was so upset when she died. It nearly broke him. He became ill. But you didn't notice, Maddy, you were too busy selling your houses and smarming around your clients. Poor Steve.'

'Was he with her the day she died?'

'Oh, that's what makes it so terrible.'

Hardly a direct answer. Maddy urged her: 'Are you saying yes?'

Bowing and bobbing, Linsey had dropped her guard on the doorway and moved down the room. Her story had driven everything else out of her head.

Clearer now, in the moonlight through the kitchen window, Linsey's body acted out the misery she was recalling. She swayed and clutched at her face and flung her arms about herself for comfort. Maddy would not have been the least surprised had she taken to wailing or ullulating. For Linsey, life was drama although she generally failed to follow the thread of the story.

Maddy badgered. 'Please, Linsey. This is important.'

'Ah, Maddy, what is important in Life is . . .'

Maddy snatched at her arm. Shook it. 'Stick to the point! I want to know whether Steve was with Beth on the day she was killed. Yes or no?'

Her outburst alarmed them both. Linsey was stilled.

Maddy was afraid it had been folly to lose control because Linsey was unstable and her disputes often ended in physical confrontation. If it came to a fight, Linsey would win. And she still might not answer the question.

'Yes or no?' Maddy's voice was thick, her heart thudding.

Linsey folded her hands together and made a quaint little bow. Finally she said: 'Yes.'

Steadying herself by holding the chair, Maddy pursued details. 'What time that day did they meet?'

'In the afternoon, late.'

'It would have been dark,' she objected, on the lookout for lies.

'No, it wasn't.'

'But it was getting dark soon after four.'

'It wasn't dark. If it had been, I wouldn't have been able to see, would I?'

'You *saw* them?'

Eager to justify her claim, Linsey described the scene. 'He came from your cottage. She walked through the churchyard and took the footpath to Wychwood.'

'But it's impossible. How could you have seen all that?'

As the words spilled out, she remembered the vantage point on the opposite hill. Yes, if Linsey had been perched up there she could certainly have watched people from Meadow Cottage and Church Cottage taking separate routes into the forest.

Linsey, though, took this to be a continuation of the argument about the level of daylight. She said: 'You read your time from clocks, Maddy. I live by the lord's clock. When it's getting dark it's late. Light was beginning to fade when Beth entered the forest. I couldn't see Steve by then because the path he was on curved away from me, but Beth was visible all the way. She was wearing a jacket with red on it. I could make out the red bits longer than anything else. In the end, she was just a few splashes of red moving towards the trees.'

Splashes of red. Blood. The last person who had seen her alive, apart from her killer, had picked her out as a few splashes of red.

Maddy shuddered. 'Did you see Steve leave the forest?'

'No, I went to the barn to meet Everard.'

A beam of light fell into the lobby behind Linsey, making her gasp. 'He's here.' She sounded delighted.

'*Steve's beguiled her,*' Maddy thought. '*He's used her for company and food and he's fooled her. She has more in common with me than I could have dreamed.*'

Linsey ran down the passage. Maddy checked the door. It remained locked. She dashed after Linsey and found her on a window-seat in the room at the front of the house, her face jammed against the pane. Linsey let out a sigh of disappointment.

Maddy shared the feeling but was also relieved. She wanted to be freed but not to encounter Steve. He had spun Linsey a yarn about collecting his property but Maddy knew it to be false. What, then, was he really up to?

They heard a sound from the rear of the house. Maddy flew to the kitchen. Torchlight fell across the table, the chair and the fridge. It was extinguished.

'Don't go!' The change of light sent her crashing into the corner of the table, tripping over her dropped bag. She threw herself at the door, rattled the handle and banged on the wood. And all the time she was pleading: 'Don't go. Please don't go!'

Behind her she heard the mocking laugh. 'A ghost,' said Linsey. 'A spirit come visiting. Perhaps it's the relic of your client, Maddy. She's come visiting, and now she's confused because you're in here and she didn't ask for her home to be sold.'

Breathless, Maddy argued. 'Mrs Laverty isn't dead. She's in a nursing home.'

'You don't know whether she's alive. You don't care, as long as you get your commission for selling her house.'

Maddy laughed a weak, hysterical laugh that was a comment on Linsey's preposterous theories. She had a better one of her own. The person wielding the torch was sure to be a professional woman who was house-hunting in the valley. It was more likely this woman was reconnoitring than that Heather's aunt's ghost needed a torch with which to go a-haunting.

She brushed past Linsey and ran to the front room. A torch flickered down the path. She bellowed: '*Come back!*'

Frenzied, she ripped off a shoe and smashed the glass. The bitterest east wind flowed through the hole. Maddy shouted and shouted, in spite of knowing her pleas were being blown away and the visitor heard only the wind threshing the trees.

Torchlight played on the gate, the wall, the roof of a car in the lane. The car's interior light came on, then its headlights. It reversed in the gateway and then moved off. Maddy went out of the room, closing the door to cut down the draught from the broken window.

Linsey was hovering in the lobby where she could keep one eye on the kitchen and the other on the front part of the house. With the door to the room closed, the hall and passage were lit only by three small rectangles of glass in a fanlight. Maddy ran her hands over the inside of the front door. Quietly she raised a clip on the lock, eased a bolt and then yanked the door open.

By the time she reached the gate, she regretted her dash. Her bag containing her telephone and car keys was in the house. Worse, her car was no longer there.

Looking over her shoulder she saw Linsey in the doorway, hands on hips. Maddy called to her: 'What's happened to my car?'

'You watched it drive away.'

She was reluctant to believe she had been misled about the identity of the person with the torch. But here she was, calling the length of the garden to Linsey and they could hear each other well enough. The wind was frisky but not so strong that it prevented voices travelling. A house viewer would certainly have heard her commotion and returned. Only a person who wanted to leave her there would have done so. Again, that presumably meant Steve.

'Where's he taken it?'

Linsey said: 'To your cottage. He can't move his things without it, can he?'

'I want my bag. It's in the kitchen.'

'Come and get it. I'm not stopping you.'

But Maddy had no intention of being trapped a second

time. She turned away from Wren Cottage towards the village.

After she had gone a couple of hundred yards and was out of sight of the cottage, she came to a halt. She was not at all sure that walking into the village was wise.

'If only I could be sure what was true. Linsey knows things but puts such a peculiar slant on them that every conversation with her becomes a guessing game. Also, she tells downright lies. Oh God, I wish I knew what to believe.'

She struggled to disentangle some strands of the story. Steve, she concluded, had definitely engineered her being lured to Wren Cottage and held captive while he stole her car. In their telephone conversation she had effectively confirmed she would be keeping the spurious appointment with Heather Laverty. She winced at the memory of telling Nesta, in his presence, that her job left her no choice about visiting lonely houses when a client summoned her.

Supposing Linsey to be correct about him moving his possessions, he was still in the vicinity. Linsey had not hinted where he was going to put them instead. The attic of Wren Cottage? If so, Maddy ran a high risk of meeting him on her way through the village.

She shrank from that, wishing he had stolen her car to drive to the furthest reaches of the country. She fantasised about him at a ferry port, putting whole countries between them.

He would not do that. She knew him a little despite all the deceptions. He would not run off when running off would draw attention to him. A properly stolen car would need to be reported to the police, while one borrowed briefly from a friend whose house he shared would not be. And look how firmly he had been set on staying under her roof until someone had been charged with Beth's murder. He had refused to go at a time when his absence would arouse interest in him. All in all, Maddy felt confident he would hang around for a while.

'*I don't know how much he's guilty of but I do know I'd give anything not to run into him.*'

She hurried back the way she had come, wondering whether Steve himself actually knew what he was going to do. A few yards short of Wren Cottage she crouched and scuttled along concealed by the wall. When she stood up again she noticed lights in the house. She ran up the centre of the lane, heading for the Dawsons' house high on the hill and glad of moonlight to guide her.

The lane was a cul-de-sac that took her only part of the way. Where it ended a footpath began. This led across a walled field and joined the lane that climbed up to Wychwood. Once she was out in the middle of the field, she felt vulnerable. Trees dotted the perimeter and a long and lonely journey lay ahead of her. She cast a worried glance at the sky, pleading for the bank of cloud over to the east to hold off and allow her the moonlight. Wind played with her hair and froze her neck.

A fox crossed the field, silent and swift. His black form skimmed over the grass, barely seeming to touch down. Maddy lumbered on. The ground was ridged and frozen. She was wearing the wrong shoes, the wrong clothes, and they hampered her progress. She knew she was obvious to anyone who looked her way, plainer even than the quickly vanishing fox. Anyone could see her, anyone could guess where she was headng. Anyone who wished her harm could cut her off.

When she reached the far side it was awkward locating the stile because the wall was shadowed. She scuffed her shoes by trying to mount in the wrong places, and took the skin off her hand when a stone rocked loose and she toppled back into the field. She picked herself up, cleaned her hands on her jacket and looked around. On the Wren Cottage side of the field something moved. She did not wait to discover what it might be, she scrambled over the wall and flung herself into the lane that led to the forest.

Trees straggled down the hill and flanked the lane, giving her cover for the uphill trudge. There was sparse foliage but the moon spread shadow beneath the boughs and she felt better protected than when she was exposed in the field. A couple of times she looked back to see whether she was being followed. She saw no one in the field, not even another fox. Soon the lane began to climb more steeply, but it was still easier walking than on the rough footpath.

The Dawsons' house was high and isolated. Although it had open views over the valley, the approach to it was masked by trees. Maddy kept thinking it was sure to come in sight around the next bend, or the next, but the trek seemed endless. Night creatures ran across the tarmac ahead of her. Dark animals moved through the moonlit landscape and light-coloured ones stirred in the deepest shadows. There was the occasional cry of a small animal come to grief, and the perpetual rustling of leaves and undergrowth that proved the countryside was a living thing, but there was nothing human to alarm her.

A great tree thrust the road out of line. '*It was about here,*' she remembered, '*that the postman saw Steve with Jay.*'

But then she was past the spot and, a few hundred yards uphill, the white posts marking the Dawsons' drive gleamed. The sight spurred Maddy on. She was tired, she ached, she had been scared and her mind was crammed with worries and suspicions, but the white posts offered respite. The Dawsons, whom she knew only slightly, would take her into their comforting home, let her telephone the Collinses and would fuss around her until a car arrived to take her to safety.

Perhaps Mr Dawson would offer to drive her home himself. On balance she thought not. Why should he risk leaving his wife at home alone, in a cottage by the forest where Beth was killed? Not everyone accepted Chris Welford was the culprit.

She reached the gateposts. The drive was black, tall shrubs crowding it. She went gingerly forward, brushing against scratching branches and catching her feet on unseen obstacles. Then the house was revealed before her, its stone palely glowing in the cool light of the moon. Curtains were open. No one answered her rings on the bell. Maddy went to a shed behind the house and helped herself to a bicycle.

She began to fly down the hill. There were no other houses up there, no point in trying to go any higher, her only hope now was to race into the village. Wind flattened her hair to her head, tore her collar away from her neck and froze her to the marrow. She sped round the bend caused by the massive tree. She was going too fast, out of control and terrifying herself.

Her speed was too fast for thought, too fast for breathing, too fast for sanity. But she could not slow, the machine seemed to have sapped her initiative. It took every ounce of her attention to hang on, to steer, to balance. Ahead, a hundred feet below, the lights of the village were a yellow smudge. Beside her the trees were a black blur. Wind hurt her eyes, made her squint. She took a bend. A light flared. A car was on the lane. She was hurtling towards it. Sometimes it was out of sight as the lane twisted. Then it was ahead of her and nearer. They were charging towards each other.

Again and again she tried to squeeze life from the brakes. At last something caught. Her speed dropped. She zigged and zagged, and slowed her progress. But the car came on. She got herself to the legal side of the road and planned to rush past the vehicle although there was a strong likelihood it contained the Dawsons returning home. At this stage, she preferred to carry on with her bike ride rather than return uphill with them and make excuses for bicycle theft.

Just below the forest, the vehicle swung across her path. She skewed, fell off, recognised her own car and Steve opening the door. Scrabbling to her feet, she fled into the forest. There was a path. No, there were dozens of paths and she knew them all. But the one she was on led into the dark heart of the forest. She needed to take another, to peel off when she reached it and cut through to yet another which would lead her into the village. The plan was her first reaction and she knew it was the best one. Others, if she had been allowed time to have them, might well be more sophisticated but the first one was the best one.

Crashing along the path, she reached the second one and went headlong down it, congratulating herself on finding it in poor light. But her triumph was brief indeed. Steve was on the path.

She did not know him well enough. She did not know how familiar he was with the forest, how much time he had spent wandering around these paths when he was pretending to be working. And so she could not gauge what advantage she might have over him. All she *could* do was pit her knowledge against his and try to outwit him.

Back on the original path she dashed ahead, deeper into the forest. '*This is wrong. This is the stupidest thing to do. A way out. I've got to find a way out.*'

She forced herself to stop, to listen, to catch the sounds of his pursuit. Somewhere close a mouse died with a lingering scream as a predator closed in. Tense, Maddy listened for the sounds of a man trailing along the path after her, or cutting through undergrowth from one path to another to head her off.

Nothing. She swallowed hard, fought against rising panic. Nothing. He might have gone back to the car. Why should he expect to find her in the dark? No, of course he would go back to the car. He had left it slung sideways across the road with its door open. How could he leave it there? He must have gone back to it.

Her reassurance ended with the sharp sound of a foot crushing leaves brittle with frost.

She did not wait to calculate how close he was, she streaked away. Further into the forest, further into the darkness, further and further from safety.

Her thoughts screamed in protest but her legs kept running. A half-plan formed. Was discarded as hopeless. Was salvaged. Was chucked out. God, she could not think, could not decide what to do, could only see herself running into the black heart of the forest.

Maddy put the hopeless plan into practice. Still running, she looked round, saw nothing, listened for a second, heard nothing and then dived off the path and crouched behind a

258

big tree. When she formed it into words, the thought was: '*If he's following me it's because of the row I'm making. He isn't close enough to see. If I hide, he might think he's fallen too far behind to hear and he might rush past me. Then I can run back the way I've come.*'

The mouldering leaves she had disturbed were releasing powerful smells of decay close to her face but she could not move away. She covered her nose with a hand and tried not to breathe deeply.

She concentrated on working out whether to choose the path he had blocked or else to dash for her car. The problem about the car, she decided, was that her own set of keys were in Wren Cottage and Steve probably had his with him. She could not rely on him having left them in the ignition.

A soft sound reached her. She peered around the tree and saw him on the path, standing still, casting around. He was just a figure the height of a man, nothing distinct. She could not even tell which way he was looking, only that his body moved as though he was looking around. She cut off imagining what might happen if he spotted her. Afraid he might sense her eyes on him, she sank back behind the tree and prayed for him to go away. She knew, in the darkest reaches of her soul, that she was in mortal danger.

Minutes later, when she judged it impossible he would still be standing there, she edged around the tree. There was no one on the path. Where was he? Which way had he gone? She had heard no giveaway sounds and it was useless trying to guess.

She tried to think as he must be thinking. Apparently he had grasped that the reason her sounds had come to a stop at that place was that she had gone into hiding. As he had waited there but not heard any sounds, except for the usual forest noises, he was probably assuming she was still near to where he had waited.

What would he do, then? Hide behind a tree and wait for her to emerge? Get ahead of her on the assumption that she would aim for the next junction and a different path? Assume she expected him to overtake her so she could head for the car, the bike or the path he had blocked?

She had no idea which he would choose. How could she guess? She just did not know him well enough.

Maddy jammed a fist into her mouth to stop herself crying out in anguish. Teeth chewed into knuckles. The pain cut through her self-pity. It took her mind away from her stupidity in ever getting hooked up with Steve. She tasted blood. She wiped the damaged hand down her jacket and, the other hand on the trunk of the tree for support, she rose to full height.

Without moving her feet, she twisted her body and gazed around. Visibility was extremely limited. Everything was dark but some things were darker. Any idea of straying from the paths was folly. And so was venturing further into the forest. She did not have much choice. She had to go back.

'*But this time I'll move quietly,*' she thought.

She tried, giving as few audible clues to her presence as possible. It was hard, when she was primed for flight, to be inching forward delicately but her footfalls were gentle now. Repeatedly, she stopped to listen for his. The forest seemed quiet, but she was not confident she could distinguish between the scurrying of forest creatures and Steve's creeping. And he might be achieving what, for most human beings, was impossible: moving without making a sound.

'*He always moves quietly. He could be upon me before I know it.*'

But as she did not dare linger she walked on, playing him at his own stealthy game.

When she had covered another hundred yards, and was anticipating the junction with the path he had once blocked, she heard a snapping of twigs on her left and spun round to see a figure diving towards her. All attempts at quietness were abandoned by both of them. Maddy spurted deep into the forest again, his footsteps thundering after her. She was fit and had several yards start which she stretched to more. But it was the wrong direction to be running.

Other plans assembled themselves in her head. She shot past the lofty tree where she had hidden. She crashed past the junction with a tiny track she knew petered out in thick undergrowth. The other plans were no good but she sifted them over and over. None of them would fool him into letting her escape to the village.

'That's it,' she realised. *'He won't let you near the village. He chased you in the car because he saw you going across the field. He cut you off from the lane to the village and then from a path to the village. So forget about the village. Go another way.'*

There were numerous paths and she knew them all. She had not always wanted to walk them but Jay had discovered them and led her wherever he chose. Thanks to him, she had a chance of getting through the forest to another road. There would be houses eventually and, with luck, passing traffic long before she reached houses. The dog, with his disobedient and adventurous spirit, had taught her these paths. She raced on into the secret depths of the forest.

The long path was a mile and more but she tried not to think about distances. Getting there was the thing. All that mattered. All that would save her life. It was chilling how readily she accepted her life needed saving.

He had not threatened her or accused her of blaming him for Beth's murder. But their peculiar telephone call, with his insistence on knowing whether she understood what was so cryptic, convinced her. His fake message luring her to Wren Cottage, and his orders to Linsey to confine her there, were all the confirmation she needed.

At one level, she realised, she did not care what he had done, whether he had by his own hand killed Beth or whether he and Beth had together been blackmailing someone. Selfishly, what she cared about was never having had the truth from him. That and being made physically afraid.

Another thought butted in. She cared, too, about Jay and the mysterious way Steve had disposed of him. He had not answered her questions about Jay, had not helped her rescue him. The dog had last been seen going into the forest with

Steve and might still be here. She had thought so on the occasion she had hovered on the edge of the trees and called for him.

'*Shout for him now*,' she thought.

But she did not do so because she was loath to lose speed. After another minute, she realised she had outstripped Steve and she slowed and recovered her breath and thought again of shouting. Steve's sounds had died away. To begin with she wanted to believe he had given up but then it occurred to her that during the time she was well ahead of him she had crossed a glade where several paths converged and it was possible he was uncertain which she had chosen.

'*If I call, the dog might not react to my voice. He usually doesn't. But Steve would.*'

She picked up speed again, and faced another thought she had been resisting. This route would lead her to the spot where Beth's body was found.

Maddy had not been near it, had not been able to stomach the idea of strolling by as though that patch of woodland were the same as any other. It never would be the same, not for her or anyone else who lived near Wychwood. It was spoiled, as badly as all their lives were damaged by the murder.

As she approached the place, she noticed her speed involuntarily slackening. She slowed to walking pace, persuaded she was not being followed. Steve could be quiet but he could not run pell-mell and be quiet at the same time. If he were to catch her he must go flat out.

'*Thank heavens*,' she thought, '*he's given up.*'

Only half convinced, she did not relax her guard. Too often she had allowed herself a premature sigh of relief only to find another hazard facing her. Alert for the signs of renewed pursuit, she walked towards the place where Beth's body had been discovered.

There was a glimmer of white, the tape the police had used to cordon off the area and which nobody had bothered to remove. The undistinguished patch of woodland it contained was very close indeed to where she would have walked on the afternoon of the murder, if Jay had not bullied her into going another way home.

She cocked her head, questioning whether she had heard a sound. Nothing.

Thoughts of Beth flooded in. She visualised her as she had known her in life, talking to a man she knew and had no cause to fear, or leaped on by one who took her by surprise. Then she remembered the Beth she had learned about from the tape, the one who demanded assignations to negotiate about blackmail.

It was hard to believe they were the same person, but casual friends and acquaintances knew only one or two facets of each other's personalities. A woman like Beth, one who had been brought up in an aura of secrecy, would have been adept at showing people only those aspects they needed to see.

The sound again. Maddy cringed.

The night had settled around her. Moonlight did not penetrate to the floor of the forest. Although her eyes had grown accustomed to the gloom, visibility was restricted to a few paces. She could not watch for Steve's approach, she had to rely entirely on her hearing.

When the sound came a third time, she had an idea it was a little to her right. But it was the wrong sound. She could not match it with the actions of a man walking extremely quietly towards her. It was . . .

A weak moan reached her. It sent the hairs on her scalp tingling. She clapped a hand over her mouth to stem her urge to scream. Her head was filled with pictures of another victim, a woman overpowered and flung down to die in the way that Beth had been. Wrong. Beth had been killed outright. The police had said so. Beth had not been left half alive to die of the cold.

Fears, ideas, skittered through her brain. Foremost was that she must be wrong about Steve. If he was the man to whom Beth had directed her recorded demand, he would have had a reason to do away with her. But Beth's case against him was unique. No other woman would have been able to say: 'You withheld justice from my murdered mother and I want money from you in recompense.' No other woman would be attacked by him. If she was listening to the groans of another victim, then Steve was not the man who had attacked either of them.

Maddy began to move when she heard the moaning again. She inched towards the area it was coming from, the area within the cordon. She had to hurry, not caring about being noisy because she had only the sounds to guide her and if they stopped, then she was lost.

She shoved the tape down and stepped over it, thrusting out of her mind any qualms about treading where Beth had lain. Instead she concentrated on discovering whatever fresh horror demanded her attention. There was a troubling smell, of animal matter and decay. Maddy covered her nose with a hand.

Drawing nearer, she experienced her first doubts. The moaning stopped, the earlier sound replaced it. A snuffling, shuffling sound. A sound unlike a human being dying in pain. A sound that reminded her of an animal in distress.

She was almost on top of him when she discovered the dog.

'Jay?' Her voice was amazed, not even pleased.

He quivered on the ground but did not struggle to come to her. Her exploring hands found he was lashed to a tree, by a rope that ran through his collar, and his muzzle was bound with tape. He let her rip off the tape. He lay panting great gulps of air, his body quaking. Maddy unfastened his collar because it was the easiest way of freeing him. He staggered to his feet, fell against her, whimpered and collapsed.

Her uppermost thought now was that she had been wrong to give Steve the benefit of the doubt. There was no doubt. How could a man who had lived with this dog in harmony for two years abandon him to die in the forest? Presumably he had been afraid the dog would give away his hideout at

Wren Cottage or elsewhere, but why had he refused to tell her where Jay was and let him be rescued? And what might he do next?

The answer to the last question was rapidly answered. She heard him approaching as she knelt by her injured pet, as he must have known she would. She just had time to wonder whether he had done something similar to Beth. Dropped or left something on the ground knowing she would stoop for it, perhaps?

Maddy began to rise but the rough ground made her unstable and she lost her footing. She saw the dark form rushing at her and this time she saw no means of avoiding him. Her attempts to outwit had culminated in this disaster. She was too kind-hearted not to have investigated the moans in the forest, too foolish to have appreciated what type of mind she was up against. And now it was too late. Steve was here and she was in a heap on the forest floor, poised to be his next victim.

She screamed with all the force of her lungs, a blood-chilling sound that expressed all her outrage and her terror, a mighty sound she had never dreamed she was capable of. He slithered to a stop, a hand outstretched but inches short of touching her.

She never knew whether he said anything or aimed a blow because in the same second utter confusion broke out. Jay had chimed in, snarling and throwing himself on Steve, ripping at clothes and leaping to sink his teeth into flesh. Maddy got to her feet, cleared the police tape and blundered after them. Steve was making a commotion. Jay was tearing him to pieces.

She marvelled that Jay had found such reserves of strength but wondered how long he could keep this up. Then she had to break into a run because they were disappearing from her sight, Steve trying to outpace the weak dog but Jay staying the course. His golden coat, harsh to her touch when she untied him, was a ghostly patch floating through the trees, a signal she could follow without difficulty. Keeping an eye on it, she ran.

She ran until torches flared among the trees and Mr Dawson, Graham Collins and two other men from the village completed her rescue.

Several hours later, at Park House, Graham said laconically: 'It was easy. I drove to Wren Cottage looking for you and met the Dawsons. They couldn't get up the hill to their house because the lane was blocked by your abandoned car.'

Maddy shut her eyes. He had answered the simple question. The rest remained a muddle of suspicion and conjecture, of events and statements open to interpretation. In the morning the village rumour mill would grind away at the story and she would not recognise her own part in it. But perhaps she did not understand what that had been, anyway, and the chatterers in the shop and by the post-box would be nearer the mark than she was.

The police had left Park House a few minutes ago. They had known where to find her, safe with her friends, not yet brave enough to be home alone.

She took a sip of brandy, thinking: *'Eventually there'll be a judicially acceptable version but that won't bring us the whole truth. Chris Welford will be let out of prison. Well, almost certainly. But if Steve hadn't . . .'*

Nesta came into the kitchen. Distracted, she reached automatically for the red apron but there was no meal to prepare and no experimental dish to cook. She dropped it on the table amid the habitual clutter. Jay, lying on a blanket in a warm corner by the cooker, raised his head and looked at her.

'If only Steve hadn't . . .' Nesta began.

Graham shook his head at her, warning her off.

Maddy, observing through sleepy, slitty eyes, completed Nesta's thought aloud: 'We'll never know exactly what and exactly why. He could never bear to tell the truth, could he? And now he's taken it to the grave.'

They fell silent. They were still numbed by the news that Steve had hanged himself in a police cell rather than give up his secrets. The story had, after all, taken one more death.

Lesley Grant-Adamson's

new novel

LIPSTICK AND LIES

is to be published
by Hodder & Stoughton
in January 1998

CHAPTER ONE

I know what I'll say when they come for me. I'll tell the tale that protects me from trouble. It's as familiar as the truth and with each repetition it grows more real. But it isn't the truth.

Each year I keep three anniversaries: the date of the murder, the date of the hanging and Sandy's birthday. I keep them involuntarily, jolted into remembrance by, perhaps, a glance at a calendar or the act of writing the date on a cheque. Without these cruel anniversaries it might have been possible to bury the truth.

I don't mark them in my diary. Look, my pencilled notes are only for appointments, shopping to do and bills to pay. There's nothing to startle anyone who peers over my shoulder.

Two more days. To the anniversary of the murder, I mean.

Oddly, I'll be spending it at the scene of the crime. Well, no, not exactly but close, visiting a cousin of mine who's settled in the town. June's older than me, lame now and clinging onto family, always begging visits. How could I refuse without her wondering whether my reasons were less to do with enjoying a busy life than with repugnance at long-ago death? Deaths. Two of them, remember: the slaughter and the hideous legal retribution.

This year it so happened it was June who alerted me to

the anniversary, in a telephone conversation hingeing on her increasing isolation. She ended a good-natured grumble by saying: 'Anna, you never allow enough time, dear. Come for a weekend and then we'll really have time to talk. How about the end of March?'

And there it was, the fatal date, falling this year on the final Saturday of the month. The murder itself took place on a Tuesday.

Without quibble I replied: 'Yes, I'll come then.'

I wrote diagonally across the space for two days on the diary page: *See June*. As I scribbled I imagined her sitting by her telephone, triumphant. Because she looks frail I underestimate her. If I were to forget how gaunt her body is and concentrate on the determined line of her jaw, which is plain now she's taken to commanding her steely hair with combs and drawing it into a knot on the nape of her neck, I'd give way less frequently. When I'm annoyed I've done so I tell myself she's selfish. We are on the whole, I think, a selfish family.

Since June's call the anniversary has hung around in my head, an impending tribulation that's all the worse for being anticipated. If only I could be sure June isn't aware of it, too. Of course, there's no means of checking without giving away what's on my mind, so I'll just have to turn up on Friday evening and hope for the best.

I could be lucky. She hasn't talked to me about the murder for ages, except for a few cautious remarks when I first went to visit her. She'd been living in the town – a run-to-seed sort of place, all history and no future – for a couple of months by then and it would have been peculiar if neither of us had commented on her coming full circle, back to what was once her parents' home and also to the town where the family drama was enacted. Every one of us had moved away in the intervening years. June's parents, too, had let their house and gone.

'The last batch of tenants were awful,' she said, and we smartly set off along the landlord-tenant byway which meant murder was kept off the agenda.

Perhaps she attempted to revive it before I left an hour or two later. Yes, I'm sure she did, but I'm adept at dodging and I had the perfect excuse for slipping away: I faced a long journey home. Presumably she registered my reluctance because she hasn't mentioned it again, not even, I think, indirectly.

Reminiscing with June is curious. As she's ten years older than me her perspective has always been different. What I saw as a child, she viewed with the sensitivities of a girl on the brink of womanhood. All the events and characters we refer to are remembered from quite different angles.

'Auntie Patch was my favourite,' I admitted once. 'I was really sad when she went to the States.'

June's face lit with humour. 'But Patch was so mean, Anna. Don't you remember what she did to Nella?'

Nella had seemed to me a dull, locked-in personality. I raised an eyebrow in query and June told me the tale of two sisters. The story didn't amount to much, not unless you were the aggrieved sister, but it justified the opinion June held. I couldn't argue with her because she was looking at it from the vantage point of her extra ten years.

'Good heavens,' I said, showing the required surprise. Privately I was sure there was bound to be another interpretation, one that favoured Patch. Bias, like beauty, is in the eye of the beholder.

On one of the other occasions that we went in tandem down memory lane I sensed June holding back rather than contradict me. It would be very easy for all our conversations to turn into mild arguments which she's bound to win because of the superiority those ten years grant her. She remembers lots of things I don't and lots more about the things I do, or so she says.

Do you know, I don't especially remember June herself when I was young. Although I struggle for a recollection of a gawky big girl, I can never bring her into focus. I recall her parents and her rather dashing brother more clearly. Naturally, I haven't said this to June because it's

3

a distancing kind of thing and she needs, very obviously needs, to feel close to someone who's family.

We have little in common apart from a few genes. She's a retired civil servant who's led a risk-free life in the lower ranks of the Ministry of Something or Other. She's a spinster who's never, as far as I know, been tempted to change her status. Her taste runs to understated jersey suits with German labels; holidays where one learns about art, opera or cookery; the *Daily Telegraph*; and scarifyingly dry sherry. I'm not like her. My life isn't like hers. That scattering of genes is the magnet that attracts her to me and I, dutifully, respond.

No doubt we had more in common when we were young, living in the same town and making Sunday afternoon outings to see the same set of grandparents. We were at the same family events, such as christenings and weddings. Not funerals, though. The family excluded children from funerals. I remember the exclusion, remember being curled on a deep bedroom window-sill and watching a black car pull away down the street, and I remember the silence in the house because everyone had gone to be sad somewhere else. But I don't know how old I was or whose funeral it was or who, precisely, was in the car. I'm left with a sensation, a symbol rather than an entire event.

To me childhood is another place, one peopled by strangers. In my mind's eye I see the little girl on the window-sill and I call it 'me', but only because it's my memory or my imagining. I have feelings about that moment she lived through, but I doubt they can be her feelings. No, I'm investing the scene with a pathos she can't have experienced because she was *in* the picture and I'm merely looking at it, interpreting it. Sometimes, at odd remembered moments in her young life, I identify with her and accept her without question as me. But it doesn't last. It's rather like recognising a friend across a street and finding, as you hurry towards them, you're facing a cold-eyed stranger.

People talk about children blossoming into adults, and

they use rosebuds as sentimental symbols of innocent child-hood, but to me the imagery seems inadequate. A gentle unfurling of petals doesn't describe the metamorphosis that separates babe in cradle from child, and child from adult. We're reinvented in a series of different forms before we're completely developed, and it's as hard to find the child in the adult as it is to see the caterpillar in the butterfly. The butterfly drinks nectar and doesn't know why the caterpillar chewed on the leaf. When we leave childhood behind, we lose a language and a system of reasoning, and there's no way back.

The child that was me and the big girl that was June are both strangers to me now. I can't put myself into the pictures June's memory paints, although I often pretend to because repeated rejections would chafe away at the weak strand that binds us.

I should say we seldom hold matching views of current events, either. For instance, I'm convinced she exaggerates when she complains about her neighbours and their garden fires and noisiness. Although I've been to her house a number of times I haven't caught a whiff of smoke or heard a peep.

And then there's this business of her local shopkeepers, who deliver groceries and meat and vegetables, even a decent bottle of wine, and appear to me to be a blessing most housebound folk can only envy. June, though, knows the worst about them: overcharging, giving short measure, gossiping about her to all and sundry.

Once, irritably, I started to say: 'Cancel them, then. You don't have to bring them to the house if they cause you so much upset.'

Just in time I bit my tongue because she has no choice but to rely on them, and it's her reliance which is her real hurt. I expect she extends the resentment to me, too, because I'm the only member of the family who visits regularly. I'm more or less certain of that. To begin with she made it sound as though several of the others came, and I believed it simply because they live nearer. Now I suspect they each made a single visit, calling on her soon after she moved in, drawn by curiosity to see her parents' old house once more. What did they talk about, I wonder? Probably the things she doesn't talk about to me.

She isn't truly old although you might be thinking so from what I've said. No, she's in her early sixties. But I notice she's behaving old, as though having a lame leg is affecting her attitude. This surprises me because the family prides itself on stoicism – or used to although I doubt any of them have said it in a long time, stoicism having gone out of fashion. Who cares about stiff-upper-lippery these days? People prefer to bare their breasts and share their suffering, wouldn't you say?

Sometimes I catch myself wondering where June and I will be in ten years' time. Will she, as she insists, be destitute and totally crippled? Will I be the only one who visits and, willy-nilly, becomes responsible for her?

But it's too soon to worry. Besides, June is most unlikely ever to be destitute and she'll come to the top of the waiting-list and have an operation one of these fine days. After that, who knows? Salsa dancing? Mediterranean cruises? A walk to the butcher and the grocer?

When we meet, June and I, we gently ruffle a few leaves of memory, swap stories of times long past, discuss her troublesome present and her fears of the future. We don't, if we can help it, dwell on murder.

Yet I feel it drawing closer, the moment when the matter becomes unavoidable. They'll come for me, you see, and I'll have to tell them something. Oh yes, I'm confident I know what's best to say. All that's required is the story that's always been my salvation. But having found me there's a chance they'll go to the old house, too, and then they'll encounter June and I don't imagine she has a story that fends off questions.

You see my difficulty? I'd like to warn her to expect questions but I'm stuck because I can't do anything without discussing the murder.

LESLEY GRANT-ADAMSON

DANGEROUS GAMES

JIM RUSH IS BACK: THE CHARMING LIAR WITH THE DANGEROUS FANTASIES, FRIGHTENINGLY CREDIBLE FOR HIS VICTIMS AND READERS ALIKE.

Dodging charges of murder and fraud in a Caribbean hideaway, the amoral Jim is trapped by the island's megalomaniac host, whose childish games are becoming ever more frightening.

But Jim can't resist playing a game of his own with a couple of hustlers who say they've found a Spanish treasure galleon. He can't seem to avoid a nosy photographer, obsessed with snatching candid shots of a passing princess but far too interested in Jim.

The edges of truth and fantasy blur. Soon the make-believe of the island combines explosively with Jim Rush's real world of dishonesty and daring.

The result is murder.

'Lesley Grant-Adamson is rapidly turning the genre into an art form.' *Cosmopolitan*

'Jim Rush is a charmer and a liar who comes at you from somewhere between an Elmore Leonard low life hustler and Patricia Highsmith's lovable, homicidal hero, Tom Ripley.' *Liverpool Daily Post*

HODDER AND STOUGHTON PAPERBACKS

LESLEY GRANT-ADAMSON

EVIL ACTS

'Evil makes us all feel a little colder. It forces us to accept how flimsy our lives and our sanity are. A crazed killer sends out shock waves. You don't have to be dead or at the graveside to suffer.'

Grace has been fooled into buying the home of a serial killer. Strange noises seem to crowd the night hours. She spurns the friends who urge her to leave and turns instead to Mike Cleary, expert on Jack the Ripper and collector of notorious addresses.

But Cleary feeds her obsession with the monster who lived in her house. Soon she is convinced of the killer's continuing presence and his efforts to destroy her as surely as he did his other victims.

'She knows how to create an atmosphere of unease and incipient horror.'
P.D. JAMES

HODDER AND STOUGHTON PAPERBACKS

LESLEY GRANT-ADAMSON

WISH YOU WERE HERE

Linda is trapped . . .

and it is her own deception that has trapped her. It was her idea to pretend to go on holiday abroad, to drive away secretively into the wintry English countryside.

Now she has met Tom, another lone traveller who lures her to Scotland. Audacious and dishonest, he exerts a strange fascination over her.

By the time she suspects he is a man who kills women, it is too late.

Her deception has made her the perfect victim.

'Among the top crime writers of our younger generation' *The Times*

'A writer with a keen eye for character.' *Mail on Sunday*

HODDER AND STOUGHTON PAPERBACKS